CW01640479

THE LIAR'S PROMISE

MARK TILBURY

First published in 2017 by Bloodhound Books

www.bloodhoundbooks.com

Print ISBN 978-1-912175-76-5

For Cassie,
who makes everything possible.

Also Mark Tilbury

The Ben Whittle Investigations Series

The Revelation Room

The Eyes of The Accused

Stand Alone Psychological Thriller

The Abattoir Of Dreams

PRAISE FOR THE ABATTOIR OF DREAMS

"This was a gritty and twisted read with so much heart and now if you'll excuse me I'll be on Amazon buying Tilbury's other books." Amy Sullivan - Novelgossip

"In terms of the plot, well OMFG, my curiosity was piqued from the start and the pace was perfect for this type of story, racing when required and slowing down at the moments where I needed it to!" Noelle Holten - Crimebookjunkie

"Hells bells what a book! Abattoir Of Dreams by Mark Tilbury Is definitely going to be one of my top reads of 2017..." Lorraine Rugman- The Book Review Cafe

"Fantastically written and chilling to the bone, this novel will sit with you longer after you have turned the final page." Samantha Ellen - Clues And Reviews

"Excuse my language but this book grabs you by the balls from page one and doesn't let go!" Helen Giles - Life Of A Nerdish Mum

"The Abattoir of Dreams is a very dark, disturbing read. It's a shockingly powerful work of fiction." Joseph Calleja - Relax And Read Book Reviews

PROLOGUE

Peter King regarded the young woman handcuffed to the brass headboard with a mixture of contempt and anticipation. It was clear she lacked breeding, and her coarse tongue left a lot to be desired, but these matters were of little consequence. This wasn't a young ladies' finishing school; not unless you took the finishing part literally. Her name was Tanya, but she would be assigned a colour and a number for the rest of her days: Purple-six. Her predecessor, Purple-five, would be a hard act to follow. Impossible, even, but now was not the time to cry over spilt blood.

Purple-six was now at the mercy of several glasses of Chardonnay and four crushed sleeping tablets. Enough to fell an average horse, let alone a lame foal like Purple-six. It was almost ten hours since she'd fallen asleep at the dining table, head resting on a plate of leftover chicken sandwiches and sweet pickled onions.

King had abducted her from his usual stomping ground at Paddington Station. He'd almost been resigned to giving up after hours of fruitless watching and waiting when she'd stepped off an incoming train from Reading like an answered prayer. The first sign she was the right girl for him had been her obvious lack of direction. After several minutes wandering around in circles, she'd sat on a bench, hunched over, hands fidgeting with just about anything they could, well, get their hands on.

King had waited a while before approaching her. His fake beard was irritating his skin, and the padding around his midriff had slipped, but these minor inconveniences would be soon forgotten once he focused on the task in hand. He adjusted his dark-grey trilby hat and sat down next to his prey, careful not to engage her in conversation too soon.

Purple-six helped things along by taking a tobacco tin from her blue coat and plugging a thin roll-up between her lips. He offered her a light with Yellow-one's Zippo lighter. Yellow-one no longer smoked. Or breathed, for that matter.

After introducing himself as Thomas Kowalski, of Polish descent, King learned that Purple-six had come to London to pursue her dream of becoming a dancer. Raised by a single mother, it was hardly surprising that she courted ambition, but, like so many before her, she would soon learn that dreams could quickly turn into nightmares.

King had invented an elderly sister, Shona, who lived in Oxford. Said he was off to visit her, and that Shona would be delighted to meet such a lovely young woman. After almost an hour's deliberation, King had finally managed to clinch the deal by telling her that Shona used to be a dancer. That she had friends in the Oxford School of Dance. Purple-six had looked like a stray dog who'd just learned its new master was a butcher.

And so they had caught the train and headed to his house on the outskirts of Oxford. He'd explained Shona's absence by telling Purple-six that his sister was likely visiting a friend. No matter. He had a key. Shona was happy for him to let himself in.

Three glasses of wine laced with sleeping pills later, Purple-six was having the longest sleep of her short life. If she'd been awake, she might well have registered shock upon learning her hands were handcuffed to a brass headboard. He hadn't bothered gagging her; the nearest neighbour was over two hundred yards away and rendered deaf by distance.

Purple-six was also unaware that her predecessor's severed head was sitting on a Queen Anne chair in the corner of the room, death lending her complexion a colour to match her name. Purple-five didn't look in great condition, which wasn't surprising considering she'd spent five days in the stocks and two days at the whipping post before death had claimed her for a soulmate. She'd lost an eye courtesy of a stone in the centre of a rotten plum, and three of her front teeth were missing after a rather nasty piece of dental work with a baseball bat.

The head was bound for a freezer in the basement as soon as it had made its acquaintance with Purple-six. The rest of her body had already been cut up in the bath and deposited in bins around Oxford.

Purple-six stirred and moaned. Her breath smelled like a bog. King folded his bony frame into a chair beside the bed, relieved to be free of the restrictions of his padded disguise. He was also now clean-shaven, his thinning grey hair slicked back with Brylcreem. He bore no resemblance to the man who'd enticed her to join him on a visit to the fictional Shona's house.

'*Sesame Street*,' Purple-six muttered. One of her eyes opened a crack, peered left and right, closed again.

'Wakey, wakey, sleepyhead.'

She muttered something about a lettuce, and opened her eyes. 'Where am I?'

'On the road to salvation.' He waited as she grew accustomed to her new surroundings.

Suddenly aware of her cuffed hands, she tugged on the restraints and kicked her legs. 'What the fuck…?'

'Please don't swear. It's both vulgar and unnecessary.'

She tried to sit up. Defeated, she flopped back, head banging against the headboard. 'Who are you?'

'Your saviour.'

Something dawned in those muddy puddle eyes. 'Where's Thomas?'

'The Polish guy?'

She nodded.

'He had to go back to his flat in Islington.'

'I don't understand.'

'No; I don't suppose you do. Let me help your brain to acclimatise. You belong to me now.'

'What the fuck…?'

'I have saved you from the wolves and the vultures.'

She rattled her restraints. 'What the fuck is this?'

King tried not to rise to the bait of profanity. 'All in good time, dear. All in good time. There's someone I want you to meet.'

She suddenly caught sight of Purple-five's head. Opened her mouth as if to scream, but no sound came out. Just frothy rabid dribble.

'That's Purple-five. I'm afraid her better days are behind her.'

Purple-six twisted her head to one side as if at the mercy of demonic possession.

'If you turn out to be half the girl she was, you'll go a long way.'

Purple-six responded by making a horrible gurgling noise in the back of her throat and belching vomit down her chin. She treated King to a revolting whiff of pickled onion and gut rot. To make matters worse, her bladder abandoned restraint and turned the crotch of her jeans from pale blue to dark blue.

Not a good sign. Unlike Purple-five, the girl lacked backbone.

CHAPTER ONE

Chloe Hollis looked at her mother, a tear hatching from the corner of one eye, breath forming foggy clouds in the freezing December air. 'I don't want to go inside, Mummy.'

Mel tried her best to dredge up a smile from that sacred place where love trumps all. It had been a long day. Nine hours working at Feelham Primary School trying to stop twenty kids from exploding with the excitement of Christmas. Not to mention a pile of marking when she got home, making dinner, and getting Chloe ready to watch the Christmas production of *Jack and the Beanstalk* at Feelham Theatre.

'Why not?'

'Be-cause.'

Mel bent down so she was at eye level with her daughter. One of her knees cracked; a painful reminder she was fast approaching forty. 'But it's *Jack and the Beanstalk.* You've been looking forward to it.'

Chloe shook her head. 'I want to go home.'

Mel tried another tack. 'Mummy's been looking forward to this all year.'

'So?'

'So… could you be a big girl and do Mummy a favour?'

'I'm not a big girl. I'm four.'

Mel wiped a tear from Chloe's cheek. 'And a half. You'll be starting school next year.'

'That's aeons away.'

Mel smiled. 'Aeons' was one of her husband, Tony's, pet words. 'Tell you what. You watch the pantomime with Mummy, and we'll get pizza after.'

Chloe sniffed. 'Tuna and sweetcorn?'

Mel moved in for the kill. 'And hot chocolate before bed.'

'Marshmallows, too?'

'Okay.'

They walked into the foyer, Chloe gripping her mother's hand tight enough to pinch. Several posters advertising a future production of *Macbeth* were pinned to the sage-green panelled walls, along with signed pictures of actors who'd made guest appearances at the theatre. Mel bought a ticket at the kiosk. She was both surprised and grateful her daughter made no demands for the sweets on sale next to the kiosk. They walked hand-in-hand across the thick red carpet to the staircase leading to the main theatre.

Half way up, Chloe stopped, jerking her mother's hand. 'Please, Mummy! I don't want to go.'

Mel summoned patience. 'But it will be fun.'

'I don't want to die.'

'What on earth are you talking about?'

Chloe looked at the stairs as if a mad axeman might be standing at the top waiting to attack her.

'Chloe?'

'I'm going to die.'

'Don't be silly. Of course you're not.'

'I am.' This came out as '*Yam.*'

'That's a daft thing to say. You're with Mummy. No one will hurt you.'

'The… Tall… Man…'

Mel stepped aside to let a couple past with a boy who looked as if he might be running on rocket fuel. She bent down and gripped Chloe's hands, looked deep into her eyes. 'What's brought all this on?'

Chloe stared at the floor.

'Chloe?'

Chloe looked up. 'I… don't… want… to… die.'

Something in the child's eyes made Mel think of possession. 'Listen to Mummy. You're not going to die. I promise.'

A voice boomed out over a microphone announcing the show, teasing the kids, getting them whipped up into a frenzy of anticipation.

Chloe screamed and dropped to her knees. She put her hands over her ears and shook her head. 'No. No. No. Go away.'

Mel's legs went weak. She reached down and tried to pick her daughter up. Chloe responded by banging her head against the floor. 'No. No. No.'

Mel remembered Chloe throwing a tantrum once in a supermarket. Refusing to get up off the floor because Mel refused to buy chocolate flakes or some such rubbish. She remembered the humiliation of all those other shoppers looking at her, waiting to see how this unfit mother would deal with her unruly little brat. That incident had been embarrassing. Humiliating, even. But this was a hundred times worse.

Mel grabbed hold of her and hauled her up into her arms. 'Stop it, Chloe. Stop it. You'll hurt yourself.'

Chloe shook her head, blonde hair flying, whipping Mel's face. 'He's going to kill us.'

Mel hugged her as tight as she could. Chloe brought her head back and looked at the ceiling.

'Are you ready?' The announcer said.

For a moment, Mel thought Chloe's outburst had subsided.

Dozens of excited voices confirmed they were more than ready.

'I can't hear you!'

'Yes.' Louder.

'Are you sure?'

'Yes.' Louder still.

And then Mel's world exploded as Chloe's head smashed into her nose, full force. A hot spurt of blood gushed over her lips and down her chin.

'I want to go home, Mummy! I want to go home, Mummy!'

Mel could hear the voice echoing around her head. She fought an overwhelming urge to drop Chloe and clutch her throbbing nose.

'Then let the show begin…'

'The Tall Man's coming. The Tall Man's coming.'

Blood ran into Mel's mouth, warm and coppery. Tears cast a veil across her eyes. Chloe was an undefined lump. She could feel the child's fingernails digging into her neck.

'Mummy… Mummy… Mummy…'

'Stop it!' Mel shrieked.

'The Tall Man's coming.'

Mel spat blood. 'All right! We're going.'

'Now?'

'Yes.'

Someone at the bottom of the stairs. Blurry. The woman from the kiosk. 'Are you all right, madam?'

'Yes. I…'

The woman walked up the first few stairs, stopped, mouth hovering in a no-man's-land between shock and speech.

'My daughter accidentally headbutted me. I'm fine.'

'Your nose might be broken. Would you like me to get you some tissue?'

'I want to go home, Mummy. NOW!'

Mel put Chloe down and reached into her handbag. 'It's fine. I've got some in here.'

'Please, Mummy,' Chloe shouted, clutching Mel's coat.

Mel held a wad of tissues over her nose. 'All right. We're going.'

The look in Chloe's eyes, that threatening storm, seemed to lift. 'Promise?'

'Yes. Come on. Let's go.'

By the time they reached the foyer, Mel felt sick and dizzy. Jesus Christ, all she needed now was to pass out and her day would be complete. The woman held the door open for her, a mixture of concern and pity in her eyes. As they stepped outside, an icy gust of wind slashed Mel's injured face. Chloe gripped her hand as if letting go might see her abducted by the Tall Man. By the time they reached the carpark, Chloe had relaxed.

'Is your nose all right, Mummy?'

'It's fine,' Mel lied.

'I'm sorry I hurt you.'

Mel removed the wad of tissues. At least the damn thing had stopped bleeding. It probably wasn't broken. Just bruised the bone. 'You didn't hurt me. It was a silly accident.'

'I love you, Mummy.'

'I love you, too, sweetheart. Do you still want pizza?'

'I'm not hungry.'

'You sure?'

'Uh-huh. I'm tired. Ruby Rag Doll will be cold if Daddy's forgot to turn my radiator on again.'

'We'll put your electric blanket on as soon as we get home.'

'Are you going to tell Daddy?'

Mel fished her car keys out of her bag. She unlocked the door. 'No.'

'What if he sees the blood?'

'Daddy will probably be asleep in the chair.'

'Daddy's a tired old bear.'

So is Mummy. 'A snoring old bear.'

'He'd better stay awake tonight.'

Mel helped Chloe into the child seat and strapped her in. 'Why?'

'In case the Tall Man comes down the chimney.'

Mel's heart skipped a beat. She climbed in behind the wheel. 'Who *is* the Tall Man, Chloe?'

Chloe didn't answer at first. Mel watched her in the rear-view mirror as the interior light faded. She seemed distracted by something outside the car. Then, she said, 'The Tall Man's going to kill us.'

'What on earth?'

'Dead, dead, dead,' Chloe chanted, in a voice that belonged to someone much older. 'Like the turkeys hanging in the butcher's shop window.'

Mel took five attempts to ram the key into the ignition.

CHAPTER TWO

When they reached home, Mel's mind was in turmoil. She hung their coats on a row of pegs inside the small porch and put their shoes in the rack. 'Go upstairs and get your jim-jams on.'

As predicted, Tony was asleep in the chair, a paperback novel resting in his lap, a snore rattling in his throat.

'I want to say goodnight to Daddy.'

'I'll wake him up when you're all tucked up in bed. Get him to read you a bedtime story.'

'Okay.'

Mel followed her daughter up the stairs. It now seemed as if nothing had happened at the theatre. As if the whole incident had been some crazy dream. The crusty residue of congealed blood on her lips and chin told her otherwise.

She waited for Chloe to go into her bedroom, and then walked to the bathroom. She filled the basin with warm water, added a splash of Dettol, and studied her face in the mirror. Dark circles beneath her eyes complimented the horror story that was the bottom half of her face. A nice long soak in a hot bath would do wonders for her aching body. Not to mention a few glasses of wine to heal her fractured mind.

She washed the blood away, cleansed her face with three face wipes, and called Chloe to come wash her face and brush her teeth.

No answer. Only the ticking of the hall clock.

'Chloe?' Mel walked along the small landing and peered inside her daughter's bedroom. Chloe was sitting on her bed, back against the pink chenille headboard, Ruby Rag Doll clutched to her chest.

'Will you go to the bathroom, please?'

Chloe didn't acknowledge her. She stared at the wall. Her eyes looked empty, as if in a trance.

'Come on, Chloe. Mummy's tired. She wants to have a bath.'

Chloe continued to stare at the wall.

Mel waved a hand in front of her daughter's face. Nothing. Not even a flicker. A thin line of dribble trickled from the corner of her mouth.

'Chloe? Sweetheart? What's wrong?'

'You don't understand me.'

Mel's heart stalled. The voice sounded older. Unfamiliar. 'Chloe?'

'You only want me to be what *you* want me to be. Just to fulfil your own stupid expectations.'

Where in God's name was this language coming from? 'That's not'

'Why can't I be myself? I want to be an artist. Why won't anyone listen to me? Everything I say falls on deaf ears with you.'

Mel backed out of the bedroom. 'Tony?'

'That's right, call the reinforcements. Gang up on me, like you always do.'

'Tony!' Louder this time.

'What?' Thick and slippery with sleep.

'Come up here. Now!'

'Why?'

'Just do it.'

Chloe looked at Mel, contempt in her eyes. Then, as if someone had suddenly unplugged her, she lay down, cuddled Ruby Rag Doll, and fell asleep.

Tony walked into the bedroom. 'What is it?'

Mel made a snap decision to just get Chloe into bed. She'd had enough drama for one day. 'Lift her up while I get the duvet out from underneath her.'

By the time they'd tucked Chloe in, Tony was wide awake. 'It's only eight o'clock. I thought the pantomime finished at nine?'

Mel left the door ajar to allow light in from the landing. 'Chloe didn't want to watch it.'

'Why?'

'I need a drink.'

'Your nose is bleeding.'

Mel walked downstairs, took a bottle of wine from the fridge and filled a large glass. She drained it without pause and refilled it.

'Whoa, there! Someone's thirsty.'

Mel flopped down in a dusky-pink armchair. 'You'd be bloody thirsty after the day I've just had.'

'What happened?'

Mel told him about the episode at Feelham Theatre, and the way Chloe had spoken to her upstairs about wanting to be an artist.

Tony sat opposite her. 'How strange.'

'First she gets hysterical about some bloody Tall Man, then she goes on about no one understanding her.'

'Perhaps she was talking in her sleep just now.'

'She was wide awake. And she damn near broke my nose at the theatre.'

'The Tall Man might be someone from a nightmare. You know what kids are like.'

Mel wasn't convinced. 'She was fine until we got there. Excited. Couldn't wait to see the giant. Asking questions. Then, she changed in the blink of an eye.'

'Kids have vivid imaginations.'

'I know. I teach them all day, remember? But this was… something else. Something I can't explain.'

'Do you want a refill?'

Mel held her glass out. 'I doubt I'll be able to sleep without the whole bottle tonight.'

'I'll join you.'

An hour later, Mel's mood had lightened enough to smile about the incident at the theatre. 'No one had better mess with her when she grows up.'

'Good for her.'

'I'm still confused about why she acted like that.'

After a short while, Tony said, 'She's probably just excited about Christmas. Kids come out with all sorts of stuff when their emotions are running high.'

Mel wanted to believe that, hang on to it for all she was worth, but it couldn't be explained away by sheer excitement. Tony hadn't seen the terror in Chloe's eyes. Okay, the headbutt had been an accident, but the rest of it? 'I'm still worried about her.'

'Let's just keep an eye on her and see how it goes.'

Mel remembered last year. Chloe had been looking forward to Christmas so much she'd made herself ill. Spent most of the day zonked out on the sofa running a temperature, barely able to open her eyes. Although a shame, at least it was a natural response to getting over-excited. But the Tall Man and the strange adult way she'd spoken upstairs? It was like something out of a horror movie.

'Only a few days until the end of term.'

Mel raised her glass. 'I'll drink to that.'

Tony taught maths at a private school in a village ten miles out of Feelham. Kingswood Preparatory School. A prestigious job, good salary, promotion in the pipeline for the New Year. Mel couldn't wait. It would give them a chance to move out of the small two-bed mid-terraced house they'd bought ten years ago. St Kilda's Close was a nice enough place to live, but the house had outgrown its usefulness. Mel wanted another child, and a dog, and a back garden big enough for them all to relax. The garden in St Kilda's was just about big enough to put up a rotary line. In the summer, they'd had to choose between putting out the washing or setting up Chloe's paddling pool.

Two refills later, Mel was drunk. Not *incapable* drunk she would never be that irresponsible with a young child to look after but drunk enough to blunt the edges of her mind and her speech. 'We should move to Cradwell.'

Tony pursed his lips. 'Hmm.'

'What's that supposed to mean?'

'I don't like the countryside.'

'What's not to like?'

'Cows.'

'No one's asking you to milk them.'

'I don't like the smell. Or the winding narrow roads with tractors everywhere. And, in case you haven't noticed, there's no shops in Cradwell.'

Mel snapped her fingers. 'S'cuse me, Mr. Hollis. Newsflash. We've got a car. Not to mention Asda home delivery. Don't give me that old cow poop about being isolated. Think of the peace and quiet.'

'It'll be anything but "quiet." Cows moo. Owls hoot. Cockerels crow. It'll be like *Animal Farm*.'

'We could have a two-hundred-foot garden. An orchard, even. Somewhere for the kids to run about, explore and build dens.'

'Or get lost and send you into a panic every five minutes.'

'It'll do us both good to get out of here.'

'I'll consider it.'

'Really?'

'I said *consider*, mind. I'm not promising.'

'Thank you.'

'Are you ready for bed?'

Mel glanced at the clock above the kitchen door. Five past ten. 'I might get a quick shower first.'

Tony took Mel's glass into the kitchen. As Mel reached the stairs, Chloe screamed. Mel's imagination conjured up the Tall Man, coming through the bedroom window, teeth bared, knife glinting in the moonlight.

The scream came again. Harsh, demanding, obliterating the effects of the wine. She rushed up the stairs. Nothing could have prepared her for what she saw upon entering the bedroom and turning on the light. Chloe was standing on the bed, her back pressed against the wall, both hands clutching her throat. Her features were barely recognisable. Her ashen skin looked like melting wax. Her eyes stared straight ahead, and her breath came in ragged gasps.

'Chloe?'

Chloe clawed at her neck, fingers digging deep into the flesh, spit foaming on her lips.

Tony rushed into the room and stopped dead. 'What the…?'

Mel gawped at her daughter. 'Chloe? Chloe? Oh, my God!'

'She's having a nightmare,' Tony said. He put a hand on her shoulder. 'Chloe?'

Chloe relaxed her grip on her throat and gasped for air. She blinked twice in rapid succession. 'Why don't you just fucking kill me and get it over with?'

'Some bloody nightmare!' Mel said, suddenly angry at Tony's insistence everything had to have a rational explanation.

'Chloe? It's Daddy.'

'Fuck off.'

Tony recoiled, as if the words had physically assaulted him.

'Put me in the cage,' Chloe shouted. 'Put me in the fucking cage and be done with it.'

Tony shook her. Chloe responded by tipping her head back and spitting in his face.

Mel noticed angry red weals around the child's neck. 'I told you something was wrong.'

Chloe glared at her father. 'You're a fucking coward.'

Tony wiped saliva from his chin. 'It's Daddy, Chloe. Can you hear me?'

'You're all fucking cowards.' Her eyes looked capable of spitting venom.

Tony grabbed hold of her and hauled her off the bed. Held her close. Rocked her from side to side. 'It's all right, sweetheart. Daddy's here. Daddy's here now.'

Chloe sobbed, body heaving, face pressed against Tony's shoulder. They stayed this way for several minutes, Tony clinging to her as if letting go might relinquish his daughter into the arms of Satan himself.

As the sobs subsided to sniffs, Mel stroked her daughter's hair, slowly, rhythmically. Chloe's breathing steadied. She closed her eyes and plugged her thumb into her mouth, forefinger curled over her nose.

'I think she's asleep,' Mel whispered.

Tony laid her on the bed. Her free hand flew up as Tony let go. Mel quickly occupied it with Ruby Rag Doll and covered her with the duvet. She told Tony to go to bed. 'I'll stay with her for a while. Watch her.'

Tony backed out of the room. He switched off the light and left the door ajar. Mel wanted to lie down on the bed with her, hold her tight, protect her from the dreadful reality of whatever was happening inside that troubled mind of hers.

Chloe stirred. She uncorked her thumb from her mouth. 'Mummy?'

'Yes, sweetheart?'

'I don't want to die.'

'You're not going to die. You just had… a bad dream. Mummy won't let anything happen to you.'

Chloe closed her eyes again, the lids fluttering like a butterfly's wings coming to rest on a delicate flower. 'Too late, Mama. Too late.'

CHAPTER THREE

Mel had managed about an hour's sleep. At least it was Friday. She could try to get her head together over the weekend. Make sense of what had happened. Keep an eye on Chloe.

'She said she didn't want to die, Tony, for God's sake.'

Tony looked as if he'd spent the whole night wrestling demons. He threw a half-eaten piece of toast on his plate, slurped some tea, banged down his mug.

'Don't look at me like that. I'm only saying.'

'I'm tired, Mel. That's all.'

'And I'm not?'

'Sorry.'

'And she called me *Mama*.'

'That's hardly the end of the world, is it?'

'But she never calls me that.'

'You're reading too much into this.'

'Really? Our child gets hysterical when I take her to the theatre. Chokes and talks about dying, and you think I'm reading too much into it?'

'It's got to have a rational explanation.'

Mel massaged her temples and tried to stop herself saying something she might regret. 'Like what? And don't tell me she was asleep. She wasn't. You saw her.'

Tony kissed the top of her head. 'It'll be all right. I promise.'

'I'm scared something really wrong with her.'

'Maybe she saw something in the theatre that set her off.'

'Like what?'

'A poster?'

Mel racked her brains, but nothing came to mind.

Tony grabbed his briefcase from the worktop. 'I've got to go. We'll talk later.'

'And in the meantime?'

'Try to relax. I'll have a word with Bernard.'

Bernard Levi was the school counsellor at Tony's school. He'd been to lunch about a year ago. Mel didn't like him. A big brash man with the manners of a rock ape. 'No. Leave it. Not now.'

'Are you sure? He's good with'

'I don't care. I don't want anyone else involved.'

Tony blew her a kiss. 'Later.'

She waited for the front door to close before going upstairs. After washing, she went to wake her daughter. Ruby Rag Doll was lying on the floor. The duvet was hanging half off the bed. Chloe lay on her back, mouth open, hair fanned out either side of her head on the pillow. Chloe never usually slept on her back because of a sinus problem which made it hard for her to breathe in this position. Mel could see faint remnants of the marks around her neck, but they no longer looked angry.

She shook her gently. 'Time to get up, Pumpkin.'

Mel was greeted by a snort and an impatient wriggle.

'Chloe?'

'Huh?'

'Come on, sweetie. It's gone seven.'

'I'm tired.'

'Me, too. But you have to get ready to go to Kerrie-Anne's.'

Chloe rubbed her eyes. 'Where?'

'Kerrie-Anne's.'

'Who's she?'

'You know who Kerrie-Anne is.'

'Don't.'

'Don't play games. Mummy's too tired.'

'I'm not.'

'Kerrie-Anne's your childminder.'

'What do I need a childminder for?'

Mel sighed. A headache tugged at the corners of her mind. 'While Mummy goes to work at the school.'

'I'm too old for child-minders.'

'Just get dressed while I make breakfast.'

'Whatever.'

Mel recoiled at the remark. It wasn't so much the actual word, but the way she'd said it. Like a petulant teenager. 'Don't speak to me like that, Chloe.'

Chloe blinked. 'Like what?'

'Like that.'

'Here we go again.'

'Chloe!'

Chloe sat up and swung her legs over the edge of the bed. 'What's wrong, Mummy?'

Mel searched the child's eyes for signs of mischief. Nothing. Blue pools of innocence. 'Get ready, please, and then come downstairs for breakfast.'

By the time Chloe was sitting at the kitchen table, Mel's head was throbbing. She swallowed two paracetamol with a glass of water and wished she had a packet of cigarettes in the house. She'd given up after she'd fallen pregnant with Chloe, much to Tony's delight and the disgust of her nerves.

She took a box of Honey Nut Loops out of the cupboard and put it on the small pine kitchen table. As she fetched bowls and spoons, Chloe's voice piped up behind her, 'I don't like cereal.'

Mel plonked the bowls down. 'You do.'

'Don't. I like pancakes for breakfast. Pancakes and maple syrup.'

'You don't like eggs, Chloe. They always give you a bad tummy.'

'Are you kidding? I love them.'

'I'm not making pancakes. And we don't have any maple syrup. It's Honey Nut Loops or nothing.'

'Suit yourself. I'm not much hungry.'

Not much hungry? 'Oh, is that so?' Mel sat down opposite her. She half-filled a bowl with cereal and added milk. 'Can I ask you something, Pumpkin?'

'Why are you calling me Pumpkin? It's babyish.'

'I won't call you it anymore if you don't want me to.'

'I'd appreciate that.'

'Can I ask you something?'

Chloe nodded, eyeing the Honey Nut Loops as if they might contain a deadly toxin.

'Do you remember what happened last night?'

'I studied and went to bed.'

'Studied what?'

'History. Anne Boleyn.'

Mel's heart picked up speed. 'Anne Boleyn?'

'Henry the Eighth's second wife. Found guilty of high treason and beheaded in 1536.'

'Where did you learn that?'

'My history book.'

'You don't have a history book. You don't go to school yet.'

'I wish!'

Mel pushed the cereal in front of her. 'Please, try to eat something.'

'I don't like cereal. I already told you that.'

'Would you like some toast and marmalade instead?'

Chloe sighed.

'So, you don't remember going to the theatre last night?'

'Nope.'

'Or headbutting Mummy on the nose?'

'I wouldn't do that.'

Mel busied herself making a cup of strong black coffee. Perhaps Tony talking to Bernard wasn't such a bad idea. She could hardly take Chloe to the doctor's, could she? *Have you got a prescription for my daughter? I think she might be possessed by the spirit of someone who studies history and doesn't like Honey Nut Loops.*

By the time Mel had made the coffee, Chloe was fixing her hair back with a bright pink ponytail. She was a practical child. Could even do a passable French plait. She also had a flair for drawing and colouring.

'We'd better hurry, Mummy. Kerrie-Anne will be here soon.'

A surge of relief. Normality! She watched her daughter tighten the hairband, shovel Honey Nut Loops into her mouth, and kick her feet against the chair legs.

'We don't want to miss the bus,' Mel said. It was their little joke after missing the bus once when they were going shopping in Oxford.

Chloe raised a hand, pretended to ring a bell, and lost a Honey Nut Loop out the side of her mouth.

'Ding, ding,' Mel said. 'Station, please.'

'I love you, Mummy.'

'I love you, too, Pum…'

Chloe frowned. 'What's wrong, Mummy?'

Mel hesitated. Christ, she didn't even know what to call her anymore. She forced a smile. 'Nothing, sweetheart. Nothing at all.'

Possibly the biggest lie she had ever told her daughter.

CHAPTER FOUR

Mel somehow dragged herself through the day. She taught Year Two at Feelham County Primary School. Every noise seemed louder, every question more difficult to answer, every child a little more demanding. She'd even raised her voice a few times, something which she normally avoided at all costs. Shouting was the first step to losing control, and a teacher who wasn't in control was, perhaps, someone doing the wrong job.

She pulled up outside Kerrie-Anne's terraced house, switched off the engine, and took a few moments to compose herself. She'd almost bought a packet of cigarettes when she'd filled up with petrol. Thankfully, she knew someone in the queue, got chatting, and the moment was lost.

Kerrie-Anne opened the door before Mel had chance to ring the bell. She gawped at Mel without speaking. Something was wrong; Kerrie-Anne was usually as hyped up as the kids.

'Is everything all right?'

'Can you come in for a minute? Chloe's playing upstairs with Harriet. There's something you ought to know.'

Mel followed her along the hallway and into the kitchen. Worry drew a picture in her mind; Chloe choking, clutching at her neck, eyes wide. 'What is it?'

'Look, this is probably nothing. It's… something Chloe said when I was brushing her hair.'

'What?' Mel asked, not sure she wanted to hear he answer.

'She said she knows how her Grandma Audrey died.'

Mel's heart stopped. The last reserves of strength drained from her body. She held onto the back of a chair for support.

Mel had never spoken to Chloe about Grandma Audrey. Ever. Mel's mother was strictly off-limits. Chloe didn't even know the woman's name, for God's sake.

'Are you all right, Mel?'

She tried to swallow, but she had no saliva in her mouth. She sat down before her legs folded. 'What… did… she… say… exactly?'

'Like I said, I was brushing her hair at the dressing table in the playroom. She seemed fine. Talking about what Santa was going to bring her. She had Ruby in her lap, and then she started talking in this weird voice. Like how ventriloquists talk with their dummies. It was as if she was a different child. Her eyes looked older. Sad. Not those of a child excited about Christmas.'

'Maybe it was just a trick of the light,' Mel said, not believing it for a minute. Kerrie-Anne wasn't a woman given to fanciful exaggeration. Enthusiastic, energetic, brilliant with kids, and highly recommended, but never prone to overreaction. That's why Mel had hired her.

'Maybe,' Kerrie-Anne agreed. She studied the table for a few moments. 'Does she have a Grandma Audrey?'

Mel ignored the question. 'What did she say?'

The childminder hesitated, and then said, 'She told me it was your fault Grandma Audrey died.'

Mel's mouth hung open. 'She… said… what?'

'I know it sounds ridiculous. But I swear on my life, that's what she said.'

This couldn't be happening. Not on top of everything else.

'Mel?'

Mel felt as if someone had set fire to her thoughts.

'I'm sorry, Mel. I just thought you should know.'

Kerrie-Anne's eight-year-old daughter, Harriet, skipped into the kitchen and ended the conversation. 'Chloe's fallen asleep on my bed. We were playing dolls, and she threw Ruby down the stairs and said she had a broken neck. Then she started crying and ran into my room. I went and got Ruby. When I got back upstairs, Chloe was asleep.'

'Wake her up,' Kerrie-Anne said. 'Tell her that her mummy's here to take her home.'

Harriet nodded and scooted out the kitchen.

They waited in silence for Chloe to come downstairs. The unspoken words were somehow louder and clearer than the spoken ones. Mel's head felt like a maze; the Tall Man waiting in the shadows for her to make one wrong turn.

Chloe shuffled into the kitchen. She looked sulky. Her bottom lip was jutting out, eyes bleary, Ruby clutched to her chest.

'Hiya, Pumpkin,' Mel said, trying to inject cheeriness into her voice.

Chloe didn't answer. She sucked her thumb.

'Busy day?'

Chloe nodded.

'Come on, let's get you home.'

Mel thanked Kerrie-Anne and carried Chloe to the car. When they arrived at St Kilda's Close, Chloe was fast asleep. Mel switched on the interior light. She decided to put her straight to bed. The trauma of the last couple of days had clearly wiped her out.

She looked so angelic with her long blonde hair tumbling forward over her purple coat. Chloe had the most beautiful long eyelashes. Mel knew she was biased, but her daughter really was going to melt boys' hearts when she was older.

If the Tall Man doesn't get her first.

Mel shuddered and took the keys from the ignition. She wrestled Chloe out of the car seat, opened the front door and managed to get her upstairs without waking her. She laid her on top of the bed and decided to leave her coat on until she was in a deeper sleep. She needed some space to evaluate what Kerrie-Anne had said. Try to put it into some kind of perspective.

Mel couldn't understand why this was happening now. Until the visit to Feelham Theatre, Chloe had been like any other normal child. Grumpy, excitable, full of energy, full of questions. No mention of the Tall Man or Grandma Audrey. Nothing.

As she walked out the bedroom, Chloe woke up. 'Where are you going?'

Shit, shit, shit. 'Go back to sleep, Chloe.'

Chloe sat up, Ruby clutched to her chest. In a strange, croaky voice, she said, 'But it's not yet six.'

A butterfly, laden with iron wings, tried to take off in Mel's stomach. 'You've had a busy day, Chloe. You need to catch up on your sleep.'

'Says who?'

'Says your mother.'

'Oh, the irony.'

'What the…?'

'What's the matter, Smelly-Mellie? Cat got your tongue?'

Mel gawped at the doll as if it had just come to life. Her mother was the only person who had ever called her *Smelly-Mellie.*

'Well you might look like that. You were nothing but bothersome from birth.'

'Shut up!'

'What are you going to do? Throw me down the stairs?'

'I never threw you down the stairs,' Mel whispered.

The doll changed. Its dark woollen hair was replaced by her mother's long unkempt grey hair. The button- brown eyes transformed into Grandma Audrey's red puffy eyes. Mouth bearing large nicotine-stained teeth.

'You always were skittish.'

Mel's heart thundered across her chest as the doll grinned at her.

'Skittish and bothersome. Never liked being told what to do. Is that why you killed me?'

'I… never… killed… you….'

'Liar, liar, pants on fire.'

Mel raised her hand, ready to strike and silence that awful croaky voice from beyond the grave.

'Didn't like it because I had all the attention, did you, Little Miss Skittish.'

Mel's hand hovered inches from the doll, shaking.

'The truth will out, Smelly-Mellie. It always does.'

'Shut up. Shut up. SHUT THE FUCK UP!'

'What's wrong, Mummy?'

Chloe's voice suddenly jolted Mel as she was about to lash out. The doll returned to its usual inanimate state.

'Mummy?'

Mel lowered her hand.

'Why are you mad with me?'

Mel clamped her fingers between her teeth, biting down hard.

'What's wrong, Mummy?'

She looked at the little girl who could melt her heart with smiles and tears in equal measures. She brushed a strand of hair out of the child's eyes. 'I'm just tired, Pumpkin.'

'I don't like it when you're mad.'

'I'm not mad.'

'Promise?'

'Promise. Do you want a bath before bed?'

'I'm hungry.'

'Didn't you have tea at Kerrie-Anne's?'

'Uh-huh. But I'm eating for two.'

Mel was thrown off course yet again. Not only by her daughter's strange voice, but by the implication of her statement. 'Two?'

'Me and my sister.'

Mel tried to keep her voice calm. 'You haven't got a sister.'

'Have, so.'

'Who told you this?'

'Grandma Audrey.'

Mel looked at Ruby Rag Doll as if she might sprout yellow teeth and a vile tongue again. 'But you don't know Grandma Audrey.'

'Do, too. She talks to me.'

'She can't talk to you, Chloe.'

'Can.'

'When?'

'At night when I can't sleep.'

'But that's impossible.'

Chloe shook her head. 'She told me I had a sister.'

A shiver rolled down Mel's spine. 'Do you see Grandma Audrey like a real person?'

'No.'

'Then how do you talk to her?'

'She tells Ruby, and Ruby tells me.'

Ruby had been Mel's childhood doll. She'd been left at the house after her mother had died and Mel had gone to live with her Aunt Cathy and Uncle John. Her father had given Mel the doll, along with a suitcase full of old drawings and clothes, a few years ago. The case had been shoved up in the attic and forgotten about until Tony had decided on a clear-out a month ago. Chloe had begged to keep her. Look after her. Love her forever. Now Mel was beginning to wish she'd sent the doll to the rubbish tip along with all the other junk.

'How long's this been happening?'

Chloe shrugged.

She'd heard Chloe talking in that strange croaky voice several times before, but had assumed it was nothing more than child's play. An imagination working overtime.

'Can I ask you something, Pumpkin?'

Chloe nodded.

Mel took a deep breath. 'You said you've got a sister?'

'Uh-huh.'

Here was the million-dollar question. The one she didn't want to ask, but had to, because curiosity always killed the cat. 'Has your sister got a name?'

'Yes.'

'What is it?'

Without hesitation, Chloe said, 'Megan.'

Mel clapped a hand over her mouth. Chloe had just named the three-month-old child they'd lost to a heart defect several years before Chloe's birth.

CHAPTER FIVE

When Tony got home from work, Mel was halfway down a bottle of wine. She'd also eaten a bag of twiglets meant for Christmas, and a mince pie which wasn't sitting too well on a near-empty stomach.

Tony hung up his coat, kicked off his shoes, and threw his briefcase on a chair. 'What a crap day. Fancy a curry tonight?'

'Hi, Mel. How are you? How's your day been?'

Tony looked at her as if she'd thrown a rock at him. 'Sorry. How's?'

'Bloody shit, since you ask.'

The weariness around Tony's eyes vanished. 'What's happened?'

Mel gulped wine, banged her glass down on the pine coffee table, and told Tony what had happened at Kerrie-Anne's.

Tony said nothing for a while. He gazed at the clock above the kitchen door, seemingly fixated by the time. 'But that's not possible.'

'Don't you think I know that?' Mel left out the part where the doll had appeared to turn into her mother; that was probably just a symptom of prolonged stress and exhaustion.

'There's got to be a'

'I've never spoken to her about that old witch. As far as Chloe's concerned, she doesn't even exist.'

'Maybe your dad said something to her.'

'No way. He hates her. And that's not all. She said something else.'

'What?'

'She was eating for two.'

Tony looked relieved. He even managed a smile. 'That's just a vivid imagi you're not pregnant are you?'

'No, Tony, I'm not pregnant. But when I asked her what she meant by it, she said she was eating for her sister. I asked her if this sister had a name. Guess what she said?'

'What?'

'Megan.'

Tony's eyes widened. The colour drained from his face. 'But…'

'She doesn't *know* about Megan.'

Tony walked to the dresser and poured himself a generous measure of Scotch from a crystal decanter. He drained the drink and poured another one. 'Someone must have told her about Megan. It's the only explanation.'

'No one's told her.'

Tony sat in a chair and focussed on his drink. 'It makes no sense.'

'You saw her last night. Saw what she was like.'

'But'

'I think she's lived before. Remembers stuff about a past life. And I think my mother's talking to her through that fucking rag doll.'

Tony drained his drink. 'That's crap, Mel. We live and we die. End of. There's no such thing as ghosts.'

'And you know that for certain, do you? Is it part of the maths curriculum? One life minus one life equals no life. Is that what it is?'

Tony put down his drink and pinched the skin on the back of his hand. 'We're just physical bodies, Mel. We die and we turn back to dust. You're just clutching at straws. Someone's been filling our daughter's head with nonsense.'

'Like who, for God's sake?'

'Your dad. Kerrie-Anne. I don't know.'

'Crap.'

'It makes more sense than thinking your mother is speaking to her through a rag doll.'

'I don't know what to believe anymore,' Mel shouted. 'All I know is something's wrong with my daughter.'

'Our daughter.'

'When it suits.'

'What's that supposed to mean?'

'It means you only ever want the good bits, Tony. The happy, smiling, bouncy Chloe. Everything else, you palm off on me.'

'That's absolute rubbish.'

An uneasy truce fell as both combatants stopped to reload their guns. Lick their wounds. Mel refilled her glass.

Then, Tony said, 'Look, I'm not trying to dismiss you. I only'

'It seems that way from where I'm standing.'

'Sitting.'

'That's not funny, Tony. Being pedantic is a side-effect of smugness, and no one likes a smart-arse.'

'I was just kidding.'

'It doesn't suit you.'

A shadow fell across Tony's eyes. 'Let's just say you're right. Chloe *has* lived before, and your mother is talking to her through the doll. What in God's name are we supposed to do about it?'

A vision of a priest with a large crucifix and a bible popped into Mel's head. 'Sorry, they don't teach A-level Supernatural in school.'

'I honestly think it will just blow over in time.'

'Is that what you thought when you threw yourself into work after Megan died?'

'For God's sake, Mel, I *had* to go to work. We had a mortgage to pay, in case you've forgotten. Bills. Car to run. Clubs. Commitments. A tendency to like wine rather too much for someone whose mother was an alcoholic.'

If Mel had claws, they would have flexed. 'I'm nothing like that bitch.'

'We all deal with things in different ways.'

Another lapse into silence. Then, Tony said, 'Look, what happened to Megan was a terrible tragedy. It kills me every single day. I've often wondered what it would've been like with the two of them running about. Who would be the dominant one. The studious one. The practical one. The loud one. The quiet one. I'm as heartbroken as you are about Megan. Please don't forget that.'

'I thought life was going too well. I should have known better.'

'Everything will be fine. I promise.'

'Don't make promises you can't keep.'

He stood up. 'I love you. And that's one promise I *will* keep for all eternity. I'm going to order a takeaway. What do you fancy?'

'I'm not hungry.'

'You've got to eat.'

'I'll have some of yours.'

He looked about to protest, then walked to the kitchen to phone the local Tandoori. When he'd finished ordering, he called through and asked Mel if she wanted a cup of coffee.

'No, I…'

'Mel?'

Mel watched Chloe shuffle trancelike down the stairs. She held Ruby to her chest, patting the stuffed toy's back as if winding it. Her hair fell across her face in tangled strips.

Mel rushed to the bottom of the stairs, afraid her daughter might trip and fall. 'Chloe?'

Chloe stopped halfway down, wobbled, and then looked at her mother.

'Chloe? You all right, Pumpkin?'

When she spoke, her voice was low and husky. 'Can't you two keep the noise down? Me and Grandma are trying to get Megan to sleep.'

Mel's heart jump-started. 'But Megan's not here. She's in heaven.'

Chloe shook her head. 'She's upstairs.'

Tears stung the backs of Mel's eyes. 'But that imposs'

'Oh, get her,' Chloe said, adopting that dreadful croaky voice. 'Anyone would think she actually cared.'

Mel walked slowly up the stairs, goosebumps hatching all over her body. 'Wake up, Chloe! It's Mummy. You're dreaming.'

'Is that so?'

Mel tried to tell herself it was just her daughter standing on the stairs. No one else. Just Chloe. Frightened, confused and sleepwalking. Dead people didn't talk through rag dolls. Not in the real world.

'You think you're in control, don't you? But you're not. Your life is just one big accident waiting to happen.'

'Stop it!'

'What the hell's wrong with her?' Tony's said, his voice devoid of its usual mathematical certainty. 'Why's she talking like that?'

'I told you,' Mel said. 'I fucking well told you.'

'Wash your mouth out with soap,' Chloe said, in her best Grandma Audrey voice.

Mel eyed the rag doll as if it might leap from Chloe's arms and attack her.

'Chloe!' Tony shouted. 'Come on. Let's get you back to bed.'

'Here he is! The knight in shining armour come to rescue the damsel in distress.'

'I'm your father, and I'm'

'And I'm the Queen of Sheba.'

Tony stopped just behind Mel. 'You stop that right now.'

'Says the man with the biggest secret ever.'

'Chloe! I'm warning you. Pack it in.'

Mel glanced at Tony. He looked as pale as the moon. He pushed past her and picked up his daughter. Chloe cried out and started sobbing. She dropped the doll. It landed face down on the stairs, silent and still, no more malicious than a cushion.

Tony walked into Chloe's room with the sobbing child. Mel thought about following him, but she didn't think her shattered nerves could cope with anything else. She poured a glass of wine and drained it in one go. After refilling the glass, she sat in the chair near the fire. The heat did little to stop her shivering.

'Jesus Christ,' Mel whispered. 'This can't be real.'

Oh, it's real, all right. How else would she know those things about Megan? About Grandma Audrey falling down the stairs? You can dismiss it all you like, call it an overactive imagination, sleepwalking, fanciful nonsense, but you can't escape the truth: she knows things she can't possibly know.

Mel had never wanted a cigarette so much since she'd given up smoking five years ago. 'What the hell are we going to do?'

The empty room had no answers. The clock above the door ticked on towards a future that terrified her more than she could have ever imagined.

CHAPTER SIX

Most of Saturday passed without incident. Chloe had slept until mid-morning after Tony had carried her back to bed. She'd fallen asleep after Tony had retrieved Ruby from the stairs and tucked them up together. Mel had finished the bottle of wine before going to bed. After a brief discussion, during which Mel had accused Tony of burying his head in the sand, Tony had retired to bed on his own. He was hiding something. It wasn't lost on Mel what Chloe had said about him being 'The man with the biggest secret in the world'.

When the phone rang late that afternoon, Mel half-expected it to be Kerrie-Anne making up an excuse not to look after Chloe on Monday. It wasn't. It was the duty doctor at the local hospital where her father was seeing out his final days with terminal prostate cancer. The doctor believed him to be close to death.

Mel walked to the kitchen where Tony was marking school books at the table.

'Can you mind Chloe for a while?'

Tony didn't look up. 'I'm busy.'

'It's Dad. He's on his last legs. I need to go to the hospital.'

Tony put down his pen and rubbed his eyes. 'Shit. Sorry. Go. Where's Chloe?'

'Upstairs playing with her dolls' house.'

Mel grabbed her bag and coat and drove the half mile to Feelham Community Hospital in a daze. A doctor introduced himself as Harry Higgs, gave Mel's hand a small squeeze as if administering a dose of sympathy, and assured her that her father was not in any pain. He then left Mel alone with the hollowed-out shell of her dying parent.

She sat down in a brown leather chair next to the bed. His chest barely rose as he struggled to draw breath. His mouth hung open revealing a black cavernous hole that had once grinned, told jokes, savoured the taste of her home-baked pies, and complimented her on what a fine woman she'd turned out to be.

His hand hung over the side of the bed. Large veins stood proud of the skin, coursing through dark brown liver spots like tiny rivers. She took it in hers and held it tight. It felt warm.

She'd never blamed him for what had happened during her childhood at Rose Cottage. He'd just been trying to earn a living. Keep the wolf from the door. Only problem was, the wolf was already inside the door her mother.

Her father was a chef on nuclear submarines. Based up in Scotland, he'd had no idea of his wife's behaviour whilst he'd been away. The days that Mel had spent locked in the basement whilst her mother had 'entertained' her male guests. Her mother's alcoholism. It was as if she had two personalities: the dutiful wife, and the drunken bitch who neglected her daughter in favour of cheap booze and even cheaper men.

Mel truly believed the only reason she was still alive was because her mother had fallen down the basement steps and broken her neck when Mel was eight years old. Because of her father's naval career, she'd been taken into temporary care, and later went to live with her father's brother and his wife. Uncle John and Aunt Cathy had helped Mel overcome her childhood trauma with patience and love, guiding her and supporting her through school, university and teacher training.

Although her life had been forever tarnished by Megan's death, it had been on the good side of bearable up until the visit to Feelham Theatre. She had a loving husband, a great job and a beautiful daughter. If she'd been offered any one of these things when she'd been a helpless child cowering in the freezing basement of Rose Cottage, she would have laughed and said she could never be that lucky.

Just being in the hospital reminded her of Megan's short tragic life. A huge part of Mel had died with the child. She visited the grave in Feelham Cemetery once a week to lay flowers and talk to her daughter. Tell her how much she missed her and loved her. Kneeling at the grave, touching the bright purple stones as if they might somehow absorb her grief and give it back to the earth.

Mel and Tony had almost lost their marriage as well as their daughter. She'd been aware she wasn't being fair, that Tony was grieving in his own way, but when it came to expressing that grief, they were like chalk and cheese. Tony threw himself into work. Fought hard to get promotion to head of year. Lived by targets. Took comfort in the stable structure of his career, and sought solace in the practicalities of mathematics. Almost seemed to accept his daughter's death as a casualty of the random law of chaos.

Mel knew this assessment wasn't fair. But what was fair? Every time you thought you'd found happiness, life threw a great big rock at your head. Time wasn't a great healer, but it did take some of the sting out of the tears.

It was almost seven years since Megan had been torn from her arms. Megan had never left the hospital. Her short life had been filled with two unsuccessful operations, medical staff testing and probing her, tubes sticking out of her tiny body, needles, unfulfilled promises, and her parents standing helplessly by as she lost her short battle for the right to live.

Mel had never believed in God. The concept of some wise old man sitting on a throne above the clouds passing judgement was too simplistic for her. But during the three months of Megan's brief life, Mel had prayed every day to the mystical man in the white robe. Begging Him to let her child live. Promising to be a better person. Wearing her own crown of thorns. Offering her soul, naked and torn.

As suspected, God had confirmed what she'd already known: He didn't exist. He was just a load of made up mumbo-jumbo to satisfy people's need for order amongst the chaos. How could He let her beautiful tiny bundle of life just slip away before she'd even spoken her first word? Taken her first step? Given her mummy her first kiss? She hadn't even held her. Cuddled her. Bathed her. Her only memory of Megan was watching her encased in that incubator attached to tubes and monitors, her tiny body trying to fight the insurmountable odds stacked against her. She would always remember that incubator as Megan's coffin.

God had gone missing once again. Just as He had when she was a child alone in the basement at Rose Cottage with the freezing cold damp air clinging to her like a second skin. Her stomach pleading for food, her heart pleading for help. But God didn't seem to be very interested in the plight of an eight-year-old child. He'd left it up to her to risk her mother's wrath by stealing a can opener from the kitchen drawer and secreting it behind an empty wooden beer keg in the corner of the basement. At least it gave her access to the dozens of tins of fruit her father brought home with him from his time away. Pineapple chunks were her favourite, along with pear halves. The sweetened juice was like a small taste of heaven to her parched throat. The huge, industrial tins of coffee weren't of much use, or the massive drums of cooking oil, but her father seemed to think storing for war was a 'necessity in uncertain times'.

God didn't seem too concerned about her drunken mother standing at the top of the basement steps, either, threatening Mel with *The Hole* for the heinous crime of knocking on the door and begging to be let out. The basement was bad enough, but nowhere near as dreadful as *The Hole:* an access hatch to a sewer pipe running beneath the house, reached only by a heavy iron manhole cover. The stench in there was disgusting. The darkness seemed to seep right inside your bones and paint your very soul black. There was a metal ladder running down to the pipe, and the only way to stop falling into the raw sewerage was to hold onto the ladder for all you were worth. After a few hours of this punishment, it was all she could do to prize her fingers free of the freezing cold ladder.

The day her mother had fallen down the steps and broken her neck, Mel had wondered if God had finally answered her prayers. Prior to the fall, the old witch had been ranting and raving about something which only made sense to her pickled brain.

For the first day, Mel had sat in the corner of the basemen, paralysed by fear. Not because of the possibility her mother might be dead, but in case she wasn't. So deep-rooted was Mel's fear of her, she believed if she so much as twitched, the bitch would spring to life and beat her black and blue with a broom handle.

By day two, she'd dared to get up and inspect the motionless body lying at the bottom of the steps. A pool of blood had spread out beside her head, and her eyes were staring at the ceiling, wide and unblinking. Her lips had turned blue, and her front teeth looked as if they were trying to eat her swollen bottom lip.

Mel never left the basement of her own volition. A paperboy had noticed the front door banging in the wind three days after the fall and had called the police. A local bobby had carried her out of that basement in his arms, her legs too weak to walk, her mind too numb to think.

Mel had never set foot in the family home again. It would be sold upon her father's death, and good riddance. Although thirty years had passed since her mother's death, the pain was like a festering wound that would never heal.

Her father made a noise in the back of his throat and opened his eyes.

'Dad?'

Breath rattled in his chest. 'Melanie.'

She squeezed his hand. 'Shh.'

'I'm… sorry.'

'Please, don't fret, Dad. You've got nothing to be sorry for.'

He shook his head. A tear trickled from the corner of one eye. He looked at the ceiling, seemingly transfixed by the overhead fluorescent light. Mel thought he was slipping away, and then he looked back at her, eyes wide, lips peeled back, tongue clacking against his dentures as if trying to prod them into life.

'Dad?'

He gripped her hand, nails digging into the flesh.

'What is it?'

'Ladybird, ladybird, fly away home, your house is on fire, and your children are gone.'

Mel was about to say something comforting, reassuring, when his grip relaxed. He slumped back against the pillows, eyes glazed over, dentures slipping from his mouth and coming to rest on his bottom lip as if to signal their life was over, too.

CHAPTER SEVEN

Peter King was in a buoyant mood. If life got any better, he would be in the company of angels and bronzed muscular men waiting to tend to his every whim. The angels were solely for the purpose of feeding him grapes and general pampering. When it came to the pleasure dome, it was strictly testicles and testosterone for him.

Part of the reason for his good mood was a young man by the name of Nathan who was currently asleep on his king-size bed. It had cost a pretty penny to secure the boy's services for an unlimited time, but money was no object. The occasional indulgence of a rent boy was healthy for the spirit. With Viagra added to the nation's libido, King anticipated a long night of sexual gratification.

He walked into the wine cellar of his large detached house. The cellar had a far more important role than just storing vintage wines. It was also home to four upright freezers, each colour-matched to their contents. Purple, orange, yellow and turquoise. A local handyman had been only too willing to spray paint the freezers for the princely sum of five hundred pounds and enough tea to cause a world shortage.

King had been sorely tempted to shoot the swine when he'd dared to stink out the downstairs loo with the aftermath of his crude proletarian diet. The man was not worthy of life, but he'd made a decent job of the freezers, and for that alone King had paid him his due and parted company amicably.

His trip to the wine cellar was not solely to select a vintage wine for the evening. It was more rooted in the contents of the purple freezer. Today was an important anniversary. One of nineteen pencilled in on his very busy calendar. It seemed even more appropriate to celebrate, because they were about to embark on a fresh game of One False Move on Christmas Day.

He opened the freezer door. In the bottom drawer, encased in clear polythene bags, the severed heads of the first two Purples King had chosen for One False Move. The first one had only lasted three months. A spineless wretch who hadn't deserved the gift of life. The other, an ugly girl with a bad complexion, had fared slightly better; she'd lasted just shy of a year. Her poor appearance had been compensated by tenacity. She'd also sported the rather pretty name of Charlotte in her former life as a free-thinking spirit with hippy tendencies. A nice warm name, Charlotte. A pretty-flower name wasted on this unfortunate toadstool. She was much better suited to her new moniker, Purple-two.

In the next drawer, Purples three and four sat in their icy tomb. Both unremarkable and fortunate to have a place in the trophy cabinet. But it was Purple-five who had brought King and his good mood to the wine cellar today. It was the anniversary of her death. Of all those who'd passed this way, Purple-five was his favourite by quite some distance. One or two of the others, particularly Yellow-one, had run her close, but Yellow-one lacked Purple-five's spunk, for want of a better word. There was a fine line between arrogance and bravery; Purple-five had stood on the right side of that line.

Not a bad looking girl. Long blonde hair. Sharp blue eyes. King sometimes thought she stood comparison with Maid Marion. Unlike the others, Purple-five had sported no ridiculous ambition to be a pop star or a film star. She'd finally succumbed to death's waiting arms courtesy of a crude attempt to recreate a French execution with a modified guillotine.

Purple-five had caught the train back to Oxford with him without fuss or fanfare. She might not have been so keen to take the journey had she known the 'execution' would turn into a disaster. The guillotine had failed to sever the head, and

Purple-five had still been breathing and gurgling when he'd hacked her head off with a carving knife.

King now had a saying to match 'Never underestimate thine enemy'. It ran something like 'Never underestimate how hard it is to sever a head with a knife'. Getting through the spinal cord and nerves, not to mention the thyroid gland, trachea, oesophagus, jugular veins and the carotid artery had taught King to invest in a chainsaw for future executions of this type. A lot messier, but a damn site easier than a faulty guillotine and a carving knife.

The whole experience of Purple-five's death had left King with an even greater dislike of the French and their inadequate means of human disposal. He'd consigned himself to more British methods from that day forth, although when you drilled down into what actually happened at some executions it was a pretty murky subject to say the least.

King opened the drawer holding Purple-five's head. Even though frozen, and as well-preserved as could be expected after losing the support of its blood supply and other vital organs, she wasn't in prime condition. Ice crystals had formed in the blood, giving her a pock-marked complexion to match that of the unfortunate Purple-two. Her remaining eye, wide and staring, looked inwards at her nose, and her lips were pulled back in a deathly rictus grin. Death had not lent beauty to Purple-five, but that didn't detract from King's admiration of her. She was of greater substance than all the purples, yellows, oranges and turquoises put together. Or taken apart, depending on which way you looked at it.

He leaned into the freezer compartment and air-kissed the frozen head, careful not to make contact with the ice. He'd made that dreadful mistake to his cost the first time he'd shown affection to Purple-five on the first anniversary of her death. His lips had become glued to the ice, and it had taken a considerable effort to tear them free. He'd had to claim cold sores for the best part of a month to stave off awkward questions regarding the damage.

He'd found Purple-five wandering around Paddington Station almost eight years ago. Unlike her successor, the dancing horse, Purple-six, Purple-five seemed like a smart girl. Educated. Decent background. But like most of the other girls occupying the freezers, at odds with a family who had no wish to see their precious pup spend an impoverished life for the sake of creative art. Van Gough's act of self-mutilation had clearly had a far greater effect than the artist could ever have imagined. A warning to all parents to crush the dreams of children if they ever dared to mention art as a career choice.

King stepped back from the freezer and gazed at the head, remembering the moment he'd first seen her. She'd been staring at the arrivals and departures boards, long blonde hair reaching down to the waistband of her faded blue jeans.

'I can never understand those things,' King had said. And then, a well-practised joke. 'I don't know whether I'm coming or going, never mind the trains.'

The girl had smiled. 'Me neither.'

'Where are you heading?'

A long pause, followed by a shrug. She ran a hand through her hair and flicked it to one side.

'Would you like a coffee? My treat.'

'I don't…'

'You'd be doing an old man a favour. I'm about to go to Oxford to visit my sister.' He stroked his fake beard. 'If I'm honest, I'm a bit apprehensive. She's rather prone to being bossy.'

'Oh.'

'She's older than me. By a day. We're twins.'

'Wow!'

'Seventy years and forty days is a long time to be bossed around by a grouchy sister.'

The girl's eyes widened. 'Seventy?'

King nodded, pleased. 'Yes.'

'But…'

'I don't look it? It's a family thing. None of us look our age. Aunty Dotty's ninety, and you'd be hard-pressed to believe she's even retired.'

'Really?'

King fought a compulsive urge to take that horrendous word, *really*, and stamp it in a muddy puddle. 'Aunt Dotty's gifted in the art of make-up. And she's a rather elegant dresser. But even so…'

'She sounds… interesting.'

'She is.' He eyed the leather satchel in the girl's left hand. 'School books?'

She smiled. 'I don't go to school.'

'No?'

They discussed this last point over coffee and scones in the grubby buffet bar. He learned that Amy May Constable was sixteen, from Woking, and she wanted to go to art school to indulge her calling.

'What a wonderful ambition,' King said, for once mildly impressed.

Her parents seemed to have other ideas. 'They want me to go to university and train to be a pharmacist.'

'A pill-pusher?' King said, shocked that any parent could have such a lowly ambition for their offspring. In more natural company, this declaration might have sparked a lengthy discussion about the evil nature of the pharmaceutical companies, and their penchant for creating illnesses to ply the human race with useless pills to contain those illnesses. He rarely took painkillers, fearful that his blood would turn to the consistency of his mother's gravy and no longer support his vital organs.

Amy shrugged. 'I don't want to be a pharmacist. I'm not doing A-levels. I don't even like science and maths.'

King had found his soul mate. He couldn't think of anything worse than crunching numbers and mixing potions, the latter of which was akin to witchcraft.

'Then you must stick to your guns, dear. Stick to your guns and fire a salvo across their foredeck.'

Amy seemed conversant with guns, but in the dark with foredecks.

'So, what are you going to do?'

She shrugged.

'Have you come to London to fulfil your artistic ambition?'

'Maybe.'

'Or just to make a point?'

Amy tossed her half-eaten scone on the chipped, china plate. 'Both, I suppose.'

'Perhaps you need a little breathing space. Time to reflect.'

'Maybe.'

Maybe. Another dreadful word. Such non-committal drivel had no place in the beautiful English language. And you could add *like* to that list, along with dozens of others spawned from illiterate minds.

'How do you fancy accompanying me to my sister's? I'm only going for three days, and your presence would make the visit a lot more bearable.'

'Oh, no, I don't'

King moved in for the kill. 'She used to teach art at a local school.'

'Really?'

God give me strength! 'Yes.'

Amy looked at the satchel sitting on the chair next to her. 'Do you think she'd take a look at my drawings?'

'She'd be thrilled.'

It took another ten minutes of persuasion, but Amy May Constable relented when King assured her that his 'sister' had connections with the Oxford Art Academy. It was doubtful whether such a place existed, but it sounded good enough to hook the fish and reel it in.

Amy hadn't reacted well to her transformation from wannabe art student to Purple-five. The girl had spirit, as his mother was apt to say before cancer had robbed her of the ability to speak. In fact, Purple-five had fought the restraints like a hellcat on heat once the drugs had worn off.

It had taken weeks to tame her. Break her in like a wild horse with a mixture of electric shocks and beatings. But rather than deter him, Purple-five had excited him. Proposed a challenge. And given a decent account of herself over the years.

King stared at the distorted icy features in the freezer. It was a terrible shame she'd lost an eye at the end, but the nature of the game left little room for caution. Purple-five had been hit in the eye with a plum stone after three days in the stocks. Another two days at the whipping post had killed any last lingering remnants of her feisty spirit.

Amy May Constable's transition from promising art student to human game piece for One False Move had been vast enough to render her unrecognisable. King had burned her drawings, which were of a reasonable quality considering her lack of tutoring. She had a genuine flair for shading and perspective, not to mention screaming and cursing. A girl of many talents, you might say.

He slid the drawer back in and closed the freezer door. 'Happy anniversary, Purple-five.'

It would be Turquoise-two's second's anniversary in ten days' time. King doubted whether he would bother to honour it this year. An unremarkable girl who'd barely given six months service before death had relieved her of her duties.

He grabbed a bottle of Château D'Yquem from the wall-to-wall wine rack opposite the freezers and headed upstairs for a celebratory drink with his latest lover. A toast to all who had gone before, particularly Purple-five, God rest her soul.

He was almost joyous enough to burst into a rendition of 'Good King Wenceslas' and hang a stocking over the fireplace for Father Christmas to fill.

CHAPTER EIGHT

Mel had stayed with her father for half an hour at the hospital, holding his lifeless hand, trying to convince herself that at least he was at peace now, free of the pain which had ravaged his dying body for the last few weeks. She'd kissed him gently on the top of his head and driven home in a strange surreal state.

She hung her coat up and walked into the lounge. Tony was sitting on the sofa, a pile of papers on the seat next to him. He looked up, pen hovering above a red text book. 'Is he all right?'

Mel shook her head. 'He's gone.'

'Oh, shit. I'm so sorry, Mel.'

His words seemed hollow. 'It's not as if it wasn't expected, is it?'

'No, but all the same...'

'Where's Chloe?'

'At the kitchen table.'

'I'll go and tell her.'

Tony busied himself tidying his paperwork. 'Would you like me to do it?'

'No.'

Chloe was sitting at the table, a large drawing pad taking up most of the surface, coloured pencils scattered about her.

'Hiya, Pumpkin.'

Chloe didn't look up. She wrapped an arm around the pad as if guarding a massive secret.

'What are you drawing?'

Chloe picked up a blue pencil and scribbled furiously.

'Can Mummy see?'

Chloe shook her head, hair whipping the sides of her face.

'Could you could put the pencil down a minute and listen to Mummy?'

Chloe responded by dragging the pencil across the pad hard enough to make the tip break. She tossed it to one side and picked up a red one, licked the tip, and then added something else to the drawing. Her face was a mask of concentration, tongue poking out, clamped between her teeth.

'Granddad's passed away,' Mel said, the last dregs of patience draining out of her.

Chloe didn't look up. 'I know. Grandma Audrey told me.'

Mel's heart fell into her stomach. 'When?'

'When he left his body.'

'But'

'It's all right. He's been a good boy and gone to heaven.'

Mel swallowed hard. 'Did she tell you that?'

'*She* has got a name.'

Mel held onto the edge of the table. 'Did Grandma Audrey say that?'

Chloe nodded. Her hair fell like a screen around the drawing.

Tony walked into the kitchen. Mel glanced at him. She wanted to grab him, shake him, demand he make all this go away. She wanted to tell Chloe to put down her pencils and stop scaring the crap out of her.

She leaned closer to Chloe. 'Is Grandma Audrey here now?'

Chloe shook her head. 'She's got better things to do with her bloody time than hang round this dump all day.'

'Chloe!' Tony shouted. 'You pack that language in right now.'

Chloe laughed. 'Right.'

Mel thought the laugh was worse than the defiance.

Chloe looked at Tony, eyes dark with mischief. 'You said, "fuck" when Mummy made you stay at home to look after me.'

Tony's eyes confirmed to Mel the validity of the claim. 'But I was upstairs and you were down here.'

Chloe returned her attention to the drawing. 'I know.'

Tony poured a glass of water.

'How did you hear Daddy if you were downstairs?' Mel asked, not really wanting to know the answer, but compelled to ask.

'Grandma Audrey told me.'

'She's lying,' Tony said.

Chloe licked the tip of her pencil and stared at Tony. 'I don't think so.'

Tony took a deep breath and sighed. 'Don't be so'

'Grandma Audrey also told me you like a teacher at your school.'

'I like a lot of people,' Tony said.

'Not the *way* you like Stephanie Wallace. Right, Daddy?'

'Who the hell is *she*?' Mel asked.

Tony drained his glass of water as if trying to cool the blush on his cheeks. 'No one. She's talking rubbish.'

'Grandma Audrey said you never could face up to your responsibilities.'

Mel banged the table. 'Stop it! Stop it right now!'

Chloe jumped and almost toppled off the chair. Tony stomped into the lounge, wiping his mouth, muttering something unintelligible under his breath.

A tear slipped from the corner of Chloe's eye. 'Why are you shouting at me?'

Mel stepped away from the table, searching for signs of Grandma Audrey in her daughter.

'Are you mad at me, Mummy?'

Mel shook her head and brushed a strand of hair out of Chloe's face. 'No.'

'I'm going to miss Granddad.'

'Me too.'

'He was nice.'

'Yes, he was. But at least he's not sick anymore.'

'No.'

'Can Mummy see what you've been drawing?'

Chloe folded her arms across the paper. 'When it's finished.'

'Do you want to give Mummy a clue?'

'No. Shut the door behind you.'

Mel thought Chloe was kidding at first. When it became clear she wasn't, she asked why.

'To give us both some privacy.'

Mel almost bit her tongue in half trying not to respond, but she was in no mood to rock a sinking ship. She walked into the lounge, closed the door, and found Tony tidying papers and rummaging through his briefcase.

'We need to talk.'

Tony didn't look at her. 'If it's about what Chloe said, there's nothing to say.'

'Is that right? So how does she know about this woman at school?'

'She doesn't.'

'How would she even know her name?'

'Maybe she's heard me mention her on the phone or something.'

'So, there is a Stephanie Wallace?'

'She used to teach English.'

Mel walked to the window. Folded her arms. Shook her head slowly. 'I see.'

Tony sighed. 'And what's that supposed to mean?'

'Nothing.'

After a lengthy pause, Tony fastened his briefcase and sat down on the sofa. 'I think you're reading too much into all this… nonsense.'

'Nonsense?'

'That's the definition of something that doesn't make sense, isn't it?'

'Don't fucking well patronise me.'

'I'm not. I'm just trying to be'

'Perhaps you ought to try honesty for once.'

'I am being honest.'

'And I'm being unreasonable?'

'That's not what I said.'

'Are you screwing someone else, Tony?'

'No.'

'Because in case it's slipped your notice, my father has just died, my daughter is scaring the crap out of me, and you're not fucking well helping.'

Tony looked at her as if swearing trumped having an affair with some tart at work. 'Chloe's only in the kitchen.'

'And?'

'Nothing.'

'Just when I thought it couldn't get any worse.'

Tony's lips moved, as if chewing over his next words before he set them loose. 'Just remember I love you.'

'You wouldn't be the first bloke to love his wife and screw around.'

'I'm not screwing around.'

Mel took a deep breath. 'You're bound to say that, aren't you?'

Chloe rescued him from having to reply. 'I'm ready.'

'For what, Pumpkin?' Mel said, momentarily thrown off track.

'To show you my picture, silly.'

Mel forced a weak smile, comforted by the fact her daughter was now talking as a four-year-old child should. 'Okay.'

They walked into the kitchen together, hostilities on hold. Chloe stood to one side of the table shuffling from one foot to the other like she needed to pee. 'Do you like it?'

At first, Mel's mind refused to accept what she was seeing. Blank out the dreadful implications of the picture. Chloe had drawn a near-perfect picture of their house, right down to the porch lantern and the coconut welcome mat outside the front door. There was even a superb illustration of their VW Golf parked in the bay. Orange and yellow flames belched from the front room window. So convincing their authenticity, the paper actually looked as if it was on fire.

'Do you like it, Mummy?'

'I…'

'Why have you drawn the house on fire, Chloe?' Tony asked.

Chloe shrugged.

As if the fire wasn't enough to render Mel mute, her mind incapable of rational thought, the giant ladybird flying away from the house with Chloe riding on its back was.

Chloe asked again, 'Don't you like it, Mummy?'

Mel wanted to tear the picture into a thousand pieces and throw it out the back door. 'I… don't… know… what… to… say.'

'It's great,' Tony said, from a faraway land. 'It's just not very nice drawing the house on fire like that.'

'What would you prefer I draw?' Chloe shouted. 'Matchstick men?'

Mel stepped back, shocked by this sudden burst of anger. 'No, it's…'

'Not to your taste?'

'Don't talk to Mummy like that,' Tony said.

'Like what? It's only a picture.'

'That's not the point, young lady.'

'It's fine,' Mel said. 'It's a great picture. Come on, let's go get some pizza.'

Chloe grinned. 'Yay! Can I have any topping?'

'You name it, Picasso.'

'Ham and pineapple?'

'Ham and pineapple it is.'

Mel left Tony studying the picture. Sod him. She needed to get out of the house for a while. Away from the picture that brought her father's last words to life in the glorious detail.

CHAPTER NINE

By Monday morning, Chloe's picture was pinned to the side of the fridge-freezer with magnetic letters, and Mel's worries were pinned to her heart with lead weights. The rest of the weekend had passed without incident. Mel hadn't spoken to Tony, apart from discussing her father's burial and paying the funeral costs out of their own pocket until his estate could settle the bill. Tony had complained that her father should have had a funeral plan in place. Mel had told him to take his sanctimonious mathematical approach to everything and jump in Feelham River.

Mel dropped Chloe off at Kerrie-Anne's and drove to school in a state of shock. She parked, watching rain bouncing off the windscreen like silver bullets. She had no idea how she would get through the day. After barely sleeping Saturday night, she'd fared slightly better last night courtesy of a bottle of wine, waking at just past 4 a.m. with a dry mouth and a bladder fit to burst.

To make matters worse, she'd slept in the spare room. The mattress was as lumpy as Tony's mashed potato. She'd tried to convince herself that Tony would never have an affair, but the more she'd thought about it, the more convinced she'd become it was true. Chloe hadn't plucked the information out of thin air. It had come straight from her mother's spiteful tongue courtesy of Ruby Rag Doll.

Mel busied herself opening a packet of Benson and Hedges cigarettes. She held the pack to her nose and sniffed. They smelled so good. So inviting. She slid one out and clamped it between her lips. Tony hated smoking, but that only acted as a spur to start again. He'd never failed to throw statistical data at her when she'd smoked. How many years the damn things took off your life.

How you breathed better when you didn't smoke. Smelled better. He'd stopped short at look better. Sod him, she didn't care about his opinions anymore.

She grabbed a cheap throwaway lighter from the glovebox and rolled the wheel.

You'll regret it! You're just doing this to spite Tony.

'And that's a bad thing?'

One puff, and you'll be hooked. Watching the clock in class, willing away the time until the next break so as you can top up your body with deadly toxins.

Mel's finger stilled on the lighter's wheel.

Not to mention getting ratty with all and sundry if you haven't had your poisonous fix.

Mel sucked on the cigarette. This action evoked a childhood memory. Thirteen. Sitting with Eileen Hislop at the back of Feelham Park, working their way through a pack of Marlboro Lights. Eileen had been as sick as a dog. Never touched another cigarette again. But Mel had been hooked. Five-a-day had turned into ten-a-day by the time she'd reached teacher training college. Ten had turned to twenty by the time she'd fallen pregnant with Megan.

She slipped the cigarette back in the packet and threw the box and the lighter in the glove box. She walked into the school, head down, rain driving against her body. Lightning slashed the sky as she closed the door against the howling, anguished cry of the wind.

She hadn't travelled to work with any other ambition than getting through the day in one piece and trying to keep her emotions in check, but as she walked along the hallway, past the wooden lockers and cubbyholes, the pictures on the wall depicting 'doing' verbs drawn by the children, rows of pegs with names of Year One pupils above them, she made a snap decision to have a word with the head. Explain things. She couldn't go on like this. It wasn't yet eight in the morning and she was already exhausted.

Charles Honeywell was a decent man. A patient man. A listening man. She removed her beige raincoat, took a deep breath, and knocked on the door.

'Come in.'

Honeywell sat behind a large mahogany desk. A slim man of average build, his intelligent blue eyes peered out from behind black-framed glasses like gems in a display case. 'Good morning, Mel. Dreadful weather. So much for a white Christmas, eh?'

'Can I have a moment?'

'Take a pew.'

Mel sat in a seat usually reserved for errant children and worried parents.

'You look as if the universe has charged you with the responsibility of having to fathom its deepest secrets.'

Mel brushed rain from her face. 'My father's just passed away.'

'Oh, dear. I'm sorry to hear that. Please accept my condolences.'

'It's not as if it wasn't expected. He's been ill for quite some time. It's just…'

'Nothing prepares us for death. The shock is never lessened by foresight.'

Tears, which had been waiting in the wings, took that as their cue and flooded Mel's face. Her body rocked and convulsed. Honeywell stood poised, as unrehearsed as a stagehand thrust into the limelight and asked to take on the leading role.

Mel leaned forward, hands clawing at her face, her body consumed by this unexpected wave of raw emotion. Honeywell plucked a tissue from a box kept on the desk. He waited for Mel's sobbing to turn to sniffles, and handed it over. Mel snorted snot and wiped her nose. The tissue turned to an instant sodden mess. Honeywell conjured another, like a magician performing tricks.

'I'm sorry,' Mel said, gesturing helplessly at her face. 'I don't know where that came from.'

Honeywell walked back to his seat. 'From your heart, Mel. It would be a stone-cold person indeed who didn't feel the loss of a loved one.'

Mel forced a smile, grateful the headmaster had a compassionate nature. She stared out the window at the skeletal trees standing naked against the darkening sky. 'Thank you.'

'For what?'

'For understanding.'

'It's part of my job, Mel.'

After a long awkward silence, Mel said, 'Can I ask you something?'

Honeywell brushed a hand across his thinning grey hair. 'Of course.'

'Do you believe in life after death?'

'Why do you ask?'

'I just wondered.'

He gazed out the window. 'I suppose anything is possible.'

'What about reincarnation?'

'To be honest, I've never given it much thought. Has something happened with your father to provoke such thoughts?'

'Not really.'

'So, what's brought this on.'

'If I tell you, do you promise it will go no further?'

'I'm guilty of many things, but being a gossip isn't one of them. What's said in this office stays in this office.'

Mel hesitated. What if he thought she was cracking up? Losing the plot. He might send her on indefinite leave and seek to have her removed from the school. The last thing she needed right now was to lose her job on top of everything else.

'Mel?'

'It's my daughter.'

'What about her?'

'She's…'

Honeywell studied her as if she might be about to go into emotional meltdown again. He plucked a fresh tissue from his diminishing stock. 'Take your time.'

Without pause, Mel told him everything that had happened with Chloe. From the episode at Feelham Theatre, to the detailed drawing of her father's deathbed message. Everything, except the part about Grandma Audrey, because she couldn't bring herself to explain her own broken childhood.

Honeywell was silent long enough for Mel to fear for her job. 'I'm sorry. I shouldn't have'

'And this all started when you took her to the theatre?'

Mel nodded. 'She was fine before we went inside. Excited about Christmas. Looking forward to the pantomime.'

'How strange. And she… choked later on that night?'

'Yes.'

'A nightmare, perhaps?'

'It was more than that. There were ugly red marks around her neck. She looked at me and Tony as if she hated us. Then she said, "Put me in the fucking cage and be done with it."'

'Good grief.'

'Said we were all cowards.'

'What a strange thing to say.'

'I want to help her. Be there for her. But how can I when I don't have a clue what's wrong with her? It's as if she's a different child. Older. In so much pain.'

'This does seem… rather bizarre.'

'The picture of the house on fire looks as if it's been drawn by an accomplished artist, not a four-year-old child.'

'Perhaps you should take the rest of the term off. Get yourself straightened out. Have a rest. Come back refreshed in the New Year.'

'What about the Christmas play?'

'Miss Hargreaves can cover that. Now, get yourself off home and take care of that little girl.'

'But'

'And that's an order.'

Mel didn't know whether to laugh or cry. 'Thank you. Thank you so much.' She left the office and walked back to the car with a head that felt as dark and full of menace as the weather.

CHAPTER TEN

Mel drove straight from the school to Kerrie-Anne's, thunder rolling across the near-black sky. She explained to the childminder that Charles Honeywell had given her some time off.

Kerrie-Anne invited her in. 'I'm not surprised. What with your dad and everything else. You need to look after yourself.'

'I doubt I'll be going back to school until next term. But I'll pay you up until Christmas Eve.'

'Thanks. I appreciate that.'

'I'd be grateful if the stuff with Chloe goes no further.'

'It goes without saying.'

After five minutes idle chat about the weather, Kerrie-Anne went to fetch Chloe from the playroom where she was playing dolls with two other pre-school kids.

Whilst she waited for her daughter, Mel tried to stop black thoughts tumbling through her mind. Tried to rationalise what had happened. Make sense of it. It was like trying to understand quantum physics. Mel had always known Chloe was bright. She'd walked at nine months. Talked in basic sentences by eighteen months. Drew pictures she had no right to draw at four years old. Mel had no discernible gift for art. As for Tony, he barely got past matchstick men. His gift for figures was strictly mathematical.

Kerrie-Anne returned from the playroom without Chloe. In her hand, a sheet of A3 paper. A look in her eyes that warned of disaster.

'What is it?'

Kerrie-Anne lay the paper on the kitchen table.

Mel stared at the picture, eyes wide, mouth hanging open. Depicted on the page, a guillotine reminiscent of those used in French executions. A headless woman in a bright purple tracksuit knelt one side of the apparatus. Blood ran down the sides of the guillotine and formed puddles either side of the base.

'Chloe drew that, Mel.'

The childminder's voice sounded as distant as the thunder rolling across the sky. Mel stared at the severed head lying in the dirt, its long blonde hair streaked crimson by the victim's blood. Although the head was facedown, obliterating the features, Mel couldn't help thinking the woman reminded her of Chloe. Older, but as she would have imagined her.

'How can she even draw like that?' Kerrie-Anne asked.

'I… don't… know…'

'It's so'

Chloe walked into the kitchen. 'Hi, Mummy.'

'Hi, Pumpkin.'

'Do you like my picture?'

Mel tried to appear nonchalant. Act as if a French-style execution was the most natural thing in the world for a child to draw.

'What's the picture about?' Kerrie-Anne asked.

Chloe shrugged.

'Why did you draw it?' Mel asked. 'What were you… thinking about?'

'I wasn't thinking nothing, silly. I was *feeling*.'

'Feeling?'

Chloe nodded and plugged her thumb into her mouth.

Mel stared at the bright-red blood splashed across the page. It appeared to move, as if coming to life. She squeezed her eyes shut, opened them again. The picture was once again still. Small mercies. 'Did you see something like this in a book?'

Chloe shook her head.

'On the computer?'

'No.'

'Where?'

'Why are you asking me silly questions?'

'Mummy's just confused, Chloe.'

'Maybe you ought to open your eyes, then,' Chloe said, in that older voice that chilled Mel's blood.

Mel looked at Kerrie-Anne and tried to apologise with her eyes. 'I'll get off.'

The childminder looked relieved. 'Okay. See you in the New Year.'

Mel told Chloe to put her coat on.

Chloe asked, 'What are you going to do with the picture?'

Mel looked at the damned thing as if might actually bite. 'I'

'Do you want me to keep it?' Kerrie-Anne offered.

'Do you want it?' Chloe countered.

Kerrie-Anne smiled. 'I'd love it.'

Chloe seemed satisfied. She walked to the hallway to grab her coat.

When Chloe was out of earshot, Mel told Kerrie-Anne to throw it away.

'I'll put it away somewhere. Just in case she asks about it next year.'

'I owe you, Kerrie.'

The childminder rested a hand on Mel's arm, much the same way as the doctor had when he'd left Mel alone with her dying father. 'No probs. Have a great Christmas.'

'You, too.'

Chloe fell asleep on the short journey home. Mel carried her from the car and straight upstairs to bed. She laid her on top of the duvet, drew her pink Minnie Mouse curtains, and tiptoed from the room. She just needed an hour to get her head straight. Rearrange the furniture as her father used to say.

She resisted an urge to go to the fridge and pour a glass of wine.

You're turning into your mother.

She sat on the sofa, tucked her feet up under her.

What are you going to do next? Lock Chloe in the basement?

No worries on that score. The poky little house didn't have one. The sooner they moved, the better. They might get a chance to relax for once without being on top of each other.

That won't solve anything. Another bedroom and a decent-sized garden won't make Chloe's bizarre behaviour disappear, will it?

Mel wrestled with an urge to go back to the car and fetch the cigarettes from the glove box. She was in danger of failing Chloe every bit as much as her own mother had failed her all those years ago.

'I'm nothing like my mother,' Mel whispered, sucking the tip of her finger and inhaling imaginary smoke. 'I'm not a cruel and vindictive bitch like her.'

There's more than one way to neglect a child.

'I'm doing my best.'

That's what they all say. But are you? Are you, really?

'Yes.' She sucked the tip of her finger again. Harder. Biting down on the nail.

What do you think the pictures mean? Fires. Guillotines. What next? A crazed axeman chopping them all to pieces?

'Shut up,' Mel shouted, half-convinced her mother had somehow got inside her head. 'I can't do this anymore. I can't cope.'

That's right. Shut up shop and run away like you always do.

Mel stared at the wall, trying to lose herself in its blank magnolia canvas, convinced that she was being punished for failing Megan. Failing Chloe. Failing herself.

You've not much going for you, have you? Even your husband's at it with some tart at school.

A scream interrupted her thoughts. She bounded up the stairs two at a time. Ran into Chloe's room and stood panting just inside the door. Her daughter was sitting on the end of the bed, Ruby Rag Doll hanging limply in her hand.

Chloe stared at her, eyes wide, the ghost of a smile on her lips.

Mel couldn't see any trace of her daughter in those eyes. The smile spoke of a thousand deadly secrets. 'Are you all right?'

Chloe nodded.

'Did you have a bad dream?'

'No.'

'Would you like some lunch?'

'Not hungry.'

'You need to eat.'

'Why?'

'To grow up into a big strong girl.'

'What's the point of growing up?'

'To have a nice happy life.'

Chloe shook her head. 'Not going to happen.'

'You'

'Why did they want me to do stupid bloody A-levels?'

'Who?'

'My parents.'

'But'

'I hate science.'

Mel walked to within a few feet of her daughter. 'Your… parents?'

'What about them?'

'What are they called?'

Without missing a beat, Chloe said, 'Jenny and Robert.'

'Do they live in Feelham?'

'No.'

'Where?'

'Woking.'

'But that's a long way away. You've never been to Woking.'

'Have.'

'When?'

'Before I died.'

Even though Mel had already considered this to be a strong possibility, just hearing it out loud made it seem more real. More terrifying. 'But you haven't died, sweetheart.'

'Have.'

'How?'

Chloe was silent long enough for Mel to wonder if her daughter had been asleep the whole time. Talking to her from somewhere deep within her subconscious. She looked up at Mel with those big blue eyes designed to steal hearts. 'Here comes a candle to light you to bed.'

Mel watched a deep red jagged line appeared around her daughter's neck. 'What the hell…?'

'And here comes a chopper to chop off your head.'

CHAPTER ELEVEN

With Chloe finally asleep at just past nine, Tony said, 'I think you should take her to the doctor's. See if he can refer her to someone.'

Mel lit a cigarette, her third since Chloe's latest outburst, and blew smoke in his direction. *That's for the bitch you're fucking.* 'No doctor's going to help her.'

'You don't know that.'

'This isn't a simple case of a cold or a dose of chickenpox, Tony.'

'I never said it was. I'

'Or have you been discussing it with the tart at work? Perhaps *she* has all the answers.'

'There is no "tart at work." For Christ's sake, Mel, I love you.'

'Is that right?'

'Yes.'

Mel took a drag of her cigarette and ground it out in a saucer. She would buy an ashtray tomorrow, along with more cigarettes. 'I don't believe you.'

'I'm telling the truth.'

'Where did Chloe get it from, then? Her imagination?'

A slight pause. 'Probably.'

'Is she pretty?'

'Who?'

'The bitch you're screwing.'

'No.'

'Then you admit there *is* someone?'

'Stop twisting my words.'

'Stephanie Wallace,' Mel said, the words tasting foul on her lips. 'Remember?'

Tony ignored her. Seemed to take a sudden interest in his fingernails.

'When did we last have sex?'

'Pardon me?'

'It's a simple enough question. When did you stop fancying me, Tony?'

'I do fancy'

'Is it because I put on a few pounds after Chloe's birth?'

'Now you're being ridiculous.'

'Am I?'

Tony walked to the kitchen, flapping his hand in the air, making a big deal of the smoke.

Mel followed him as far as the doorway. 'Is she thinner than me?'

He took a bottle of Budweiser from the fridge and removed the top.

Mel fired another salvo. 'Even your over-rational brain must be able to see that Chloe is picking up stuff she can't possibly know.'

'I never said she wasn't.'

'You admit she knows things, then?'

Tony swallowed half the beer before answering. 'Maybe.'

'About my mother?'

'It seems that way.'

'About Megan?'

'Yes.'

'So, why the hell am I expected to believe the one thing she says about you knocking off a tart at school is a load of crap?'

'Because it is.'

Mel walked back into the lounge, lit a fresh cigarette and sat on the arm of the sofa. 'If you were any sort of man, you'd tell me the truth.'

He poked his head around the door as if coming into full view might leave him open to a fatal wound. 'What's the point, Mel? As usual, you've already made up your mind. Just like you decided to shut me out after Megan died.'

'I was grieving.'

'So… was… I.' Tony banged the door frame with each syllable.

'Maybe I *was* selfish. Too consumed with my own grief. I'm just a heartless bitch. I should have been more considerate when our three-month-old daughter's heart stopped beating.'

'I never said'

'Is that what drove you to that tart?'

Tony stood by the kitchen door. 'Why are you so certain I'm having an affair based on a child's hysterical outburst.'

'You think that's what this is?'

'I think she's been having bad dreams, and they've somehow affected her. She a bright kid. An imaginative kid.'

'Imaginative enough to draw a picture of the house on fire after what my dad said at the hospital?'

'She's gifted at art. I've heard of plenty of cases of child prodigies. Kids that can play the piano like Mozart at Chloe's age.'

'You saw the drawing.'

'It was spooky, I grant you, but not unheard of.'

'How do you explain it tying in with what my dad said?'

'It could just be a coincidence.'

'Piss off, Tony. It's not a bloody coincidence.'

Mel told him about the picture Chloe had drawn at Kerrie-Anne's. 'Where did she learn about guillotines? Or was that just a coincidence as well?'

'She might have seen one sometime. On telly. The computer. In a book.'

'She hasn't. And it was in fine detail. She even drew the grain in the wooden frame, for God's sake.'

'Like I said'

'I know what you said. Our child is a coincidental prodigy, right? One that draws a near-perfect depiction of a scene from the French Revolution.'

'But'

'She's four years old, Tony.'

Tony stared at his empty beer bottle, rotating it between his thumb and forefinger. 'So, you reckon she lost her head in the French Revolution, do you?'

'Why not?'

'Because it's bloody absurd.'

'You didn't see the picture.'

'Then show it to me.'

'I left it at Kerrie-Anne's. It was too disgusting to bring home. Too graphic. When she woke up screaming this afternoon, she started talking about having other parents. Jenny and Robert. Said they lived in Woking.'

'Not a very French-sounding name, is it?'

'Don't mock me, Tony. I'm only repeating what she said.'

'It sounds like a load of mixed up mumbo-jumbo.'

Mel resisted an urge to hurl the makeshift ashtray at him. 'Guess what else she said?'

'What?'

'"Here comes a chopper to chop off your head."'

'Like I said, she needs to see a doctor. Get something to calm her down and stop the bad dreams.'

'Haven't you listened to a single word I've said?'

'Yes. And it's only convinced me more that our daughter's suffering from an overactive imagination.'

'You saw the marks around her neck.'

'Marks can appear because of the subconscious mind. They've proved it using hypnotherapy. I watched a programme once where they hypnotised a bloke and told him they were going to touch his arm with a Japanese bay leaf. The leaf causes an allergic reaction. The hypnotist then touched the subject's arm with a harmless dock leaf. Guess what happened?'

'I don't care.'

'He had the same reaction as he would have had with a Japanese bay leaf.'

'Chloe said she lived with this Robert and Jenny before she died, for fuck's sake. And you're prattling on about leaves.'

'What do you want me to say, Mel? Do you want me to lie and say I believe all this nonsense?'

'I want you to open your mind for once. She had a deep red mark around her neck. It looked as if…'

'What?'

Mel fumbled for the words to describe the ugly wound around her daughter's neck. 'It… looked as if she'd had her throat cut.'

'Maybe she scratched herself in her sleep.'

'Fuck you, Tony. You're in denial.'

'Me?'

'Yes.'

Tony fetched another beer. He slammed the fridge door and stomped back into the front room. His eyes looked almost black. 'There's no such thing as reincarnation. It's crap. We have one body, and when we die, that's it. Into the ground or the furnace. It's crazy to think we might somehow survive. Or come back. Why on earth would we?'

'I don't fucking know.'

'Surely, if your soul theory is right, everyone would be born with a brand new one. It just doesn't add up.'

'I wondered when we'd get around to that,' Mel said. 'If you can't divide it by the square root of bugger knows what, it doesn't exist, right?'

'I'm only'

'Saying? And I'm sick to death of listening. I want you to go.'

'Don't be ridiculous. I'm not leaving you on your own while you're like this.'

Mel picked up the saucer and threw it at her husband. 'Get out, Tony. Get the fuck out before I do something I really regret.'

CHAPTER TWELVE

Peter King walked down the twenty-two concrete steps leading into the bowels of Feelham Theatre. His current good mood lent a spring to his step, banishing, albeit temporarily, the arthritis plaguing his right knee. Two glasses of red wine had also helped to soften the blow.

King had bought the theatre at the knockdown price of sixty thousand pounds some twenty years ago when it had been little more than a derelict shell. It had once thrived as a cinema in the small riverside town before the word multiplex was even invented. He'd bought it to indulge his love of Shakespeare and to fulfil his lifelong ambition to direct some of the great man's finest works.

King's ambition to act had been thwarted by the twin handicap of a stammer, which surfaced only when faced with pressurised situations such as auditions, and a father who'd done everything in his power to suppress his son's natural inclination in favour of forcing him to learn the skills necessary to run the family's clothing empire.

King's father was a brutal man who seemed to make no distinction between cruelty and discipline. He ruled the family home in Knightsbridge with a rod of iron. Literally, considering his propensity to use a poker to enforce some of his more bizarre rules and regulations. King would often find himself subject to severe beatings and acts of barbaric humiliation under the dubious guise of making a man of him. Albert King was a possessive man. A jealous man. One who believed the only way to achieve faithfulness was by locking his wife away and denying her contact with anyone other than him.

Florence King was what Peter would later describe as a free-thinking spirit. A short woman, plain as a rice pudding, with small, round glasses and black hair streaked grey and scraped back in a bun, she looked nothing like the threat to fidelity King senior seemed to imagine.

But every cloud had a silver lining, and the long days locked away with his mother in the family library whilst King Senior was away on business had forged a deep bond between them. One which was enhanced by a mutual love of the written word. Most notably Shakespeare. He wasn't a mere writer, in young Peter's opinion; he was a sculptor of words. A creator of a language so rich and so empowering that, as Florence King read to him, he would often weep tears of joy.

Through Shakespeare, King had discovered a deep range of emotional states, visiting torment, suicide and triumphant vengeance in such a compelling way as to make Hamlet the greatest creation of all time, both real and fictional.

His father had started sexually abusing Peter when he was nine years old. The beatings had inspired Albert King to a state of sexual frenzy, sated only by sodomising the boy and threatening him with death if he so much as talked about it in his sleep.

King had endured twenty-two years of virtual hell on earth, relieved only by his mother's kindness, before fate had dealt him the first decent break of his life. His father had dropped dead from a heart attack whilst wielding a poker and threatening to kill his long-suffering wife. King had kept that poker to this day. Secreted at the back of his wardrobe, and brought out on the anniversary of his father's death each year, it was one of his most treasured possessions. A symbol of justice. King had forged a phrase of his own to pay his respects to the implement: *Who shall live by the poker, shall also die by the poker.* King wasn't too concerned he'd largely stolen the words from the Gospel of Matthew; plagiarising religion was perfectly acceptable considering it was all a lie to control the weak and gullible masses with threats of hellfire and sin.

King had inherited the chain of high-end menswear shops located in such prestigious places as Bond Street and the King's Road no connection to the family. King had flourished upon his father's death. Setting aside an allowance for his mother who'd inherited the house and nothing else, King had sold the family business, become an instant millionaire, and followed a natural path towards the arts.

He'd been forced to abandon his dream to act just shy of his fortieth birthday. No one seemed willing to employ an actor with a stammer. To make matters worse, his mother had succumbed to lung cancer after a long and fruitless battle with Mother Nature's nasty streak. She hadn't helped herself by smoking like a chimney after her husband's death, but she'd hardly deserved such a rotten pain-ridden end.

He'd sold the house, complete with the body of a young man encased in a concrete tomb beneath the basement, and left London with a renewed purpose. A small market town was just what he needed to get his creative juices flowing again and put some colour in his cheeks.

He'd bought a beautiful four-bedroom detached home on the outskirts of Feelham, and spent the next three years renovating the old cinema and turning it into Feelham Theatre. It was a project which excited him. Somewhere he could indulge both passion and fantasy in equal measure.

Now, King unlocked an oak door in the bowels of the theatre and swung it open on rusty hinges. An overbearing stench snuffed out his good mood. Excrement, with a dose of damp and a splash of halitosis. He pegged his nose between his thumb and forefinger and stepped into his kingdom. He hadn't been down here for the best part of a week because he'd been planning a new game of One False Move. He'd also been involved in the Christmas pantomime, a distraction which did little to enhance his mood, and everything to remind him of the poor taste and questionable intelligence of the masses. Still, everyone had their cross to bear, and this year, *Jack and the Beanstalk* was his.

The room was thirty feet long and twenty wide. Lined up along one wall: a metal cage that had once housed a pet chimp according to the eBay advert; a set of wooden stocks, made to order and of less dubious origin; and a wooden post bolted to the concrete floor by way of a metal bracket.

There was a large oak table pushed against the opposite wall, with two dark-red leather chairs sitting either side of it. King walked to the table and sat down. The leather creaked beneath his weight. He stretched out his legs, rubbed his dodgy knee, and surveyed the game board set out on the floor in front of him.

One False Move was his brainchild. His baby. A concept nurtured and fostered over many hours of fantasy. The game was beautiful in its simplicity. Two players moved around four sides of the life-sized board painted on the floor. Each side comprised twenty-five coloured squares painted purple, orange, yellow and turquoise. The contestants moved to the value of a dice, and answered questions related to Shakespeare depending on which colour they landed on. Twice around the board before moving along the five squares leading to the large centre stage. Then the chance to answer the Encore Question and win the game.

To set the scene of One False Move, King dressed as Shakespeare, and his partner as the playwright and poet, Christopher Marlowe. The game was mined with punishments and forfeits, including the cage, the stocks and the whipping post. Two squares were also marked as Death Squares, but death was pardonable at the discretion of the opposing player.

King's current crop of game pieces were housed beyond a locked door in the far wall. Known only as Purple, Yellow, Orange, and Turquoise, these real-life pawns were his longest serving pieces. Purple-six had been with him for five years now. An extraordinary feat when you considered the dangers inherent in playing One False Move.

To date, King had lost three pieces to the Death Square, two to the stocks, and four to the punishment cage. It was not a record he was proud of, but his opponent had lost far more than him.

Six to the Death Square in the last three years alone, if memory served him correctly.

King and his partner spent many evenings trawling websites in search of new and interesting riddles. Once asked and answered correctly, the question was always destroyed. Anything was fair game. Direct quotes from Shakespeare's many plays, the history of the characters, scenes, settings, plots.

Tomorrow, the game pieces could clean the place ready for the new game. Decontaminate their living quarters with disinfectant and bleach. King had been sorely tempted at times to reconsider his decision to use female game pieces in One False Move. Apart from the fact that they were cursed with menstruation and all the monthly mess incurred by that ghastly freak of nature, they seemed to be largely preoccupied with mood swings, petulance and bitchiness. Not to mention that he found them about as attractive as thorn bushes laden with poisonous berries. But it was largely for this reason that he'd elected to use the fairer sex a wholly inappropriate name, considering they'd shown themselves to be anything but fair. The last thing he needed was to be distracted by young lithe men moving around the board and leaving him in a permanent state of arousal.

"'O mischief, thou art swift to enter in the thoughts of desperate men,'" King said, quoting the great man to reinforce his resolve.

An image of men wearing nothing but leg irons shuffling around the One False Move board popped into his head and treated him to a fantasy which was almost enough to tip the balance in favour of their use. Just for one game. Indulgence, in moderation, was a sin which was good for the soul.

King turned his mind to other thoughts to alleviate an overwhelming urge to masturbate and leave his seed on the Death Square. He would need to provide the game pieces with buckets of water and soap to wash themselves. The last thing he wanted was the stench of their poor hygiene putting him off his game. He'd won the last four straight, and he wanted to make it five out of five. He couldn't think of a more splendid way to spend the twelve days of Christmas. Uninterrupted bliss.

His numerous yet brief affairs in London had taught him a lot about the frailty of commitment. He'd long since learned that a fool and his heart were easily parted. He'd also learned that promiscuity was rife, security scarce. He'd lost two lovers to AIDS, one to a skulking weasel he'd believed to be a friend, and another who'd expired due to an ill-fated bondage session which had resulted in fatal asphyxiation.

This unplanned death had both terrified King and excited him in equal measure. He'd kept the body in the bedroom at his mother's house for almost two months, preserving it as best he could with embalming fluid and liberal doses of his mother's perfume and make-up. His name was Alex. Or Big Al, as he'd preferred to be called in his more articulate days.

King had learned at an early age, thanks to his father's terrible example, to mix pain and pleasure in a deadly cocktail of sexual desire. King could only achieve orgasm through inflicting extreme suffering on others. It proved to be a difficult combination to satisfy, but Big Al seemed more than willing to be tortured to within an inch of his life. Not that King was excited by having pain inflicted upon him; that street was strictly one-way with a no entry sign strategically placed to thwart any ideas of two-way traffic.

Sadly for this fledgling relationship, King had brought a permanent end to proceedings by handcuffing Big Al to the bed, stuffing a sock down his throat, hacking lumps out of his naked body with a razor blade, and throttling him with his bare hands to achieve orgasm without penetration. This fantasy had proved reliable. King had ejaculated as Big Al had breathed his last.

By then, King's mother wasn't in the best of health. She mostly stayed in her own room, attended to her by her dutiful son. Keeping Big Al's corpse in his room had posed little risk. He'd bathed him daily, tended to him as only a lover could, and read Shakespeare to him every night.

He'd had to move Al to the basement when the stench of his decaying body had proved too much for Dettol and deodorant. After much deliberation, King had hired a concrete cutter and fashioned Big Al a coffin beneath the basement floor. After saying his goodbyes, he'd filled in the hole with cement. It had taken him the best part of a week to complete the task after electing to mix the blessed stuff himself. He'd sworn from that moment on to never embark on manual labour again. Cement dust had all but destroyed his lungs, and a pulled muscle in his back had forced him to walk with a stoop for days.

Comfortable, and at peace in the familiar surroundings of the theatre, he leaned back in the chair and folded his hands behind his head. Life hadn't turned out too bad, all things considered. He had an understanding lover, a beautiful home, the theatre, and enough money in the bank to indulge his taste for the finer things in life.

It was true to say he would have swapped everything he owned for just one night on the stage playing Macbeth or Hamlet, but life was as fate had seen fit to arrange it. Peter King was not one to look to the heavens and curse his rotten luck.

Quite the contrary.

CHAPTER THIRTEEN

Chloe went to bed at just past eight o'clock on Christmas Eve. There had been no further incidents. It was as if the real Chloe had come back for Christmas, and Mel wasn't about to upset the apple cart by asking questions about the events of the past few days. Hopefully, this was the end of it.

So, you're just going to let your marriage crumble because of something Chloe says?

Mel sipped her first glass of wine that evening and tucked her feet up beneath her on the sofa. She lit a cigarette. On the face of it, it was insane. Absurd. But then, so was what Chloe had said about Megan and Grandma Audrey, along with the picture she'd drawn.

Mel wanted to rip the damn thing off the fridge, burn it, scatter the ashes from the top of Beaconsdale Hill. Cast them to the wind. Give them back to the universe, or whatever the hell it was all those New Age hippies believed in.

But why now? Everything had been fine until the trip to Feelham Theatre. Not one hint her daughter was anything other than a normal, bright, happy little girl.

The Tall Man's coming, Mummy. The Tall Man's going to kill us.

Mel shivered as she remembered Chloe's haunting prophecy. Who the hell was the Tall Man? Mel racked her brains. The only tall man she knew was a teacher who'd taught at Feelham Primary School about five years ago. John Hardy. Nice guy. About as threatening as a blackboard. Apart from him, zip. No one at school. None of her friends had tall partners. Tony was five-eight in his shoes.

Maybe the Tall Man's not really tall. He just looks tall to Chloe because she's little.

Of course! All men would look tall to a child.

The doorbell chimed making her jump. If that was Tony, he could get lost. She didn't want him spoiling Christmas with his denials and lies. It wasn't lost on Mel how Chloe's behaviour had improved since she'd thrown him out.

She opened the front door, heart beating a little faster, mind crammed full of responses to possible attempts by Tony to reconcile. She wasn't in any mood to forgive a philanderer. Especially a lying, smug, self-righteous one who couldn't think beyond algebra and equations.

Charles Honeywell stood on the doorstep, black Burberry coat buttoned to his chin, a parcel tucked under one arm. 'Merry Christmas, Mel.'

She gawped at him, half-expecting Honeywell to morph into her husband at any moment and shout *fooled ya!* 'Charles?'

'How are you bearing up?'

She invited him in, took his coat, offered him a drink.

'That would be most welcome, thank you. I'll have a small Scotch. Neat on the rocks if you've got it.'

Mel poured his drink and handed him a crystal tumbler.

'I've got a little present for Chloe.'

'You shouldn't have.'

'Nonsense. You've been through a lot. It's the least I could do.'

Mel put the present under the artificial tree by the front window. She didn't return to her place on the sofa, electing to sit on the arm of the chair near the kitchen door. 'How did the school play go?'

Honeywell sat in Tony's chair near the fire. He busied himself wiping his glasses on a small polishing cloth. 'Brought the house down.'

'That's good.' Mel took a mental measurement of his height. About five-six. 'Everyone remember their lines?'

He perched his glasses back on the end of his nose and returned the cloth to his glasses case. 'Miss Stobie had to prompt once or twice, but apart from that…'

'I'm sorry I wasn't there.'

'You've got nothing to apologise for.'

'I'll be back in the New Year.'

Honeywell sipped his drink. 'Take all the time you need. How's Chloe?'

'She seems okay.'

'I must confess to having given this quite a lot of thought these past couple of days. I'm rather intrigued by what you told me. I've been looking into the phenomena of past-life experience. It seems a rather common occurrence. Much more so than I imagined.'

'Really?'

Honeywell swirled ice around the bottom of his glass. 'Extraordinary stuff, some of it. There was one child who remembered being burned to death.'

'That's awful!'

'Isn't it? Burned to death in a bakery where she worked. Over a hundred years prior to her birth. This child was born in Brighton. Her memories were rooted in Lancashire. How on earth could that be?'

'I don't'

'The child knew the minutest details of her other birthplace. A small village. The layout. Where her home was at the end of a towpath. The bicycle she rode to work. Her husband. Five children.'

'But that's… impossible.'

Honeywell nodded. 'They found the village. Found the towpath, too. The cottage was long gone, but records showed it had once stood on that plot of land. They even traced the child's former name through church records. Everything turned up true, Mel. The bakery, the fire, the whole tragic episode.'

'Bloody hell!'

'You say Chloe acted strange when she went to Feelham Theatre?'

Mel nodded. 'She didn't want to go inside.'

Honeywell was silent for a moment, stroking his chin. 'This a complete shot in the dark, and forgive me if it sounds preposterous, but I can't help wondering if perhaps something once happened to your daughter inside that theatre.'

'Like what?'

'I don't know. I'm just thinking about the fire in the bakery.'

Mel excused herself, walked to the kitchen, and retrieved Chloe's picture. She held it up before the headmaster like an auctioneer's assistant displaying a fine work of art.

'Did you draw that?'

Mel shook her head. 'It's the one I told you about.'

'Chloe drew it?'

'Yes.'

'But… she's only four, isn't she?'

'Yes.'

'She couldn't possibly draw something of that standard.'

'I wish she hadn't.'

'It's… incredible.'

'She drew another one at her childminder's.'

'What of?'

'A guillotine.'

'For cutting paper?'

'No; for cutting off heads.' Mel described the grisly detail of the bloody execution.

'Where on earth would she get such an idea from?'

'You tell me.'

He was silent for a moment, thoughtful, and then he said, 'It does appear your daughter has lived before, Mel. What does your husband think?'

'He's not here. We've… had a bust-up.'

'Over Chloe?'

'Sort of. I don't want to talk about it. This whole thing's been a nightmare.'

'You said Chloe had marks around her neck?'

Mel nodded. 'At first, I thought she'd been strangled. But then…'

'Mel?'

'They could have been made by a guillotine.'

'Like in the drawing?'

'Yes.'

'It might be prudent to look at the history of Feelham Theatre. See if there's ever been a fatal accident. I'll look into it if you like. See if I can trace its history right back to its construction.'

'You don't have to do that.'

'I want to. I'm intrigued. I wonder if there's ever been a fire there?'

'She drew this house on fire, not the theatre.'

Honeywell put his empty glass on the coffee table and stood up. 'I'd better be going. Things to do and people to see. I'll pop back in a few days' time if I manage to dig something up.'

Mel escorted him to the door. 'I don't want you to put yourself out.'

'Quite the contrary. It will give me something to get my teeth into.'

Mel thanked him and let him out into a night intent on delivering rain and spoiling every kid's dream of a white Christmas.

CHAPTER FOURTEEN

Purple-six sat on the edge of her bunk, massaging the back of her neck with her manacled hands. A three-foot long chain between the wrist restraints afforded her limited movement, just enough to perform bodily functions, eat, stretch, wash. Leg restraints, joined by a shorter chain, allowed her to shuffle around the cell and just about keep the blood circulating around her body.

The Game Master's voice, muffled by the heavy door, but no less threatening, said, 'I have left six buckets of water and cleaning equipment for you in the theatre. Four are for personal use. The others for scrubbing the floors. Is that clear, Purple-six?'

'Yeah.'

'I want this place spick and span for tomorrow, okay?'

'Yeah.'

'And try to inject some enthusiasm into your voice. It's Christmas Day tomorrow. A day to celebrate.'

I can't fucking wait. 'Right.'

'I want you to make an effort. The new game starts tomorrow.'

'Okay.'

'I'll unlock the door now. I want you to wait a full five minutes before opening it. If you defy me, I will shoot you. Understand?'

Purple-six, more than aware the Game Master was incapable of making idle threats, confirmed she understood. Yellow-four made a face and spat on the floor. Orange-seven lay on her bunk, staring at the mouldy ceiling as if it might reveal a way out.

'I wish I could kill the cunt,' Turquoise-six said. 'Wrap these chains around his fucking neck and throttle him.'

Purple-six, formerly known as Tanya Wichello, resident of Lower Spittle, shuffled to the door and listened to the Game Master's retreating steps.

'Why don't we just go for it,' Turquoise-six persisted. 'If we all rushed him at once, we'd'

'All be shot,' Yellow-four snapped. 'There's no way out of here. Except in a body bag.'

'What have we got to lose?' Turquoise-six said. 'Absolutely fuck all.'

Tanya turned to face the others. 'Will you be quiet? I'm trying to listen.'

Turquoise-six rolled her eyes and chewed on her index finger as if it was of great nutritional value. 'I'll fucking kill him.'

'Is that right,' Yellow-four said. 'So, how come you haven't done it already? You've been here for ages.'

Turquoise-six shrugged. Her chains rattled and echoed around the bare walls. 'Just waiting for the right time.'

Yellow-four shook her head. 'Yeah, right. And I'm Father Christmas.'

Orange-seven leaned over the side of her bunk. 'Always thought you looked like a bloke.'

Yellow-four laughed. 'That's me. All body hair and bollocks.'

'More like a big butch lesbian, if you ask me,' Turquoise-six said.

'No one's asking you,' Yellow-four retorted.

Tanya moved away from the door. 'I think he's gone.'

Turquoise-six clapped her hands, rattling her chains. 'Give the girl a prize.'

Orange-seven climbed off the top bunk. 'You going to open the door, then?'

Tanya thought the woman's bright orange tracksuit made her look like a traffic cone. 'Okay. But I don't want everyone squabbling. We'll do the chores, and then we'll wash.'

'What I want to know,' Turquoise-six said, 'is who made you the leader of the fucking Teletubbies?'

Yellow-four rounded on her. 'Who made *you* the biggest whinger in the world?'

'What the fuck do you expect, locked in this freezing cold shithole?'

Tanya said, 'We're all in the same boat, in case you hadn't noticed.'

She snorted and zipped her turquoise tracksuit top up as far as it would go. 'Boat? Fucking dungeon, more like.'

Tanya took a deep breath. 'The sooner we get this done, the sooner we can relax.'

'Are you for real? The only thing you can do down here is freeze your tits off.'

Orange-seven walked over to the door and stood next to Tanya. 'I hope to God she gets picked tomorrow.'

Turquoise-six flipped her the bird. 'I heard that!'

'Good.'

'Just in case you've forgotten, they pick two for each game.'

'I know,' Yellow-four said. 'But at least there'll be a fifty-fifty chance you'll wind up out of my life.'

Tanya turned to her friend. 'That's a bit OTT.'

'I don't care. She does my head in.'

'And you do my head in,' Turquoise-six said. 'But I don't keep going on about it.'

Yellow-four rounded on her. 'Don't you ever shut up?'

'That's enough,' Tanya said. 'Come on. Let's get this done.'

Turquoise-six looked at Yellow-four as if she was trying to set fire to her with her eyes. 'And you needn't bother to ask me to wash her. Unless you want me to wash her mouth out with soap.'

Tanya shook her head. She wasn't one to wish ill on anyone, but she'd be lying if she said she'd never wished Turquoise-six would be chosen to play One False Move and never return. She knew it was a terrible thing to think, and she hated herself for doing so, but this place did all it could to destroy every last ounce of compassion.

She didn't know how long she'd spent locked away down here. It might have been one year, might have been ten. Time no longer existed. Minutes bled into hours, hours haemorrhaged into weeks. It was a completely different Tanya Wichello who had travelled from Paddington Station to Oxford with the tall, bearded, pot-bellied man.

She remembered little about the house he'd taken her to. By the time she'd drunk her third glass of wine, everything in the room had presented itself in twos. Two Thomas Kowalskis, two wine glasses, two tables, two chandeliers swinging above the dining table. If there was one piece of advice Tanya could give to women, it would be this: never surrender control to a man. Give him your time. Your money, even. But never your mind. Once you gave that away you were as vulnerable as a fawn in a valley full of wolves.

She remembered a sensation akin to being on a fairground ride, followed by euphoria, and then darkness, thick and black as an oil slick. When she'd regained consciousness, she was chained to a bed, and a severed head had been sitting on a chair in the corner of the room. After her initial burst of hysteria, the man had hit her with a baseball bat and knocked her unconscious.

She had no recollection of how she'd got from the bed to her basement prison. The other three girls, dressed in turquoise, yellow and orange tracksuits, had all long since perished playing One False Move. One, Yellow-two, had been so helpful and caring during those first few months that without her Tanya might well have taken her own life.

Tanya opened the door. The Game Master had left polish, dusters, brooms, four bottles of bleach, Flash sprays and six buckets of water as promised. After a long debate about who was going to do what, they set about sweeping the floor, polishing the oak table, dusting the stocks and cleaning the cage.

Tanya elected to clean the game board, getting on her hands and knees and scrubbing the orange, yellow, turquoise and purple squares with hands almost as rough as the concrete.

Turquoise-six leaned on her broom. 'I don't know why you're bothering to do that. We'll only be treading all over it tomorrow.'

Tanya climbed to her feet. 'Because if we don't, he'll punish us.'

'Like he's not doing that already?'

'You want him to put you in the cage?'

'I couldn't care less.'

'You want to get electrocuted by the cattle prod?'

'I'

'Or perhaps you want to be tied to the whipping post and have forty lashes with the leather whip?'

Turquoise-six didn't answer.

'I didn't think so. Now get on with it. The sooner we're done, the sooner we can relax.'

Turquoise-six rolled her eyes and made a point of pushing the broom as slowly as she could across the floor.

After finishing the Game Room, they set about cleaning their living quarters. Wiping down the bunks, folding blankets, sweeping the floor, rolling up sleeping bags. Tanya sprayed bleach into the toilet and cleaned the rim with Flash. After washing themselves, they returned the equipment to the theatre.

Turquoise-six wasted no time complaining about aching limbs and hunger.

'All right,' Tanya said. 'We'll eat now if everyone's ready.'

Food was supplied by an upright freezer stocked full of microwave meals. A fridge contained bottled water. There was no kettle or facility for heating water. The waste was collected once a week, along with dirty laundry; and the bin was emptied at the same time.

'Can't fucking wait,' Turquoise-six. 'What's on the menu tonight? Let me guess; curry or lasagne?'

Tanya slammed the door. 'Just give it a rest, for fuck's sake. In case you haven't noticed, it's the same for all of us. We all have to live in this shithole, eat the same crap every day, and suffer.'

'I'm only saying.'

'Well, don't. If I have to listen to your whining a minute longer, I'll put you in the bloody cage myself.'

Turquoise-six looked about to say something else, then seemed to think better of it.

They ate in silence, washing down their microwave meals with water. At least the aroma of the spicy food masked the stench of damp and excrement.

'Who do you reckon will get chosen tomorrow?' Yellow-four said, as they settled down on their bunks.

'Does it matter?' Orange-seven said. 'We're all fucking dead, anyway.'

Tanya lay on her bed and stared at the mouldy ceiling. Cobwebs decorated the peeling paint with ghostly veils. Her top bunk put her within two feet of the spores. Mostly black, but with occasional red and pink blooms, the mould sometimes invited her to make out random shapes and faces.

A bare bulb hung on a short length of flex in the middle of the ceiling, making deep sleep impossible unless someone removed the bulb. There was no switch inside the room, and Turquoise-six was terrified of the dark. The electric fan heater barely took the chill off the ten feet square room. The bare stone walls were constantly wet with condensation. A rotting black beam running along the centre of the ceiling looked as it was about to fall away at any minute and bring the ceiling crashing down with it.

Tanya had spent so much of her time locked in this stinking room contemplating death. Would it be quick? Would it be final? Was there such a thing as an afterlife? Heaven or hell? Sometimes, lost in fantasy, she imagined being in heaven, tasked with deciding the fate of her captors. She had brief respite from the horrors of her existence by condemning them to burn in hell for all eternity. She would have gladly stoked the fires herself.

The man who had lured her away from Paddington Station bore no resemblance to the man who now ruled her life. He was clean shaven and slim. His height, well over six feet, lent an awkwardness to his gait. His sharp features reminded Tanya of a bird of prey. How could she have been so stupid? How could she not have noticed the padding around his stomach? The fake beard?

Blinded by ambition. Hearing what you wanted to hear. Seeing what you wanted to see. Believing what you wanted to believe.

And wasn't that the truth? Following a stupid dream to be a dancer. Well, she'd got her wish now, hadn't she? She danced to the Game Master's tune every single day of her miserable life. As for his side-kick, his opponent in this pathetic game of life and death, she'd never seen him out of costume. The Game Master always referred to him as Mr. Marlowe. They both dressed in old-style costumes, possibly Elizabethan, but history had never been her strongest subject.

Many times during her captivity, she'd considered ending her own life. Fashioning a makeshift noose from her tracksuit bottoms and hanging herself from the beam. Or tearing the wires out the back of the microwave and electrocuting herself. The only thing that had stopped her was a determination not to let the Game Master win. Her life meant nothing to him. Less than nothing. And she owed it to herself to fight him with every ounce of strength left in her body.

Yellow-four, lying on the top bunk next to Tanya's, rolled onto her side. 'Merry Christmas.'

'Merry Christmas.'

'Any New Year's resolutions?'

Tanya laughed. 'To stay alive.'

'Why would you want to stay alive?' Turquoise-six interrupted. 'I can't wait to die.'

Tanya sighed. 'You don't mean that.'

'Fucking well do. I couldn't bear another year in this shit-tip living with a bunch of losers like you.'

Tanya didn't have an answer to that.

CHAPTER FIFTEEN

King woke up on Christmas morning with a thumping headache. Too much wine, too much Viagra and too much sex. He rolled onto his back and was joined some moments later by his throbbing head. He reached out for his lover, but the bed was empty. He stared at the space beside him, unable to comprehend his lover's absence. And then he realised he was in the spare room, lying in the single bed normally reserved for guests and childish fallouts.

Memory seeped through the fog of last night's action. The rent boy, Nathan, doing things to his cock which he didn't believe possible. King had fed himself Viagra like a child feeding itself smarties.

Sometime around midnight, his partner had joined them on the four-poster bed in the master bedroom for a threesome that had lasted long after Santa had climbed down his final chimney. All good, so far. But something was tearing a great big hole in this happy memory. He tried to sit up, but his head was in no mood to go vertical. Not yet.

He massaged his forehead. A thought suddenly roared through his head like a stunt rider on a motorbike.

The rent boy's dead.

King groaned.

Dead and lying naked in the wine cellar.

For a moment, King thought his mind was playing tricks on him, attempting to spark him back into life with wild claims. Why on earth would he want to kill the rent boy? It wasn't as if Nathan was being held there under false pretences. He'd been paid handsomely for his services. Unlike the nine homeless men, two hitchhikers and one drunk they'd lured back to the house. In fairness, the drunk hadn't exactly been lured; he'd been rescued from a thorn bush where he'd been sleeping as soundly as a man in a five-star hotel room.

As he did not hold these sorry losers in as much esteem as the owners of the heads in the freezers, King had settled for carving a notch on the four-poster bed for each of them. To be fair, he had fond memories of one hitchhiker. Colin. A virgin, too, which was always a bonus. They'd systematically abused Colin with a variety of implements ranging from a broom handle to a cattle prod. Colin had taken five days to go past his expiry date, and King had been rather sorry to see him go when the time had come to turn him into Colin cutlets ready for disposal.

But the rent boy was different. Nathan had given him the best sex he'd ever had, no offence intended to his lover, and King had been rather keen to engage the young man's services for the rest of time he'd paid for, possibly beyond. So why in damnation had they killed him?

King's cock was still under the influence of Viagra; it peeked out of his boxers and almost castrated itself on the edge of his open fly. He crammed it back inside and cursed his weakness for alcohol.

Another memory. This one in full colour. His partner securing the rent boy's wrists to the wooden bedposts with two silk scarves. King cutting the young man's balls from their sac with a craft knife. Then cutting him across the chest. Just tiny nicks at first, then frenzied slashes, tearing at the skin, peeling it back in large, bloody flaps.

Nathan had screamed loud enough to tear plaster from the walls as they'd both set about mutilating him like a pair of hungry lions ripping into the carcass of a kill.

'Shit.'

And shit was about right. They were meant to be starting a new game of One False Move today. It would have to be postponed. There would be no time to do anything after clearing up the mess.

Although Mr. Plod was hardly going to come knocking on the door looking for runaway rent boys, even ones as beautiful as the delectable Nathan, he didn't particularly like the aftermath of a kill. It was as off-putting as cold congealed sperm on the bedsheet after a burst of red-hot passion.

'Where are you?' He called to his lover. 'Can you hear me?'

No answer. Just the ticking of the hall clock marching up the stairs. Light spilled beneath the floral patterned curtains. For one wild moment, he wondered if he was still asleep. Perhaps the Ghost of Christmas Past would appear any minute now and remind him of things best left forgotten. He touched his head to make sure he wasn't wearing a hideous nightcap fashioned by Dickens' pen.

He caught sight of himself in the mahogany dresser mirror. His eyes looked haggard and red, his face as pale as the sheet clutched in his right hand. Bloody mirrors. They rarely took account of light and angles and nights of frenzied passion.

He tried to console himself with the fact that on a good night, in the right light, he'd get away with claiming fifty, perhaps younger if the recipient of this white lie was visually impaired. Thankfully, he'd inherited none of his father's bullish features, and one or two of his mother's better ones. Although not a looker, his mother had possessed a pleasant face and a mannered tongue. He was grateful for her simple acts of kindness during the trauma of his childhood. He would always honour her memory, and cherish her love of Shakespeare, which had taught him so much about the human condition, and educated him in a way school never could.

There were times, particularly when playing One False Move, when he felt possessed by Shakespeare's spirit. Dressed and made up to look like his idol, he was sometimes driven to higher plains of existence and compelled to speak in a tongue which was sometimes both alien and, if honest, a little scary. He sometimes wondered if Shakespeare lived on through him. He was more than aware of the expression *suffering delusions of grandeur*, but this rather derogatory term was mostly born of jealous minds and lowly beings who never got beyond the realms of soap operas and Jeremy Kyle.

To say he lived for the theatre, even if it was currently bogged down with housing a cheap and nasty production of *Jack and the Beanstalk*, would draw no argument from him. The Shakespeare productions were an absolute joy. The Oxfordshire audience seemed both knowledgeable and appreciative. In the New Year, rehearsals were due to start for the summer production of *Macbeth*. It was hard to have a favourite among Shakespeare's many masterpieces, but *Macbeth* was certainly a peak in his humble opinion.

The New Year promised to be an exciting one. Fresh games of One False Move, the new production of *Macbeth*, and a holiday in the Maldives at the onset of winter. But the untimely death of the rent boy had put a black mark on the calendar. The boy would have a pimp. And pimps didn't like it when one of their prized assets went missing. He knew nothing about whore-handlers, having never met one, but you didn't need a degree in depravity to figure out they didn't take kindly to the murder and mutilation of one of their charges.

'Damn and blast it. Why did we have to kill him?'

With no answer forthcoming, he stared at his manhood, almost tempted to rip the bloody thing from its berth. Why couldn't he exercise restraint? It was one thing to challenge the limits of sexuality with a stray homeless person; quite another to risk liberty with a prostitute from Boys R Us.

Fearing a police visit, King attempted to get off the bed and begin the process of mind rehabilitation. One step at a time. Find his dressing gown. Go downstairs and swallow as many painkillers as possible without damaging his liver. Find out where his absent turtle dove had flown to.

King hoped he was in the bathroom chopping Nathan into bite-sized chunks ready for disposal.

CHAPTER SIXTEEN

After a lengthy phone call, a lot of heart-searching, and a mutual agreement that it would be in the best interests of Chloe, Mel allowed Tony to come home for Christmas Day. With Chloe sitting in front of the TV watching her new Disney DVD, *Finding Dory,* Mel and Tony sat at the kitchen table peeling sprouts and drinking coffee.

Tony scored a cross on the top of a sprout. 'I'm sorry.'

'What for? I thought you'd done nothing wrong?'

Tony studied the steam curling from the top of his coffee cup.

'Well?'

'I want you to promise me you won't get mad.'

Mel lit a cigarette. 'I'm not promising you anything.'

'I want you to think about Chloe, okay?'

Mel didn't answer. She was beginning to see Tony for what he really was: a spineless liar. 'You'd better just spit it out, Tony.'

Tony took a deep breath. He didn't make eye contact. 'It was years ago. I swear. Just a one-off. I was messed up and confused.'

'Stephanie Wallace, right?'

Tony nodded.

'You screwed her?'

'Once.'

'Oh, well, thank heavens for that. There was me thinking you'd been unfaithful. You bastard. You absolute shit!'

'I'

'Why did you do it? My body not good enough for you?'

'Of course it is. I'm sorry. What else can I say? I'm trying to be honest. I didn't have to tell you.'

'You didn't fucking well need to. It was already written in your eyes for everyone to see.'

'I'm sorry.'

'Stop saying that! You're not sorry. If you had one shred of decency, you wouldn't have gone anywhere near that bitch in the first place.'

'I know.'

Mel stared at her half empty mug of coffee, tempted to hurl it at his head. 'Are you still fucking her?'

Tony shook his head. 'It was ages ago.'

'When?'

'I don't remember exactly.'

'Last year? The year before? I want the truth. One more lie, and we're finished.'

'It's hard to say.'

'You tell me now, or else you're out the door and you won't come back.'

'About six years ago.'

Mel's heart fell to the floor.

'It was just the once. I swear. It meant nothing. It was just a stupid fling. A heat of the moment thing. It was'

'That's not long after we lost Megan.'

Tony looked away.

'We lost our baby, and you went to another woman?'

'It wasn't like that. I was just as heartbroken as you. But you shut me out. I'

Mel ground out her cigarette and lit another one. 'I didn't shut you out. We were both grieving. You threw yourself into work and then threw yourself at another woman.'

'I'm sorry.'

Mel sucked on the cigarette as if drawing strength from it. 'Was she good?'

'No.'

'Better in the sack than me?'

'No.'

'You would say that, wouldn't you?'

'I'

'Better body than mine?'

'No.'

'Bigger tits?'

'No.'

'You bastard.'

'I'm sorry.'

'You apologise one more time and I will swing for you. So help me, I will.'

'I'

'Are you still fucking her?'

'No.'

'Look at me.'

'I'm not fucking anyone. She's not even at the school anymore.'

'Hallelujah. Where's she gone? Soho?'

'I don't know, and I don't care.'

Mel wanted to grab Tony by the throat and throttle him. Their marriage was over. Kaput. She hated him as much as she hated her mother. She opened the back door and threw her cigarette into the garden. It landed on the path in a spray of tiny red sparks. 'I want a divorce.'

'For God's sake, Mel. You're angry. I get it. But'

'You don't get it at all. Not one bit. But you will. One day when you're sitting all alone with nothing but a headful of what-might-have-beens, you'll get it.'

'Please don't do this.'

'What did you expect me to do? Throw my arms around you?'

'No.'

'Be grateful for your honesty?'

'I just wanted to put the record straight.'

'Are you for real? The record's broken, Tony. Beyond repair.' She slammed the back door. 'You can stay for dinner. I don't want Chloe upset. Not today. But as soon as we've finished dinner, you make an excuse and leave. We'll work something out regarding access in the New Year.'

'One meaningless screw, and you want to throw everything away?'

'And what happens next time poor little Tony gets himself all mixed up?'

'Nothing. I swear.'

'But that's the whole point, isn't it? You can swear until you're blue in the face, but I'll never believe a word you say ever again.'

'But'

'You broke your vows, Tony. And with it, you've broken my fucking heart. So, you remember that when you go crawling back to your mother to explain why it's over. You tell her what you've done.'

Tony stood up. 'I'm going.'

'Really? Do you want to explain to Chloe why you're leaving?'

'Of course I bloody well don't.'

'Then stay and eat your dinner.'

'What's the point?'

'Because you owe it to your daughter. Then, get the fuck out of my life.'

'Please don't do this.'

'I've done nothing, Tony. This is all down to you.'

They lapsed into an uneasy silence. Mel's head was in danger of spiralling out of control. Now she understood why Tony had thrown himself into work after Megan's death. The reason for all those late nights. The widening gap between them. Taking his electric razor to work. Expensive aftershave. Little telltale signs that went unnoticed because of the tsunami of grief swelling inside her. If he thought she believed it was just a one-off, a throwaway screw, then he was more stupid than he looked.

A sudden scream rescued Mel from an urge to dig her nails into Tony's face. Gouge his skin, let him feel some of the pain she was suffering. She rushed to the lounge door and yanked it open.

Chloe was kneeling on the floor in front of the TV, head twisted to one side, strands of hair pasted to the side of her face.

'Chloe?'

Chloe's breath came in laboured pants. She held her hands straight out in front of her, balled into fists.

'What's wrong with her?' Tony asked.

Mel ignored him. 'Chloe? Can you hear Mummy?'

Chloe's head snapped to one side as if in receipt of a heavy blow. She screamed loud enough to shatter Mel's heart. Mel squatted down in front of her. There appeared to be a huge bruise beneath Chloe's left eye. She touched the child's hand.

'No. No. No. No more!' Chloe screamed. 'No more. NO MORE!' Her head jerked back.

'Come on, sweetheart. Wake up. It's Mummy.'

Chloe's head flopped forward, chin resting on her chest.

'What the hell's wrong with her?' Tony shouted. 'Wake her up.'

Mel leaned forward. 'It's all right, sweetheart. Come on. Mummy's got you.' She was just about to take Chloe into her arms when the child's head jerked up. One of Chloe's eyes looked at Mel, the other gawped wildly to the left at the TV.

'Oh my God. Chloe?'

Chloe smiled. She tilted her head back and spat into her mother's face. 'Fuck you. Fuck you all.'

Mel wiped the spit away with the back of her hand.

Chloe's head jerked to the right. She screamed again. Mel took a chance and lunged forward. She grabbed her daughter and held her as tight as she could. 'It's all right, baby, I've got you. Mummy's got you.'

'What's wrong with her eyes?' Tony asked.

Mel didn't hear him. She rocked back and forth, comforting Chloe as best she could. She stayed this way until she could no longer feel her legs. After about half an hour, Tony told Mel that Chloe was asleep.

'Put her on the sofa.'

'She might be better off in bed.'

'Just do it, Tony. I want her down here where I can see her.'

Whilst Tony laid Chloe on the sofa, Mel reclaimed her legs and switched off the TV. She walked back into the kitchen, sat at the table, lit a cigarette.

Tony joined her a few moments later. 'What the hell happened with her eyes?'

'I don't know.'

'I'm not going anywhere while she's like this.'

'This doesn't let you off the hook, Tony. Our marriage is over.'

CHAPTER SEVENTEEN

When Chloe woke up an hour after the episode in the front room, her face was unmarked and her eyes had returned to normal. They ate a Christmas dinner of turkey and all the trimmings, followed by mince pies and brandy butter. Mel did her best to pretend to be hungry, set an example to her daughter, but her stomach felt cramped and full after just a few mouthfuls.

Tony, to his credit, put on a good act, joking with Chloe and working his way through his dinner as if nothing was wrong. But he was good at pretending, wasn't he? When the time came to leave, Chloe asked him why he had to go back to Nanna Vicky's house.

'Because Nanna's not well, darling. She needs Daddy to look after her.'

'Why can't we all go and look after her?'

'Another time. She needs some peace and quiet at the moment.'

'I won't be noisy.'

Tony put his coat on and ruffled Chloe's hair. 'I know. But we have to do what Nanna Vicky wants at the moment. Deal?'

Chloe raised her hand, palm out. 'Deal.'

Her lifted her up and kissed her forehead. 'Be a good girl for Mummy.'

'I will.'

As he put Chloe back on the floor, Mel could see tears glistening in his eyes. She almost changed her mind, but then thought about Stephanie Wallace and Tony at it like a pair of dogs on heat whilst she sat at home pleading with God to make her heart stop hurting.

They watched Tony's VW Golf pull out of St Kilda's Close. Chloe waved and blew kisses until the car vanished from sight. They walked back into the lounge and sat on the sofa.

'You want to watch *Finding Dory* with me, Mummy?'

'Again?'

'Uh-huh.'

'After Mummy's done the dishes, okay?'

'Shall I help?'

Normally, Mel would have said no. But today, she wanted to keep Chloe close. 'That would be fab. I'll wash and you can dry. How does that sound?'

Chloe smiled. 'Okay.'

After doing the dishes, they watched the film together, Chloe wrapped in Mel's arms. When it ended, Mel switched off the TV and lifted Chloe onto her lap, facing her. She brushed electric strands of hair out of her face and looked deep into her eyes.

'Are you all right, Mummy?'

'I'm fine, Pumpkin. You?'

'I wish Daddy was here.'

'You'll see him again soon.'

'When?'

'When Nana Vicky's better.'

'When will she be better?'

'Soon. Can I ask you something?'

'Yes.'

'Remember when we went to the theatre?'

Chloe's sapphire-blue eyes, beautiful enough to elicit compliments from strangers, looked away. 'Yes.'

'Do you remember what happened when we went inside?'

Chloe shook her head.

'Do you remember being upset?'

'You had a nosebleed.'

'That's right. Mummy had a nosebleed. Do you remember why?'

'No.'

'What about the Tall Man?'

'Who?'

'The Tall Man. You said he was coming.'

Chloe frowned. 'Maybe I meant Father Christmas.'

Mel stroked her daughter's hair. 'Do you remember talking about Megan?'

Chloe's eyelids fluttered and drooped. She didn't answer.

Mel stopped stroking her hair. 'Chloe?'

'Huh?'

If Tony was here, he might have insisted Chloe say 'pardon'. But he wasn't. He was at his mother's, no doubt sulking, licking his wounds and plotting a way back into her life.

Or back to his tart.

Mel's heart double-locked itself. Fuck him. He could rot in hell for all she cared.

'Mummy?'

Mel jerked back to reality. 'I was just wondering if you remembered talking about Megan?'

Chloe nodded. 'Megan lives in the graveyard.'

'How do you know?'

'Grandma Audrey told me.'

'Oh.'

'I see her sometimes.'

'Who? Grandma Audrey?'

'And Megan.'

'Really?'

'She's got black hair like you. And brown eyes. Not like me. I look like Daddy, don't I?'

'Do you see Megan for real, or just in a dream?'

Chloe shrugged and fell silent.

'Chloe?'

'What's with all the questions?'

Stunned by the sudden change in demeanour, Mel dropped the subject.

'I don't keep a bloody diary.'

'Okay. That's enough. Don't use that language in front of Mummy.'

Chloe blinked twice in rapid succession. 'What language?'

'Swearing.'

'I didn't.'

Mel's heart was beating so hard she could see it pulsing through the thin fabric of her tee-shirt. They sat together in silence. Mel knew she couldn't just ignore this behaviour any longer. She would have to find someone who could help to unravel this mess. But who?

A psychiatrist?

But this was hardly a mental disorder, was it? It was as if Chloe became momentarily possessed, and then flipped back to an innocent little girl again.

Chloe leaned her head back and smiled. 'I love you, Mummy.'

'I love you, too.'

'You're the best Mummy in the world.'

'And you're the best little girl in the world.'

'The angels helped me to choose you, Mummy.'

'Really?'

'Uh-huh.'

'Why?'

'They said you would be the best Mummy to help me.'

'With what?'

Chloe shrugged. 'They didn't say.'

'Did these angels have wings?'

'Yes.'

'Like fairy wings?'

'Bigger than fairy wings.'

'How big?'

'Bigger than the whole world. And they were all pretty colours.'

'Not just white, then?'

'Nope. Pink. Purple. Yellow. Like rainbows.'

'Wow.'

'They had light shining out of them.'

'Double-wow.'

'They know everything.'

'Clever and beautiful, then?'

'Yeah.'

'Like you, Pumpkin.'

'No way. I can't even fly anymore.'

'Did you used to?'

'Yeah. Really fast. Just by shutting my eyes. I could go anywhere I wanted. Even a chocolate factory.'

'How brilliant.'

'Real chocolate.'

'Cadbury's or Galaxy?'

Chloe made a face to suggest Mummy was as dumb as mud. 'I said *real* chocolate.'

'Like *Charlie and the Chocolate Factory*?'

'Better.'

'Crikey! Are you joking?'

Chloe shook her head. '*Charlie and the Chocolate Factory*'s just made up stuff. This place is real.'

'How long were you with the angels?'

'Don't know.'

'Days? Weeks?'

'There's no time in heaven.'

'Really?'

'Uh-huh.'

'How do people know when to do things?'

'They just do.'

'Do the angels tell them?'

'Not really.'

'God?'

'No.'

'Did you go to heaven after you died?'

A shadow passed in front of Chloe's eyes. She shrugged. 'Maybe.'

'When you lived in Woking?'

'I'm tired, Mummy.'

'Do you remember telling me your other parents' names?'

Chloe shook her head and put a thumb into her mouth.

'You told me they were called Jenny and Robert.'

Chloe didn't acknowledge this. Her eyes drooped.

Mel let it go. She didn't want to push her over the edge again. She needed to find someone who could give her advice. Guidance. Someone who had no emotional link to them.

Chloe's thumb slipped from her mouth. 'Daddy's been bad, hasn't he?'

'What do you mean?'

Chloe shrugged.

'Daddy's fine.'

'Why isn't he here?'

'You know why. He's looking after Nanna Vicky.'

'That's just an excuse.' Chloe put her thumb back into her mouth and fell asleep instantly.

CHAPTER EIGHTEEN

Dressed, and in better shape than when he'd risen from the ashes of his drug-induced slumber, King sat at a large oak dining table sipping his second mug of strong black coffee. His hangover had dulled to a steady throb courtesy of two paracetamol washed down with a glass of fresh orange juice.

For the second time in his life, he wished he possessed the power to turn back time, revisit his actions, and plot a different course. The first such time had involved the lover he'd killed in London. Big Al. Not because of the murder itself, but because he'd lived on a knife-edge for months worrying that someone might dig up the basement and reveal its dubious contents.

He ran his fingers through his hair and swore to God, the empty dining room, the spirit of his mother and anyone else who might be compassionate to his suffering, he would never drink to excess again. He would keep his fantasies on a leash unless there was no chance of his actions coming back to haunt him.

To make matters worse, if they could get any worse, they would have to postpone the new game of One False Move. It was almost midday already, and he was in no fit state to get into costume, let alone pit his wits against his opponent. The only bright spot, on this darkest of days, was that his lover had already dismembered the unfortunate Nathan with a chainsaw in the guest bathroom, and separated him into manageable chunks by the time King had made it downstairs.

Now, they would have to waste precious time going out in the early hours of Boxing Day morning to distribute the parts in bins throughout Oxford. By the time that mundane task was complete, the following day would have to be spent catching up on lost sleep. It was as if fate had conspired to ruin the new game before it had even started.

His lover strode into the dining room, looking in far better shape than King. Five years his junior, Charles Honeywell had a remarkable capacity for recovery.

'All finished?' King asked.

Honeywell adjusted his spectacles. 'He's bagged. I've scrubbed the bathroom.'

'Why the negative tone?'

'The sheets are ruined. And blood's seeped through onto the mattress.'

'Is that all? I was beginning to imagine he'd reconstructed himself and was in the guestroom making demands for croissants and coffee.'

'I think it's fair to say he's well and truly lost his appetite.'

'We'll take him to Oxford tonight.'

'Okay.'

'Try to cheer up, Charles. You look as if you've just lost your virginity and discovered a dose of syphilis. If you're worried about the boy, then don't be. Even if someone saw him getting into my car, it doesn't prove a thing, does it?'

'No; of course'

'So, relax.'

Honeywell made a mug of coffee and perched on a chair opposite his lover. He squinted at King through a veil of steam. 'Do you believe in life after death?'

'Every time I look in the mirror.'

Honeywell didn't seem to be in any mood to share the joke. 'I'm serious. Do you think we can survive death?'

'What's brought this on? Do you think Nathan will come scooting up the plughole when you're in the bath and demand his pound of flesh?'

'No, but'

'If he does, you must tell him it's scattered in the bins around Oxford.'

'Please take me seriously for a minute.'

King sobered. 'What is it?'

Honeywell cleared his throat. 'I think something is amiss.'

'There's a lot "amiss" in this world.'

'There's a girl. She's… oh, I don't know. It all seems rather stupid when I say it out loud.'

'What girl?'

'The daughter of a teacher at school.'

'And?'

'She's showing signs of having lived before.'

In spite of his headache and frazzled nerves, King grinned. 'Don't tell me. She was Queen Victoria.'

'Of course not.'

'Anne Boleyn?'

'No one like that.'

'Why are you even bothering my intellect with such rubbish? No one has lived before. Reincarnation is a fanciful whim dreamt up by those with fluffy clouds for brains.'

'I'm inclined to agree, Peter. But…'

'What?'

'The child talks of being executed.'

'And?'

'Beheaded.'

'By whom?'

Honeywell put his mug down and shrugged. 'I'm not sure.'

'I'll ask you again: why are you telling me this tripe?'

'Because the child claims to have been executed by guillotine.'

'Is she French?'

'No.'

'Then who in heaven's name executed her by guillotine? An overzealous teacher?'

'It's no laughing matter. She's also talking about a tall man.'

'That narrows it down to half the population.'

Honeywell marched on. 'The girl became hysterical when her mother took her to the theatre.'

'Theatre?'

'Here at Feelham. To watch *Jack and the Beanstalk.* Said she got hysterical the minute they walked through the door.'

'She has my deepest sympathy. I don't understand why we even bother with that nonsense each year.'

'I think the child was one of ours.'

'A game piece?'

Honeywell bobbed his head.

'Why on earth would you think that?'

'She remembers dying. She had all these marks around her neck. Then she said, and I quote, "Put me in the fucking cage and be done with it." What kid says that to her mother?'

'One that is being ill-treated by the sound of it.'

'The theatre? The cage? The guillotine? All just coincidences, Peter?'

King was thoughtful for a moment. As far as he was concerned, human beings were nothing more than physical entities. They were born, they led mostly miserable lives, they died. 'All that supernatural stuff is hogwash. I'm surprised an educated man would even contemplate such drivel.'

'I have an open mind.'

'Open minds are gateways for corruption. I suggest you close it at once. We've a body to dispose of that poses a much more imminent threat to our liberty than a silly child who's had an attack of the heebie-jeebies.'

'I still don't like it.'

'How old is this child?'

'Four.'

'Good God, barely able to talk.'

'Exactly.'

'And the mother's a teacher at the school?'

'Yes.'

'Of a sound nature?'

'She's a good teacher. Bright. Committed.'

'Just goes to show a mask of sanity can camouflage a devious mind.'

'I don't think she's trying to deceive anyone. And there's more.'

'What?'

'The child has drawn stuff.'

King sighed. 'That's why they invented crayons.'

'These pictures are extremely detailed. There's no way on earth a four-year-old child could have drawn them.'

'Have you seen them?'

'The house on fire, yes.'

King's interest was piqued. 'What house?'

'Theirs.'

'Perhaps the mother drew it.'

'No way. She's terrified. And then there's the picture of the execution.'

'Have you heard yourself, Charles? You sound like Hecate.'

Honeywell didn't seem put off by being compared to a witch in *Macbeth*. 'Purple-five was good at art, wasn't she?'

'What of it?'

'This child is gifted at art,' Honeywell said, laying the statement on the table like a trump card.

'That's an illogical leap. Next, you'll be talking of one-eyed hags and boiling cauldrons.'

'We tried to execute Purple-five by guillotine.'

'How could I ever forget? I'm still baffled as to why it didn't take her head clean off.'

'It's a lot of coincidences.'

'Life is littered with coincidences, Charles. People are always looking to join the dots, but from my experience, random events and unexplained happenings are always prey to supposition.'

'I don't like this at all.'

'And I don't like having a body to distribute around Oxford. I like it even less that we have to postpone the new game whilst we cover our tracks.'

'It was you who took it upon yourself to kill the boy.'

King stood up. Took full advantage of his six-foot two-inch frame. He looked down at his lover turned nemesis. 'Do you think throwing ill-founded accusations at me reinforces your argument about reincarnation?'

'It's nothing like'

'Do you stand before me, trying to render my intellect mute by nefarious means? Did you not take part in the mutilation of that boy?'

'Yes.'

King felt Shakespeare's blood flowing through his veins. 'Then still your tongue, lest it talks itself into an early grave. Are we clear on that at least, sir?'

'Yes.'

'Good. And we'll have no more talk of this reincarnation nonsense. It's made up fodder to feed feeble minds.'

Honeywell stared into his coffee cup. King made a mental note to watch his lover carefully over the coming weeks. He was more than aware of the dangers inherent when love turned to liability.

CHAPTER NINETEEN

The rest of Christmas Day and the whole of Boxing Day passed without incident. Chloe enjoyed playing with her presents, especially the ballerina princess Tony and Mel had bought her whilst they'd still been a proper couple getting ready to enjoy the festive break.

Mel's friend, Susan, a teacher from Feelham Primary, had popped in earlier that day. Mel hadn't told her about Tony. She'd fudged her way through three cups of coffee, explaining that Tony was at his mother's looking after her. Yes, she'd had a wonderful Christmas, and yes, Chloe was loving it. Life was perfect. If it got any better, she'd burst into song and tap-dance into the future.

After Susan had left, and while Chloe was having an afternoon nap, Mel had sat at the kitchen table and cried for almost half an hour. She'd followed this emotional breakdown by going into the garden and smoking two cigarettes, freezing half to death in the icy wind blowing across St Kilda's Close.

How could everything go so wrong in such a short space of time? Two weeks. A fortnight. Fourteen lousy days. Hadn't she suffered enough with her mother? Losing Megan?

They say it comes in threes.

She sat at the kitchen table sipping a large brandy. How could Tony could do this to her? Not only had he destroyed her trust in men, he'd left her to deal with Chloe on her own.

You've got to get a grip. If you're not careful, you'll end up losing Chloe. Failing her, just like your mother failed you.

She lit a cigarette, blew a stream of smoke at the ceiling and blamed it on the tears in her eyes. 'I'm nothing like that bitch.'

That glass of brandy sitting on the table begs to differ.

Mel drained the drink, trying to block out the voice in her head. Her life was in free-fall. Her marriage was over and her daughter was possessed. And now she was turning into an alcoholic.

'I haven't got a clue what to do anymore,' she whispered.

The doorbell rang. She ignored it. She couldn't face anyone right now.

Maybe it's Tony.

If it was, he could jump in the river. She never wanted to see him again.

The bell rang again.

She walked to the window and peered out. The Golf wasn't parked outside. She was about to turn away when Charles Honeywell peered through the glass. He raised a hand to tap on the window, saw Mel, grinned, looked sheepish.

Mel cursed. What did she do now? She didn't want to see him, but she could hardly ignore him now he'd seen her, could she? She opened the front door and noticed a large purple bruise around his right eye.

'I thought I'd drop by and see how you were getting on.'

Mel invited him in. 'What happened to your eye?'

'I walked into a cupboard door at my sister's. She left it open, and I didn't look. I suppose you could flip a coin to apportion blame.'

'It looks nasty.'

'Injuries always look worse than they are.'

'Have you put anything on it?'

Honeywell hung his coat on a peg and sat in the chair by the fire. 'It's fine. It's superficial.' He accepted Mel's offer of a brandy. 'Just a small one, mind, I'm driving.'

She poured his drink and handed it to him.

'Thank you. Just what the doctor ordered. Did Chloe like my present?'

'She loved it.' She didn't tell him Chloe hadn't even touched the Winnie the Pooh jigsaw puzzle. Would you like me to put a steak on your eye?'

'No. It's fine. Really.'

'I've got some in the freezer.'

'Doesn't it have to be defrosted?'

'I can thaw it out in the microwave.'

'Please don't fuss. I'm fine. Honestly.'

Mel sat down on the sofa. 'So, apart from walking into the cupboard door, did you have a nice time at your sister's?'

'Yes, thank you. A most pleasant day.'

'Does your sister have children?'

'Two.'

'How old are they?'

He looked away. 'Six and eleven.'

'Boys or girls?'

'Boys.'

'Bet they were excited.'

Honeywell fiddled with his glasses and changed the subject. 'How's Chloe bearing up?'

'She's been all right for the last couple of days.'

'I sense a *but*.'

'It's just…'

Honeywell leaned forward. 'What is it?'

'Something else happened on Christmas Day.'

'What?'

'She was watching a Disney film in here. Me and Tony were in the kitchen prepping the dinner. Then she let out this awful blood-curdling scream. We rushed into the front room and she was kneeling on the floor with her arms held out in front of her. Then, it was as if something hit her in the face. It was like…'

After a short pause, Honeywell prompted, 'Like what, Mel?'

'Something was attacking her. She had a huge bruise on her face. Then her head snapped back and fell forwards. Her eyes were all wrong. One was staring at me, the other was looking at the TV. Then she spat in my face and said, "Fuck you. Fuck you all." Or words to that effect. It was as if she was reliving something... something from a past life. Sounds absurd, doesn't it?'

'Not at all.'

Mel took a cigarette out of the packet. 'I don't know what to do, Charles.'

'For what it's worth, cigarettes won't help. A friend's mother was a smoker. Brought about an early demise through lung cancer. A lesson for us all, perhaps?'

'That's easy for you to say. My life's falling apart at the seams. On top of everything else, me and Tony have split up.'

'Because of this?'

Mel lit up. 'Partly.'

'Do you know where he's gone?'

'Off the edge of a cliff for all I care.'

'You're still angry. It will pass.'

'It won't.'

'I'm here for you if you ever want to talk about it, okay?'

Mel nodded.

'Nothing's ever as bad as we imagine.'

It fucking well is. 'I'm just lost at the moment. Confused. My head's in a spin.'

'You need to focus on your daughter for now. She's the most important thing.'

'I know.'

'What about taking Chloe to the doctor's?'

'That's what Tony suggested. But they don't have pills to cure reincarnation, do they?'

'He might be able to prescribe her a mild sedative.'

'I'm not having my daughter drugged up to the eyeballs.'

Honeywell opened his mouth to say something else, but was interrupted by Chloe walking down the stairs, eyes wide as if in a trance.

Mel rushed to the bottom of the stairs. 'Chloe?'

She stopped halfway down and held her hands out in front of her, palms up. 'I don't want to be a bloody pharmacist.'

Mel walked towards her. 'Wake up, sweetheart. It's Mummy.'

Chloe looked at her hands. 'Why won't anybody listen to me? I want to be an artist.'

Honeywell walked to the foot of the stairs, head cocked to one side.

'Look at Mummy, Chloe.'

'My name's not Chloe. It's Amy. Amy May Constable.'

'It's not,' Mel corrected. 'It's Chloe. Chloe Marie Hollis.'

Honeywell gripped the bannister as if drawing strength from it. 'Ask her how old she is.'

Tears filled Chloe's eyes and spilled down her cheeks. 'Here comes a chopper to chop off your head… here comes a chopper to chop off your head… here comes a chopper to chop off your head… here comes a chopper to chop off your head… here'

Mel grabbed Chloe, pulled her close, held her tight.

Honeywell's lips were pressed into a thin line, his face as white as the frost-covered ground outside. 'I'll get going. Leave you two to…'

Mel didn't hear him.

'You're hurting me,' Chloe protested, her voice muffled by Mel's chest.

Mel walked down the stairs. *Not as much as you're hurting me, Pumpkin*, she thought. *Not half as much as you're hurting me.*

CHAPTER TWENTY

'For the headmaster of a school, your gift for babbling whilst under pressure intrigues me,' King said. 'What if there was a fire at the school?'

'That's irrelevant. You're not listening. The kid said her name was Amy May Constable.'

King fell silent as his brain processed this new information.

'Purple-five,' Honeywell added.

'Do you consider me of sound mind?'

'Of course.'

'Then don't bring my memory into question. I'm well aware of who Purple-five is was.'

'And?'

'She's dead, Charles. Deceased. Kaput. No more.'

'So, how do you explain the child's assertion that she's Amy May?'

'She could be talking about anyone. There's more than one Amy May Constable in the world.'

'*Here comes a chopper to chop off your head?* How do you explain that?'

'It's one of those silly nursery rhymes. "Oranges and lemons, say the bells of St Clement's". Ring any bells?'

'It's too much of a coincidence. Plus what happened on Christmas Day with Chloe kneeling in the front room. It brings to mind the stocks.'

King shook his head. 'I disagree. You're taking all these random things and assembling them as paranoia sees fit. It's the way those fake astrologers work; throw out a load of old guff and let the masses make the facts fit the fiction. Or the fiction fit the facts, if you prefer.'

'I think the child has lived before as Purple-five. And she's been sent back to punish us.'

King laughed and fiddled with a new red cravat given to him by his lover in more rational times. 'At what point did Gypsy Rose Lee possess you, Charles?'

'She was a dancer and a stripper, not a fortune teller.'

'Don't split hairs. You come back from that woman's house laying claim to wild supposition, and you expect me to fall into line and accept that some teacher at your school has given birth to the reincarnation of Purple-five?'

'Yes.'

'Are you aware of how fanciful that sounds?'

'I believe it's true.'

'And I believe one day Jammie Dodgers will inherit the earth, but belief and reality are distant cousins. Just stop and consider what you're saying for one moment.'

'I've done nothing but,' Honeywell protested.

'It's outrageous.'

'And she speaks of a tall man. You're over six feet.'

King changed course, lest they hit an iceberg and the conversation went the way of the Titanic. 'We need a holiday.'

Honeywell removed his glasses and rubbed his injured eye. 'I thought you wanted to start another game tomorrow?'

'It can wait.'

'I don't want a holiday. I want to sort this mess out.'

'Would you like a thump in the other eye?'

Honeywell hastily returned his glasses to their rightful place. 'No.'

'Then stop being so objectionable.'

'I'm not. I'm scared.'

'"Cowards die many times before their deaths; The valiant never taste of death but once." Julius Caesar.'

'I'm aware who said it.'

'Then take note of it.'

'I'm at my wits end, Peter. You didn't see the girl.'

'Then perhaps I should.'

Honeywell looked doubtful. 'I can't just turn up on Mel's doorstep with you in tow.'

'Do I look as if I've taken leave of my senses?'

'No, but'

'Then stop alluding to it. I know someone who might be able help with this matter. Put it to bed once and for all.'

'Who?'

'Gavin Westwood.'

'Who's he?'

'An acquaintance. He's a trained hypnotist. He could regress the girl.'

If Honeywell had been a chicken, he might very well have leapt onto the table and started scratching and pecking. 'But… but… but… what if he finds out?'

'If, by some miracle, your fears about the girl are justified, rest assured Gavin won't say a word.'

'I've not heard you speak of him before.'

'That's because I don't gossip.'

'We can't just hypnotise her. Mel might not want that.'

'It's not about what she wants. It's about what *we* want.'

'But'

'It's your job to persuade her, Charles.'

'How?'

'For God's sake, man, use your imagination. Tell her that Gavin is a reputable hypnotherapist, and promise her that no harm will come to the child.'

'And if Chloe really was Purple-five?'

'Then we'll have little option but to kill her.'

'We're not killing a child.'

King smiled. It didn't touch his eyes. 'We will do what is necessary. Death shall lie "on her like an untimely frost".'

'It's all very well quoting *Romeo and Juliet*, but we're talking about a four-year-old child, Peter. Not a fancy line from a fancy'

'Be careful of words, Charles; they may form themselves into a sentence of death.'

Honeywell snapped his mouth shut.

'No one is indispensable.'

'But'

'What doesn't kill you will make you wish it had.'

'I don't like this. What if Westwood turns out to be untrustworthy?'

'He won't.'

'How can you be so sure?'

'I know things about him.'

'Such as?'

'What he likes to do with patients under his care.'

'What do you mean?'

'Do you need everything spelling out? He commits acts of gross indecency whilst they are under his spell. He also films these rather distasteful episodes for his own perverted gratification and shares them with other like-minded souls on the Dark Web. Satisfied?'

Honeywell didn't look it. His bruised eye stood out on his ashen face like a plum in the snow. 'How do you know this?'

'Because he told me.'

'Why?'

'He trusts me.'

'Is he aware of what we do?'

'No.'

'Why would he confide in you?'

'His tongue tends to loosen when he's had too much wine.'

'Why have you never spoken of him before?'

'Is that a tinge of green I see in those blue eyes?'

'I'm not jealous; I'm curious.'

'And we all know what that did to the cat.'

'I don't like this.'

'You're beginning to irritate, Charles. Perhaps you ought to go for a nap. See if you can't wake up in a more genial mood. I'd hate to see this petty disagreement escalate into something regrettable.'

'I'm just worried.'

'And jealous.'

'I'm not.'

'Your eyes tell a different story.'

'Perhaps they'd look otherwise if you hadn't walloped me.'

'They'll look even worse with pennies on the lids.'

'I still don't understand how I'm supposed to persuade Mel Hollis to bring her child to a complete stranger and allow her to be hypnotised.'

'By convincing her that Gavin Westwood is a trusted family friend. That he is a reputable hypnotherapist, and she is at liberty to stop the regression any time she wishes.'

'And if she does stop the regression?'

'She won't. I'll get Gavin to put her under before we start.'

'You're going to be there?'

King smiled. This time, the smile sparkled in his blue eyes like sunshine glinting on an ocean. 'I wouldn't miss it for the world.'

'But how will I introduce you to Mel?'

'You won't have to. I'll stay out of the way until she's put under. Anyway, stop fussing. By the time school rings the bell for the new term, they'll both be dead.'

Honeywell looked about to object.

'Yes?'

'Nothing.'

King watched him walk out the room. Charles was letting emotion and sentimentality stand in the way of good reason.

'"Though patience be a tired mare, yet she will plod,"' King said. 'Though in this case, I fear she plods straight to the knacker's yard.'

CHAPTER TWENTY-ONE

Chloe was in her room having a nap when Honeywell turned up unannounced two days before New Year's Eve. Chloe seemed to be tiring so much more easily than she used to, almost regressing back to when she was a toddler, but Mel put it down to the trauma of the last couple of weeks. The last thing she wanted to do was force her to stay awake and cause another problem.

Mel was pleased to see him. She'd had a long argument on the phone with Tony about what he'd described as his 'forced exile'. A ridiculous term for what amounted to self-pity on his behalf, justice on Mel's. She'd disconnected the call, unplugged the phone and switched off her mobile.

Having allowed Chloe to speak to her father before the ill-fated attempt at civil conversation, Mel had spent half an hour answering questions and pretending to miss Daddy, too, when all she really wanted to do was stick pins in the bastard's eyes.

She invited Honeywell in and made them both coffee. She'd made a vow that morning to lay off the booze. Its healing power lasted for about two hours after climbing into bed. Weighed against thumping headaches and half the night spent at the kitchen table smoking far too many cigarettes, Mel had sought solace in chocolate for the foreseeable future. She'd rather be fat than turn into her booze-addled mother.

Charles Honeywell sipped his coffee and drummed his fingers on his knee.

'Are you all right, Charles?'

'Me? Yes. Fine. Worried about you, that's all.'

'I'll survive.'

'I'm sure you will. That's not the same as living, though, is it?'

'I suppose not.'

'Any news on the husband front?'

'No. And good riddance.'

'That bad?'

'Yes.'

'Beyond repair?'

'Yes.'

'From my experience, nothing is ever truly extinguished. A spark can sometimes be found in the deepest pile of ashes.'

'I doubt it.'

'I have a proposition for you, Mel. Don't feel obliged to accept.'

'What is it?'

'I have a friend who's interested in trying to help Chloe.'

Mel's eyes widened. 'Who?'

'He's a hypnotherapist.'

'How's a hypnotherapist going to help her?'

Honeywell took a deep breath. 'He specialises in regressive hypnotherapy. It's perfectly safe. He's highly reputable. He could take her back, Mel. Back beyond this life. See if her outbursts really are linked to a past life.'

'Isn't that dangerous?'

'I wouldn't dream of suggesting anything that might harm Chloe.'

Mel shook her head. 'She's far too young.'

'He assures me it's better that she *is* a child. She hasn't got so far to go back.'

'What if something terrible happens to her?'

'Such as?'

Mel gnawed her index finger. 'She died a terrible death if the picture of the guillotine is anything to go by. What if this hypnotist takes her back and she dies again? What then?'

'He's extremely experienced.'

'That's not an answer, Charles.'

'Gavin's regressed lots of children. He'll be in complete control at all times. First sign of any trouble, he'll bring Chloe straight out of the hypnotic state.'

'Can I ask you something?'

'Of course.'

'What would you do if it was your child, Charles?'

Honeywell looked hesitant.

'All you had left in the world?'

'I'd want to help her.'

'By putting her in the hands of a stranger?'

'Gavin Westwood's not a stranger, Mel. He's a friend.'

'He's a stranger to me.'

'I'm sorry. It was only a suggestion. I didn't mean to upset you.'

Mel lit a cigarette. 'I'm sorry. I'm just at my wits end. We have two days where nothing happens, and I think everything's gone back to normal, then, BAM! It's as if Chloe is two different people, switching from one to the other in the blink of an eye.'

'It must be awful for you. Beyond awful. I've never had children, but I've been lucky enough to nurture young talent in my capacity as both a teacher and a headmaster. I care deeply about children, Mel. My job allows me to fulfil a wish that my personal life does not. I understand how frightened you must be, with the added responsibility of being Chloe's parent, but you can't afford to sit back and hope this will all go away.'

'I know.'

'You're an intelligent woman, Mel. A great teacher. Blessed with a gift. I'm just trying to help you.'

Mel almost told him she thought Chloe would die if someone didn't help her. But a hypnotist? How on earth was taking Chloe back to the most traumatic situation imaginable going to help her? It might end up doing the exact opposite.

'Would it help to sway you if Gavin regressed you first? Let you experience it for yourself.'

Mel shrugged and put out her cigarette. 'I've never been murdered before as far as I know.'

'It might help you to see the procedure is harmless before you allow Chloe to go ahead.'

'I need time to think about it. It's too much to take in.'

'I understand.'

'Mummy?' Chloe shuffled down the stairs, one hand clutching the bannister, the other holding Ruby Rag Doll.

'Hey, Pumpkin.'

Chloe sat on the sofa next to her mother. 'You woke me up.'

'I'm sorry. Mummy was just talking to the headmaster from school.'

Charles Honeywell smiled. 'Hello, Chloe.'

Chloe stuck her thumb in her mouth.

Mel wrapped an arm around her daughter. 'Say hello to Mr. Honeywell.'

Chloe pulled Ruby Rag Doll close to her.

Mel rolled her eyes. 'She's tired.'

'I'll get off. Leave you two lovely ladies to it. Give me a ring and let me know what you decide.' He took a card from his pocket and handed it to her. 'That's got my mobile number on it.'

'Thanks.'

'I don't like him, Mummy.'

'Chloe! Don't be so rude.'

Honeywell walked to the porch and put his coat on. 'It's all right. I'd be grumpy if someone had just woken me up.'

Chloe lifted her head and turned to face Honeywell. '"Out, out, brief candle! Life's but a walking shadow."'

Honeywell's mouth hung open. He stared at Chloe Hollis as if she'd just sprouted two heads.

Chloe buried her head in her mother's chest.

Mel looked at Honeywell, stunned. 'Isn't that *Macbeth*?'

'I believe so.'

'But she doesn't know any Shakespeare.'

'I don't suppose she does… please, consider my offer, Mel. I fear inaction might lead to something neither of us want.' He let himself out the front door.

Mel shivered as a gust of icy wind blew through the house. She held Chloe tighter. 'Why were you rude to Mr. Honeywell?'

'I don't like him.'

'Why not?'

'He's bad.'

'He only wants to help.'

'And you believe the liar's promise, do you?'

Mel's brain started spinning like a centrifuge. Where the hell had that just come from? Not from the mind of a child. 'He's the headmaster at Mummy's school.'

Chloe buried her head deeper into Mel's chest. When she spoke, her words seemed to pass right through Mel's body and into her heart. 'Then I pity the children.'

And with that, she was asleep again.

CHAPTER TWENTY-TWO

Charles Honeywell found his lover, after a frantic search of the house, including the wine cellar, garden, and several outbuildings had failed to locate him, secreted in the bowels of Feelham Theatre dressed as Shakespeare, in padded Elizabethan attire, strutting about in the centre of the painted game board squares like the hammiest actor ever known to man.

'"Out, out, brief candle! Life's but a walking shadow, a poor player that struts and frets his hour upon the stage and then is heard no more: it is a tale told by an idiot, full of sound and fury, signifying nothing."'

'It's all true,' Honeywell babbled. 'All of it.'

King jumped and spun around as if Macbeth had transcended both time and possibility and joined him on his imaginary stage. 'Good God, you stupid man, you almost gave me a heart attack.'

Honeywell didn't seem perturbed by this news. In fact, his natural nervous state seemed to thrive on it. '"Out, out, brief candle."'

'Are you mocking me?'

Honeywell's eyes snapped to attention in their sockets. 'That's what she said.'

'Who?'

'The girl.'

'What girl?'

'Chloe.'

'She quoted *Macbeth*?'

Honeywell bobbed his head like one of those silly nodding dogs that once adorned parcel shelves across the land to satisfy a need for cheap novelty.

'Why in heaven's name would she do that?'

Honeywell looked as if he'd just been asked to explain deep space. 'I don't know.'

'She must have learned it from the mother. People like to teach their offspring tricks to impress.'

'Mel's not like that.'

'How do you know? Have you had an intimate relationship with her?'

'On a professional level, yes. But that's beside the point. She wasn't just quoting Shakespeare.'

'Don't tell me; she was dressed at one of the Three Witches.'

'She was quoting from the exact passage you were when I walked in.'

King was about to dismiss this latest drivel with the contempt it deserved when Honeywell repeated the text. '"Out, out, brief candle."'

'She actually said that?'

'Yes.'

'Word for word?'

'Yes.'

'How peculiar.'

'It's bloody well scary, Peter. It's as if she knows things. And…'

King waited, confidence dented by the spooky relationship between the child's words and his own. When nothing was forthcoming, he said, 'And, what?'

'She told her mother she didn't like me.'

King sighed. 'Is that all?'

'It's enough,' Honeywell squawked. 'For God's sake, it's as if she remembers me.'

'How could she? Even if I were to buy this ridiculous notion that the child was once Purple-five, how in all that's sane would she remember you? You always dress as Christopher Marlowe when we play One False Move.'

'She just *knows*.'

'Don't be ludicrous. She simply doesn't like you. Children don't possess a filter for expressing what's on their minds. They are all narcissistic brats.'

'I don't agree.'

'Perhaps her honesty sits unwell with your vanity?'

'I'm not vain,' Honeywell protested.

'You're the headmaster of a primary school. You're vain. Stop sulking and tell me what the mother said regarding hypnotherapy.'

'She'll think about it.'

'Is that all?'

'What do you expect? She's hardly going to surrender her child to an unknown entity just like that. I told her to phone me and let me know.'

King raised his eyebrows. 'And in the meantime?'

'I don't follow.'

'We simply wait and see what else the child lets slip?'

'I thought you said this was all stuff and nonsense?'

'It is.'

'Why the urgency, then?'

King walked to within a foot of his lover. The fake moustache was tickling the bottom of his nose, inciting an urge to sneeze. The clip-on gold hooped earring was also pinching his lobe. 'Because Gavin Westwood is a busy man.'

'A man with secrets can always make time.'

'Don't play with words, Charles. Gavin Westwood and favours are difficult to come by. And we have a new game of One False Move waiting.'

'I can't force her to bring the child.'

'Are you aware of the word, *coercion*?'

'Yes. But I didn't want to push too hard in case she got all defensive and dismissed the idea out of hand. You've got to understand, Peter, she's emotionally wrecked by all this. Her husband has walked out on her.'

'Are you my partner or the woman's defence barrister?'

'I'm just saying we need to tread lightly.'

'The husband's leaving is a blessing.'

'If you say so.'

'Did you tell her Gavin would regress her first? Put her mind at rest?'

'Yes. But what if something goes wrong?'

'It won't. Gavin can put her in a deep trance whilst we go about our business with the child. He can program the mother's mind to forget the whole thing once she gets home.'

'Seriously?'

'Yes.'

'And then what?'

'If it turns out the child was Purple-five, we'll simply work out the best way to eliminate the pair of them.'

'I'm not comfortable with killing them.'

'I'm not concerned with your comfort, Charles. If you want to play with wolves, you must also be prepared to howl at the moon.'

Honeywell's good eye adopted a sly confused look King didn't care for. 'If she hasn't phoned by tonight, I want you to go back and put on your best salesman's head.'

'My career has been in teaching.'

'What is teaching if it's not selling the myth of education?'

'It's'

'If you want my opinion, most of the stuff scratched onto blackboards is a lie. The classroom is the greatest propaganda tool known to man. The establishment have just seized upon the perfect opportunity to brainwash the masses.'

'I must object.'

'Mind control, Charles.'

'Without education, no one would be able to read and write.'

King adjusted the woollen padding in his black, laced doublet. He'd not been able to dress properly because the drawstrings were at the back. He'd just wanted to connect with Shakespeare's character for an hour before returning to the murky business in hand. First the rent boy, now the child. It was as if fate was conspiring against him.

'You might not have encountered Shakespeare's works without an education.'

'I have my mother to thank for my affinity with Shakespeare.'

'Education is a gift.'

'It's a curse. And so is your irritating manner. Stop defending the indefensible. I want you to arrange a meeting. Tomorrow at noon. You can pick them up and take them to Gavin's office.'

'His office? Where?'

'It's in Oxford. I'll give you the postcode for the satnav.'

'I don't even know the man.'

'I'm not asking you to form a meaningful relationship with him.'

'Have you?'

King pursed his lips. 'Have I what?'

'Formed a relationship with him?'

'He's merely an acquaintance from way back. Long before I met you.'

'Was he a lover?'

'He's not my type.'

'What *is* your type?'

'I'm with *you*, am I not?'

'I sometimes wonder.'

'Take charge of your emotions, Charles. Envy is so off-putting.'

'I'm'

'"O, beware, my lord, of jealousy; it is the green-eyed monster which doth mock the meat it feeds on."'

King watched his lover turn around and stomp up the basement steps like a child refused its supper. He waited for him to close the door, took a deep breath, and exclaimed to the empty basement, '"Good night, sweet friend: thy love ne'er alter, till thy sweet life end."'

CHAPTER TWENTY-THREE

When Honeywell turned up at the house just after breakfast, Mel was in acute danger of losing her sanity. She'd spent half the night comforting Chloe after another screaming fit, and the rest of it lying awake watching shadows on the ceiling, waiting for another outburst, hand tracing the space beside her that Tony had occupied before infidelity had got the better of his weak and useless mind.

Chloe was watching a *Little Mermaid* DVD, giggling every time Sebastian the crab appeared. She seemed oblivious to last night's events, and Mel was in no mood to remind her. The poor kid was traumatised enough already.

She invited Honeywell into the kitchen and made him a strong black coffee. She opened the back door and lit a cigarette.

'Are you all right, Mel? You look as if you didn't get much sleep.'

'I didn't get any.'

'Do you want to talk about it?'

'There's not much to say. Chloe woke up screaming. It took me ages to get her back to sleep. Then I couldn't shut off my mind.'

'It must be hard for you, on your own with no one to talk to.'

'You could say that.'

'I've had a word with Gavin Westwood. He's free today.'

Mel hesitated. Too many unanswered questions were still running around inside her head regarding hypnotism. It was virtually impossible to know which way to turn. Finally, she said, 'I'm scared it will do more harm than good.'

'Think of Gavin as the man who can open the door to Chloe's mind.'

'And what if he can't close it again?'

'He's done this hundreds of times, Mel. No one's ever come to any harm.'

'There's a first time for everything.'

'He'll be in complete control at all times. And he'll be able to bring Chloe straight back to the present with just a click of his fingers.'

'What if he can't?'

'I understand your apprehension. But sometimes you just have to take a leap of faith. If Chloe was ill, you'd trust her to the care of a doctor, wouldn't you?'

'That's different.'

'How so?'

'Because doctors know what they're doing.'

'You only say that because you're more familiar with doctors than hypnotists. But it's only a perception.'

'I'll bear that in mind if Chloe ever needs an operation.'

'Maybe revisiting the past will help to bring closure. Exorcise the ghost within her. Help her to heal, move on, fulfil the wonderful life she's been given with you.'

Mel flicked her cigarette butt into the garden. 'How long will it take?'

He shrugged. 'I'm not sure. But you'll be with her at all times. If there's anything you don't like, you can ask Gavin to stop immediately. He'll bring Chloe straight back to the here and now.'

Mel fiddled with her cigarettes, pulled one halfway out, slid it back in. 'And you're certain no harm will come to her?'

'I promise.'

'She's all I have left.'

'I know.'

Mel looked out the kitchen window at the naked trees standing proud beyond the wall separating the house from the park. They looked as if they were giving thanks to the heavens, skeletal arms raised skywards.

Sometimes you just have to take a leap of faith.

'I've already lost one daughter. I don't want to lose another.'

Honeywell's uninjured eye widened. 'I'm sorry. I had no idea.'

'No, well… I don't make a habit of announcing it.'

'How dreadful.'

'She was three months old. Three lousy months. What sort of life is that?'

Honeywell's Adam's apple bobbed up and down in his throat as if trying to dredge up words from his heart.

'She was so tiny. So vulnerable. So helpless.'

'Life can be unbearably cruel.'

'I had to stand by, useless, and watch her fight for the right to live. Three months. Barely a school term.'

Honeywell fiddled with his glasses. 'I'm so sorry.'

'All that poor little mite ever knew was that incubator. Tubes and needles. Do you know what she looked like?'

Honeywell shook his head. He didn't make eye contact.

'A fucking experiment.'

'I can't imagine how'

'And then she died.'

'I have no words to comfort you, Mel. No experience to draw upon. I can only'

'And what does Tony do? What does my super-supportive husband do? Screws the first bitch on heat he can find.'

Honeywell looked visibly shaken.

'Stephanie Wallace. A teacher at Tony's school. The very thought of the two of them together makes me feel sick to the stomach. All the time I was crying myself to sleep, those two were at it like they didn't have a care in the world.'

'I can see why you're angry.'

Mel snorted. 'Angry? You think I'm angry? I'm fucking heartbroken. I lost my daughter, for Christ's sake. How could he be so callous?'

'I struggle to comprehend his actions, Mel. I truly do.'

'I wanted him to support me. Understand me. Love me. Is that really too much to ask?'

'Not at all.'

'But oh no, not Tony. He throws himself at the first bitch who'll have him. Not a care in the world. It was as if Megan's life counted for nothing as far as he was concerned.'

'I'm sure that's not true.'

'It is. I've a good mind to report him to the school. Expose him for what he is. A dirty, worthless, gutless liar.'

'I think you need to try to let it go, Mel. Focus on the future.'

'That's easier said than done. I've already lost virtually everything. I don't want to lose Chloe as well. She's the only reason I haven't thrown myself off the top of a cliff. Believe me.'

'I understand.'

'Do you? Do you really?'

Honeywell nodded, lips pressed into a thin line.

After a lengthy silence, Mel said, 'Okay. We'll do it.'

'You won't regret it.'

'I will hold you personally responsible if anything goes wrong.'

'It won't.'

'I wish I shared your optimism, Charles. I really do.'

CHAPTER TWENTY-FOUR

King, back home and once more dressed as himself in a smart black suit, crisp white shirt and a pink tie more designed to make a statement than draw compliment, greeted the news that Mel Hollis had agreed to surrender her child to regressive hypnotherapy with a rare authentic smile. 'Wonders shall never cease.'

'I don't like doing this to her. Deceiving her.'

'We spend most of our lives carrying out unfavourable tasks. Do you think God should grant you immunity?'

'No, but'

'You've done a splendid job by getting her to agree. Don't spoil it by pursuing a career in doubt.'

'I'm'

'I take it she's not waiting in the driveway?'

'I'm picking her up at eleven-thirty.'

'Good. Gavin's expecting you at midday. There's a parking bay behind the office. For heaven's sake make sure you park in the correct one. The charity shop and Boots are most objectionable if you dare to use their space. Gavin's is marked *The Wellbeing Clinic*.'

'Considering Westwood's true nature, the title's a rather contradictory one.'

'Wit and your tongue seem to have made a casual acquaintance since we last met. Perhaps Mel Hollis brings out the best in you?'

'She scares the hell out of me, if you want the truth.'

'Gavin has a secretary. Olivia. She's complicit. She knows the regression of the child is for the greater good.'

'Can she can be trusted?'

'Olivia started life as plain old Oliver. She's got enough skeletons in her cupboard to challenge Feelham Cemetery to a head count. She first came to Gavin for therapy about ten years ago. It soon transpired she'd suffered a very troubled childhood, resulting in several years in a young offenders' institute after beating a classmate unconscious. Apparently, Olivia's somewhat effeminate nature seemed to attract merciless bullying at school. The time spent locked up gave her a chance to discover her true nature. She never looked back after gaining boobs and an artistic flair with a makeup brush. She also likes to take part in therapy sessions.'

'What do you mean?'

'Let's just say she has a gift for performing sexual acts on male subjects whilst the camera is rolling. She's a very dutiful secretary. And a grateful one. So, please don't worry about loyalty as far as that one's concerned.'

'If you're sure.'

'I am. And don't stare at her hands; they look more suited to bricklaying than typing.'

Honeywell nodded. His Adam's apple bobbed up and down, reminding King of another of Olivia's little discrepancies. 'And don't stare at her throat, either. She's very conscious of her male heritage.'

'I'll just avoid looking at him… her, period.'

'*Period*? Is this another example of American terminology leaking into schools in the twenty-first century? I thought you qualified as an English teacher?'

'I did.'

'Then kindly adhere to its roots. Anyway, back to the delightful Olivia. The child can wait with her whilst Gavin puts the mother under.'

'What if Mel doesn't want to be hypnotised?'

'Hypnotists don't need permission. Gavin will work his magic whilst she answers his preliminary questions. She won't even be aware anything's happened. Nor will the brat. She'll think Mummy is still as normal as apple pie.'

'The child's extremely sensitive.'

'So are my teeth. What of it?'

'She might not react the way you expect her to.'

'What do you suggest, Charles? We offer her a lollipop and a good-girl sticker?'

'I'm just saying she needs handling carefully.'

'Gavin can put her into a state of compliance just by greeting her. He's a natural. Relax.'

'And if it turns out Chloe really was Purple-five?'

'Then we make plans to eliminate her.'

'Can't Westwood just re her mind? Plant a false memory or something?.'

'Any suggestions? Dorothy from *The Wizard of Oz*, perhaps?'

Honeywell cocked his head to one side. 'I'

'If we give her a false memory, the girl might end up with multiple personalities, all willing to tell tales. Is that a risk worth taking?'

'It was only a suggestion.'

'Stop trying to take charge. You might be the head honcho at your kindergarten, strutting about like a preening peacock, but you'd do well to remember your place when at home.'

'Don't forget whose idea this was if it all goes wrong.'

King turned on his heel and walked along the oak-panelled hallway to the front door. 'And don't *you* forget which side your bread is buttered; it can so easily turn to burnt toast.'

The journey to Oxford did little to lift his spirits. After electing to drive the scenic route and getting stuck behind a tractor, he'd then suffered the humiliation of the tractor driver reacting badly to his constant blaring of the horn to let him past. The oaf, large enough to bale hay with his bare hands, had climbed out of his medieval contraption and offered King the chance to take part in an illegal boxing match. Or, more to the point, and truer to the script, rearrange his face into an unrecognisable pulp. King had declined, and spent the rest of the journey to Oxford trying to stop his knees knocking together and his hands shaking on the steering wheel.

Gavin smiled and shook his hand upon arrival. King made minimal eye contact, wary of the powers lurking behind those sly brown eyes. He was alarmed to learn the hypnotist still seemed capable of reading his mind. 'You look as if you stole the Honey Monster's Sugar Puffs and he came after you to get them back.'

King told him about the tractor driver, leaving out the part where he'd pleaded for his life, and embellishing the tale by telling Westwood he'd sent the brute packing with threats of the police and prison.

'Prison?'

'Told him I was a high court judge.'

'Good for you.'

'Bloody Neanderthals. Be better for all concerned when we don't need them for manual labour.'

Gavin smiled, and led him up a narrow wooden staircase to his first-floor office. A large mahogany desk dominated the room, complete with a computer and paper tidy. A six-foot tall rubber plant added a touch of greenery to the corner of the room. Various plaques and framed certificates were hanging on the pine-panelled walls declaring Gavin Westwood's expertise in his chosen field. Not one offered evidence of his greatest speciality: perversion.

Gavin stroked his dyed black moustache and treated King to a stare that seemed to peek deep into his soul. 'What's the score, Peter? You say the child is exhibiting past-life memory?'

King tried to look nonchalant. He still felt shaky from his brief encounter with Cro-Magnon Man's primitive relative, the farmer. 'I don't. Charles does.'

'Your headmaster friend?'

King nodded. 'As I told you, the girl's mother is a teacher at his school. He's trying to help her.'

Westwood nodded. 'This headmaster friend of yours? What have you told him about me?'

'Nothing. Other than you're a fine hypnotist.'

'Is he aware of our… arrangement?'

'No. And I'd prefer it if we keep it that way.'

Westwood tapped the side of his nose. 'Discretion is my middle name.'

'I want you to put the mother into a trance whilst you regress the child.'

'Okay.'

'I don't want her interfering if it all turns nasty. Programme her to believe all is well with the kid. Oh, and I want her to have no recollection of the session.'

'Any special reason?'

'I'd appreciate it if you'd just carry out my instruction. Once mother and daughter are both under control, I want to sit in and observe.'

'If I didn't know you better, I'd assume you were trying to avoid this woman.'

'Assumption is the plaything of the ignorant.'

'Is there anything you're not telling me, Peter?'

'It's personal.'

'No nasty surprises waiting to hijack the session?'

'No.'

'The twitch in your left eye suggests otherwise.'

'The twitch in my left eye is due to the stress of having to keep my true association with you a secret from Charles.'

'Why would you want to do that?'

'Because he's given to bouts of jealousy.'

'What on earth for?'

An invisible hand slapped King's pride. He noticed, with some satisfaction, specks of dandruff on Westwood's shoulders. 'I'm a handsome man. It can elicit insecurities.'

'Your modesty knows no bounds, Peter. Anyway, down to business. The child's past-life experience. Do we know how she died?'

'Executed by guillotine apparently.'

Westwood whistled. 'Sounds as if she was involved in the French Revolution.'

'Sounds more like fanciful nonsense. You just drill down and see what you can find.'

'I'll do my best.'

'And I want this done in the strictest confidence.'

'My lips are sealed.'

'I'll wait in the stockroom. Come and get me when you're ready to regress the girl.'

CHAPTER TWENTY-FIVE

Honeywell took Mel and Chloe up the stairs to Gavin Westwood's small waiting room. A light-oak coffee table in the middle of the room offered magazines. Venetian blinds, coated with dust, carved the large window overlooking the carpark into slices of silver-grey light.

Olivia walked out from behind a reception desk at the end of the waiting room. She offered refreshments. Mel and Honeywell declined. Olivia turned her attention to Chloe, treating the child to a set of white teeth which looked capable of glowing in the dark. Copious amounts of black eyeliner and mascara made her eyes look predatory rather than pretty.

'Would you like a biscuit and some lemonade, sweetie?'

Chloe didn't answer. She buried her head in her mother's side, holding onto Mel's coat with one hand and Ruby Rag Doll with the other. They sat down on padded red leather chairs. Mel hoisted Chloe onto her lap.

'I want to go home, Mummy.'

'We won't be here for long, sweetheart.'

'We've got cake left over from my birthday,' Olivia tried. 'It's got jam and cream.'

Chloe clutched her doll as if protecting it.

'Do you want some cake?' Mel prompted.

Chloe shook her head. She didn't look at Olivia.

'I'm sorry. She's left her manners at home today.'

Olivia returned the smile and walked back to the reception desk. 'She's young. She's allowed.'

Chloe said, 'I don't like her.'

'Don't be rude,' Mel warned. 'She's just being nice.'

Gavin Westwood walked into the waiting room. He offered a hand to Honeywell. 'Hi Charles. I trust you are well?'

Honeywell took his hand and shook it limply. 'As well as can be expected .'

He turned his attention to Chloe. 'So, this is the young lady I've heard so much about?'

Mel answered for her. 'She's not in the best of moods today.'

Westwood knelt down so as he was at eye level with Chloe. 'Don't want to be here, right?'

Chloe fiddled with Ruby's head as if picking her brains for an answer.

'My name's Gavin. What's yours.'

Chloe didn't look up when she spoke. Her lips barely moved. 'You know what it is.'

'Do I?'

'Yes.'

'Is it Ethel?'

Chloe sighed.

'Primrose?'

'I want to go home, Mummy.'

'Martha. I'll bet it's Martha.'

Chloe looked up. 'Go away.'

Westwood held up a hand. 'Okay. You're the boss.'

Mel apologised.

'It's no bother, Mum.' He looked back at Chloe. 'You're all right now, aren't you?'

Chloe stroked Ruby's woollen hair. Seemed to relax. 'I suppose.'

'Just been a long day, hasn't it, Chloe?'

'Long as Mummy's nose.'

Mel smiled. 'Hey, that's rude!'

Westwood looked over at the receptionist. 'Olivia? Be a dear and show Chloe one of those funky games on the computer.'

Olivia looked less certain of herself than when she'd greeted them a few minutes ago. 'Is that all right with you, Chloe?'

Chloe jumped off her mother's lap. 'Cool.'

'Me and Mummy are just going to have a little chat in my office,' Westwood said. 'You okay with that?'

'Uh-huh.'

Mel watched Olivia take Chloe's hand and walk back to the desk. It was as if Westwood had waved a magic wand over her daughter and transformed her into a different child. Normal, compliant, happy.

'Come on through to the office. We can have a little chat about what will happen and so forth.'

Seated at his desk, Westwood formed a steeple with his fingers. 'Charles tells me your daughter's been experiencing some rather disturbing memories?'

Mel almost laughed at the understatement. 'You could say that.'

'From a past life?'

'Yes.'

'How about you? How are you coping?'

'Not too good.'

'I can imagine.'

'It's as if my whole world has been turned upside down.'

'Who cares for the carers, eh?'

Mel thought his voice had a velvety texture to it. Soothing. 'You could say that.'

'It's important you take some of the responsibility off your shoulders. You're not built of stone.'

'More like bloody glass.'

'I want you to close your eyes now.'

Mel did.

'Isn't it wonderful to shut out the material world?'

'Yes.'

'To blank out all those distractions which constantly seek our attention?'

'Wonderful.'

'I'd like you to take deep even breaths. Then I want you to count slowly backwards from ten to zero. As you do so, cast your worries to the wind. Give them all back to the universe.'

Mel counted backwards while Westwood gazed out the window. Finished, he returned his attention to her. 'Are you relaxed?'

'Yes.'

'Is anything troubling you?'

'No.'

'I want your mind to stay open to everything I suggest.'

'Okay.'

'You can open your eyes now.'

Mel stared at Westwood, eyes wide.

'How do you feel, Mel?'

'Fine.'

'You see that leather chair in the corner of the room?'

'Yes.'

'I want you to sit in it and stay there until I tell you to get up.'

Mel walked to the chair and sat down, her mind completely at peace for the first time since before Megan had died.

'I'm going to have a little chat with Chloe in a minute.'

'Okay.'

'Are you happy for me to talk to her?'

'Yes.'

'You won't remember anything about the conversation, apart from Chloe is a very healthy and happy little girl, and that she has no problems. Do you understand?'

'Yes.'

'When you go home, you will have no recollection of your visit here.'

'Okay.'

'No more needless stress and worry. Just a long and happy life.'

Mel smiled.

'I'm going to get Chloe now. You remain seated and relaxed. '

'Okay.'

'I don't want you to react to your daughter in any way.'

'Okay.'

'You must only respond to my voice if I address you directly, understand?'

'Yes.'

'You will remain this way until I instruct you otherwise.'

'Okay.'

'Thank you, Mel. You may go into a deep sleep now.'

Mel closed her eyes. Her jaw slackened. Her chin fell onto her chest.

Westwood waved a hand in front of her face. She didn't react. He traced the outline of her lips with his index finger. Nothing. He reached out and touched her left breast.

Mel sighed.

Westwood straightened up, thrust his hands in his pockets, and walked back to the waiting room to fetch his latest subject.

CHAPTER TWENTY-SIX

Westwood told Olivia he was ready. Before they walked into the office, he crouched down in front of Chloe. 'How's the number one girl?'

'I'm okay.'

'Now, listen carefully, Chloe. When we go into the office, Mummy will be sitting in a big leather chair. She's just going to be with us while I talk to you, but it's important that we don't speak to her, okay?'

'Yes.'

'Good girl.'

Once seated behind the desk with Chloe sat opposite, he asked her if she was comfortable.

Chloe nodded, clutching Ruby to her chest.

'Big chair for a big girl.'

Chloe giggled.

'How old are you?'

'Four.'

'Wow! You're a clever girl for that age. Bet you're going to be famous when you grow up.'

'Like Barbie?'

Westwood grinned. 'Just like Barbie. How would you like to go on a journey with me?'

'Where to?'

'Back to when you were a baby.'

'I don't want to be a baby.'

'We're only visiting.'

'Like when I go to Aunty Carla's?'

'Exactly.'

'Okay.'

Westwood held up his right hand, palm facing Chloe. 'Look at the pretty pattern on my hand. What do you see?'

'It looks like Daddy's dart board.'

'Daddy has a dart board?'

'He says it's good for maths.'

'Daddy sounds like a lot of fun.'

'He is.'

'Look at Daddy's dartboard. Can you see the pretty swirling pattern?'

'Yes.'

'See how it's like a tunnel if you look closely?'

'Uh-huh.'

'The pattern will make your eyes sleepy in a minute. Don't worry. Just close them when this happens.'

Within a few seconds, Chloe's lids drooped, fluttered, came to rest.

'It's nice to close our eyes when we're tired, isn't it, Chloe?'

'Yes.'

'I want you to concentrate on the top of your head. The bit you scratch when you've got a problem.'

Chloe giggled.

'Imagine a bright light coming down through the top of your head, going down into your body, right to the bottoms of your feet. The light will make you happy and peaceful. You won't have a single care in the world.'

Chloe's breathing slowed.

'Your body is getting warmer. The warmth is spreading all the way through your body. Down your neck, into your chest, your arms, hands, tummy and legs.'

'Nice,' Chloe slurred.

'We're going to go into a beautiful garden in a moment. But first, I want you to let your mind go completely blank. You will hear nothing else until I tell you, Okay?'

Chloe nodded, head falling forward, hands resting limply on Ruby.

Westwood walked to the door keeping half an eye on his charge. 'Olivia?'

'Yes?'

'I'd like you to fetch Mr. King. He's in the storeroom.'

'Okay.'

King peered around the door a few moments later. 'Is it safe?'

'Of course.'

He stepped into the room and regarded Mel as if she might be a bomb capable of detonating at any minute. 'Is she still awake?'

'She's in a deep trance.'

King looked dubious. 'Are you sure?'

'Of course I'm sure.'

'And the girl?'

'Same. She's prepped and ready to go into a deepening state. I'm on the verge of taking her back. Now, I want you to keep quiet whilst I settle her on the mother's lap.'

'Won't the mother grow agitated if the girl experiences… difficulties?'

'The mother is programmed to respond to me and me alone. Unless I ask her a direct question, she'll be passive.'

'I hope you're right.'

Westwood lifted Chloe out of the chair and put her on her mother's lap. Mel, oblivious to this action, wrapped her arms around her daughter's waist by reflex.

King folded his tall frame into the empty chair. 'And you're sure neither of them will remember a thing?'

'The mother will believe her daughter is healthy and not suffering any past-life recollection.'

'And the child?'

'That's a different matter. Although I can program her to forget this meeting, I can't wipe her memory banks clean. What she's experienced in this life and beyond will have left an indelible mark.

Rather like a computer hard drive. You can delete your search history, but you can't get rid of it altogether.'

'Do you actually believe in all this past-life nonsense?'

Westwood picked up a pencil from the desk and sucked on the tip. 'Yes, and no.'

'Wonderful answer, Gavin. You ought to consider a career in politics.'

'I've regressed enough people to believe there's something to it. Dead lips don't lie. I mean, how can you remember things in such vivid detail from many years ago, often centuries, without having experienced them? Most cases I've come across are just too elaborate to be fabricated. I once had a man babble in ancient Hebrew.'

'He was probably Jewish.'

'He was a dustman and an atheist. I had another who appeared to have lived in Elizabethan times.'

King's interest was piqued. 'Not related to Shakespeare by any chance?'

'Not as I recall. Another died in a mining accident in 1886. The pit shaft collapsed and buried him alive, along with twenty other miners. It went some way to explaining his extreme fear of tunnels and lifts.'

'But surely he could have read a book or watched a film depicting a mining disaster?'

'His details were extraordinary. He had a vast knowledge of his life in a northern village. Considering the furthest north he'd ever ventured was Banbury, it was quite remarkable.'

'He might have studied the mining disaster in history at school.'

'Maybe,' Westwood agreed. 'Right, I want you to remain quiet once the regression gets underway. You can't interrupt me. That's vitally important.'

'What if I want to ask a question?'

Westwood pulled a pad and pencil out of a drawer. 'Write it down and show me.'

'But I'm talking now. What's the difference?'

'Think of the child as an idling engine at the moment. But once the regression starts, it will the same as slipping her into gear and pressing the accelerator pedal. Her senses will be alert to any outside influences.'

'Like a dream for you, eh, Gavin?'

'What?'

'Disturbed people coming to you with all their fears and phobias.'

'I'd be lying if I said the job didn't have its perks.'

King looked nervously around the office. 'You've got no cameras running now, have you?'

'No.'

'You sure about that?'

'Why would I waste film on something that has all the appeal of a runny dog turd?'

'What a dreadful turn of phrase. Shakespeare would spin in his grave if he could hear you.'

'Then thank goodness he can't. Right, any more questions before we begin?'

'How long will this take?'

'It depends on the detail and the depth of the regression.' He walked to within a couple of feet of Mel and Chloe. 'Right, let's get this show on the road.'

CHAPTER TWENTY-SEVEN

'Can you hear me, Chloe?'

'Yes.'

'Are you nice and warm?'

'Yes.'

'I want you to imagine you are standing at the top of ten large stone steps leading down into a beautiful garden.'

'Okay.'

'There's a handrail to hold onto. Can you see it?'

'Yes.'

'We're going to walk down the steps now. I will count each step. As I do so, I want you to concentrate on my voice. Deeper and deeper down, until we reach the garden. Okay?'

'Uh-huh.'

'Hold the rail tightly. Ready?'

'Yes.'

Westwood counted down from ten to one with a five second pause between each number. With each step, he told Chloe she was going into deeper and deeper levels of consciousness.

King caught his attention with the pad. On it, written in barely legible writing: *How does she even understand that???*

Westwood grabbed the pad and scrawled. *Because I'm not talking to her four-year-old brain. I'm talking to a much deeper level of consciousness.*

King snatched the pad back, seemed about to write something else, then put the pencil down.

Westwood returned his attention to the child. 'Okay, Chloe. I want you to step into the garden. Can you see all the lovely flowers?'

'Yes.'

'All the pretty pinks, blues, yellows and reds?'

'Yes.'

'This is where God lives. This is where he answers prayers. We're going to walk through the garden and sit by a lovely lake.'

'Okay.'

Westwood walked her through the garden and sat her down at the edge of the lake. 'Isn't this the most wonderful water? So clear? So blue?'

'Like my eyes.'

'Just like your eyes. Can you see all the fish swimming in it?'

'Yes.'

'You're safe here, Chloe. I won't let any harm come to you. You see the bridge leading across the lake?'

'Uh-huh.'

'In a minute, we will walk across it.'

'Where to?'

'A place where you used to live before you were born. But don't worry, we can come back any time. Is that all right with you?'

'I…'

'It doesn't matter for now. Let's just enjoy the water for a while. Go for a paddle if you want. Would you like that?'

'Yes.'

Westwood looked at King and put a thumb in the air. King returned the gesture with a look that spoke of sour taste.

After a few moments, Westwood spoke to Chloe again. 'Is the water nice?'

'Uh-huh.' Chloe kicked her legs. Her feet hit against Mel's shins, but her mother didn't respond.

King held up the pad again. *Can't we just cut to the chase?*

Westwood shook his head.

Chloe's eyes darted left and right beneath the lids. 'I don't want to go across the bridge.'

'Why?'

'I'm scared.'

'There's nothing to be afraid of. I'm here to protect you.'

'But'

'God won't let anything bad happen to you. I promise.'

King stared at Chloe, shaking his head. 'I knew this was'

Westwood rounded on him and shoved a finger against his lips so hard he jabbed a nostril. 'Shush.'

King closed his mouth, but his eyes did their level best to carry on the conversation.

'Chloe?'

'Yes?'

'I know this seems scary. But I'll be right there with you.'

'What about the Tall Man?'

Westwood hesitated. 'Who?'

Chloe pushed herself back against Mel. 'He's… bad.'

Westwood ignored the pad King was waving at him. 'Don't worry about him. No one can hurt you. I control everything that happens in the garden. I won't let anyone in. The Tall Man's banned. And that's a promise.'

'What if he sneaks in?'

'He won't. God's garden is protected by angels. They won't let the Tall Man anywhere near us.'

Chloe seemed to settle a bit. 'You sure?'

'Absolutely. We're all here to help you, Chloe. God, the angels, me. We all want what's best for you.'

'Okay.'

'Get out of the water now. Stand in the warm sunshine and take my hand.'

'Okay.'

'And remember you are loved and protected at all times, okay?'

Chloe nodded.

'Do you trust me, Chloe?'

'Yes.'

'Thank you. When you're ready, we'll walk over the bridge.'

'I don't like the trees. The Tall Man might be hiding.'

'No one's hiding. I told you, no one else is allowed here.'

'Promise?'

'I promise. Take my hand. We'll walk over the bridge together.'

Chloe's eyes darted about behind their closed lids. 'Okay.'

Westwood spoke about the sunshine, the clean fresh air, and how brave Chloe was as they crossed his imaginary bridge. Once over, he reassured Chloe that she was in no danger. She could let go of his hand.

'I don't like it here.'

'That's only because you're afraid of the unknown. But you've nothing to fear, Chloe. You're safe.'

'Where am I?'

'Just in another time. Another place. You see the path leading between the trees?'

Chloe nodded. 'It's like the one in Hansel and Gretel?'

'Exactly. We're going to walk along the path now, through the trees.'

'I don't want to.'

Westwood rolled his eyes and stroked his moustache. 'How would you like to fly over them instead?'

'I can't fly.'

'You can do anything you want to.'

'I haven't got wings.'

'Don't need them. You've got an imagination.'

'How will that make me fly?'

'Just close your eyes. I'll count to five, and then we'll take off.'

'Like Dumbo?'

'Exactly. Only smaller ears!'

Chloe giggled. 'Okay.'

'Ready?'

'Uh-huh.'

Westwood counted, reassuring Chloe once more that she was safe.

After several moments, Chloe gasped. 'I can see the tops of the trees.'

'Do you like flying?'

'Yeah. It's cool.'

'In a minute, we're going to land in a big field. It might make your tummy go funny as we come down, so hold on tight to my hand.'

'Okay.'

'As we come down, I want you to go back in time. Right back to before you were born, okay?'

After several seconds, Chloe jolted in her mother's lap, as if she'd just landed there in the midst of a dream.

Westwood waited a while before speaking again. When he did, his voice was soft and soothing. 'That wasn't so bad, was it?'

'No.'

'You can go back anytime you want.'

'Okay.'

'But it's important we stay for a while.'

'Why?'

'To find out who you are. Look at your feet. What are you wearing?'

'Nike trainers.'

'Nice!'

'Not really. They're too tight. Mum says if I want another pair, she'll get some off the market. Reckons money doesn't grow on trees. I never said it did! She only buys me good stuff when I do what I'm told.'

'What's wrong with that?'

'It's bribery.'

'What clothes are you wearing?'

'Dungarees and a white tee-shirt.'

'What colour are the dungarees?'

'Red.'

'That's a nice bright colour. Do you like bright clothes.'

She nodded. 'Grey is for grannies.'

'What colour is your hair?'

Chloe picked up her hair and held it in front of her closed eyes. 'Blonde.'

'I like blonde hair.'

'I prefer pink.'

'That's a strange colour.'

'It's not. I'll dye it as soon as I get away from home.'

'Why do you want to leave home?'

'Because my parents don't have a clue.'

'They probably only want what's best for you.'

'That's what my gran says. But it's not true. They only want what's best for them. So as they can show me off when their friends ask about me.'

'What's your name?'

'Amy.'

'That's a pretty name.'

'It's a granny name.'

'You seem to dislike old people.'

'Not really. I just don't want to be one.'

'What's your surname?'

'Constable.'

'How old are you, Amy?'

'Sixteen.'

'Do you still go to school?'

'Worse luck. But I'm leaving this summer.'

'What are you going to do?'

'Go to art school.'

'You like art, then?'

'Obviously.'

'Do you paint or draw?'

'I sketch stuff and then paint it in after.'

'You must be very talented.'

'Deluded, more like. That's what my parents reckon, anyway.'

'Maybe they don't understand.'

'They want me to be a pharmacist.'

'Sounds like a good job.'

'More like a waste of life.'

'Pharmacists are important.'

'So are toilet cleaners, but I don't want to be one.'

'If you could have one wish, what would it be, Amy?'

'To leave home.'

'Can't wait to be grown up, eh?'

'Something like that.'

'Where are you right now?'

'In Keeble's field.'

'What are you doing there?'

'I've been drawing a horse.'

'Oh, yes, I can see that now. It's superb.'

'Thanks.'

'Whereabouts do you live, Amy?'

'Woking.'

'Do you like Woking?'

'No. It's boring. I want to go to London one day.'

'Why?'

'Because… London is like Saturday night; Woking is like Monday morning.'

'That's a rather poetic way of describing it. Could you do me a favour, Amy?'

'What?'

'I want you to imagine you're a little older now.'

'Okay.'

'What's the oldest you can imagine yourself being?'

'Twenty-one.'

'Why twenty-one?'

'Don't know.'

'Did something happen to you when you were that age?'

A slight pause. 'I'm not sure.'

'Did you get to leave home?'

'Yes.'

'When?'

'When I was sixteen. In the summer. I packed up my art stuff in my satchel, took my savings, and caught a train to London.'

'That was a brave thing to do.'

'Dumb, more like.'

'Why?'

'That's where I met him.'

'Who?'

'Don't know what his real name was, but he said it was Thomas Kowalski.'

'That's a strange name.'

'Said he was Polish.'

'What did he look like?'

'He had a beard and moustache. Tall. Pot belly. But it was all a disguise.'

'Why would he be wearing a disguise?'

'So no one would recognise him. There's cameras everywhere these days.'

'Why wouldn't he want anyone to recognise him?'

'Because he lured me away to Oxford. Reckoned he had a sister in Oxford. Said she used to teach art and had connections to the Oxford Academy of Art. I couldn't believe my luck.'

'But he was lying?'

'Oh, yeah. A lying piece of scum. But like a gullible fool, I trusted him. It was as if all my dreams had come true. I would finally get a break. Show my parents they were wrong. Get enrolled at this academy and my life would take off like a hot air balloon. Trouble is, that's all it was: hot air.'

'How does that make you feel now?'

'Stupid. Cheated. Worthless.'

'So, you went back to Oxford with this Thomas Kowalski?'

'We caught the train.'

'What happened then?'

'He had a car parked at the train station. We drove back to his house.'

'Do you know where the house was?'

'It was about half an hour away from the station. He said it was his sister's house, but that was a lie.'

'No sister?'

'No. The house was all dark. He said she was visiting friends or something. But it just didn't feel right.'

'In what way?'

'I don't know. All I kept thinking about was how I would get to live my stupid dream. How I would make my parents eat their words when I returned home and told them about my enrolment at the art academy.'

'Nothing wrong with having a dream.'

'There is if you wind up dead.'

'What happened after you got back to his house?'

'He was being nice. The perfect gentleman. He allowed me to have a shower. Let me use his supposed sister's bathrobe. Treated me like frigging royalty. But it was all an act.'

'He sounds very devious.'

Chloe laughed. A harsh sound that had no business in a four-year-old child's throat. 'That's the understatement of the year. But how was I to know? He spun me a load of crap about his family being wiped out in the Second World War. How most of them got gassed in the concentration camps. Only him and his sister survived after getting smuggled out of Poland in a cattle truck. I doubt if he's even been to Poland.'

'Really?'

'He didn't even have an accent. Reckoned he was grateful to England for giving him the chance to live a free and fair life.'

'I take it you never got to meet his sister?'

'I told you, there wasn't one. It was all just a part of his lies. He made me tea. Chicken salad with new potatoes. And then he offered me a glass of wine. Taking that glass of wine was the biggest mistake of my life.'

'Why?'

'Because I was no longer in control. By the time I was halfway down the third glass, my head was spinning. At first, I felt great. Happy. About to do what I'd always wanted. I spilled some of the wine down my chin. When I tried to wipe it, I couldn't coordinate my hands properly. He moved in and out of focus. One minute he was sitting opposite me, the next, he was on the far side of the room.'

'How did that make you feel?'

'Scared.'

'What happened next?'

'I must have passed out. Next thing I remember is waking up on a bed wearing a hideous purple tracksuit. My hands were cuffed to the headboard. I felt as sick as a dog. My head was thumping. My eyes were stinging. I've no idea what he put in the wine. Enough to knock me out.'

'So much for dreams.'

'Tell me about it.'

'What do you remember about the room?'

'It was full of old stuff. Antique furniture. Dark blue curtains. An ornamental thing around the light. The carpet was dark blue like the curtains. The bed was soft. There was a picture on the wall. An oil painting of a woman.'

'His sister, perhaps?'

'Who knows?'

'I want you to rest for a while, Amy. Enjoy the sunshine. I'll be back in a minute.'

'Okay.'

Gavin Westwood turned away from Chloe and sat at the desk. He took a fresh pad out of the drawer and wrote, *Jesus Christ, Peter, that's your spare room she's describing.*

King looked as if he'd just witnessed the Second Coming. He scribbled on his own pad and held it up. *She can't know this. It's not possible.*

Westwood followed suit and held his pad up. *Are you Thomas Kowalski?*

King didn't respond..

Are you?

King nodded, lips pressed into a thin line.

What have you done to her?

That's my business.

For goodness' sake, Peter. Murder?

Do I question your sordid activities?

Westwood didn't respond.

Then kindly refrain from questioning mine.

At least I've killed no one.

No; you just molest them and film it for your perverted friends to drool over.

It's hardly the same.

How can a kid barely out of nappies know all this?

Because she's lived it.

King shook his head. *But dead is dead. Kaput. Ashes to ashes.*

The Lord moves in mysterious ways.

Don't you dare bring religion to my door. God's little more than a scare tactic dreamt up to keep the masses in line.

Do you want me to stop?

No.

Westwood sighed and dropped his pad on the desk.

CHAPTER TWENTY-EIGHT

Chloe appeared to be asleep when King and Westwood finished their short notepad conversation. Her head had flopped to one side, and Ruby Rag Doll had fallen onto the floor. Mel stared, unblinking, at the blades of light slicing through the venetian blinds.

King sat at the desk, pencil and pad at the ready, eyes fixed on Chloe.

Westwood addressed the child. 'Hello again, Amy.'

'Hi.'

'Are you enjoying the sunshine?'

'Yeah.'

'You remember we were talking about the man who handcuffed you to the bed?'

Chloe nodded and fidgeted in her mother's lap.

'Apart from telling you his name was Thomas Kowalski, did he mention any other names?'

'No.'

'Can you describe him?'

'Clean shaven and thinner than when he picked me up at Paddington Station. Tall. Not much hair. Long face.'

'Did he tell you why he'd tied you up on the bed?'

'No.'

'Did he say anything?'

'He said, "Good morning, Purple-five. I trust you are well." Then he left. I wanted a drink. My throat was parched. My whole body ached as if I had flu. Next time I saw him it was pitch-dark. He turned the bedroom light on and pointed a gun at me. He told me that if I so much as moved a muscle without his permission he would blow my head off.'

'That must have been terrifying for you. What happened next?'

'He released me and made me walk downstairs to the garage. He then forced me into the boot of his car.'

'Was it the same car he brought you back from Oxford in?'

'No. That was a small one. Maybe a Fiesta or a Nova. This one was a shiny dark blue BMW, I think. Posh-nob's car. I remember the first part of the registration number. It was X13. Unlucky for some! I kept telling him I was claustrophobic and suffered from panic attacks, but he just laughed and told me he wouldn't charge me for curing phobias.'

'All heart!'

'He doesn't care about anyone but himself. He's a selfish, evil piece of work. All I kept thinking about was how I'd ended up in the deepest shit possible because of my stupid dream to become an artist.'

'It's not stupid, Amy. It's what you wanted to do.'

'And look where it got me.'

'You weren't to know that.'

'And that makes it all right?'

'We all make mistakes.'

'Not like this. I don't want to talk about it anymore.'

'It's all right. You're safe now. I promise.'

'Men always make promises they can't keep.'

'Not all men, Amy.'

'I had a boyfriend once. Danny Clayton. He promised he would love me forever. Said I was beautiful.'

'That's a nice thing to say.'

'Next thing, he's going out with my best friend.'

'People change, Amy. That's just part of growing up.'

'You can't trust anyone.'

'You can trust me.'

'My parents only liked me when I was doing what they wanted me to do. Soon as I dared to want something for myself, they tried to bully me. Bribe me. Threaten me. But I didn't want to be a bloody pharmacist. It's what *they* wanted.'

'I'm sure they only meant well.'

'If they'd only supported me, encouraged me, I'd never have run away from home in the first place.'

'Where did the man take you?'

'Don't know. It felt like forever locked in that boot. He made me get out at the back of a big building. Apart from a security light, it was pretty dark. He unlocked a small white door next to a fire exit and forced me inside. Then we walked down some stone steps to a large wooden door. He unlocked it and made me walk through this huge room with all these coloured squares painted on the floor. There was a large cage and some old-fashioned wooden stocks pushed against one wall. I kept begging him to let me go, but he ignored me. He unlocked another door at the far end of the room and told me to go inside.'

After a long pause, Westwood asked what happened next.

'I did as he asked. He had a fucking gun, for Christ's sake.'

'What was in the room?'

'Three other women. All asleep on bunk beds. He told me to take the vacant bottom bunk beneath Turquoise-three.'

'*Turquoise-three?* What sort of name is that?'

'Everyone had a colour and a number.'

'But why *three*?'

'Because the two previous ones were dead. Murdered.'

'By this man?'

'Him and his sick game.'

'What game?'

'One False Move. He plays it with another man. They sit at the side of the painted squares and roll dice. We were used as game pieces to move around the board to the value of the dice. Then they ask each other questions.'

'What sort of questions?'

'About Shakespeare. If they answered correctly, they were allowed to move to the value printed on the question card. The whole idea is to reach the centre of the stage in the middle of the squares. It's like Trivial Pursuit, only, well… evil. To make it more… interesting, there are Death Squares and Punishment Squares, so God help you if you land on one of those.'

'What happens if you do?'

'The Death Square's obvious, isn't it? The Punishment Squares can mean anything from spending a day in the stocks, to being tied to the whipping post or tortured in the cage.'

'Good God!' Westwood said, his voice losing its smooth buttery texture.

'They dress up like something out of a history book. They call each other Shakespeare and Marlowe, and keep scores on cards with quills dipped in blood. They're fucking sick.'

'That's rich!' King shouted.

Chloe stiffened in her mother's lap. 'Who's that?'

'No one,' Westwood assured her.

'He's here.'

'He's not, Amy. It's just your mind playing tricks.'

'You promised me I was safe.'

'You are.'

'You lied.'

'I didn't. You're only hearing him because your memory is triggering the sound of his voice. He's not here for real. He's not allowed.'

'I don't believe you.'

'God wouldn't allow such a man to come to His special place.'

'I'

'Let's have a break. Relax and enjoy the lovely sunshine for a while.'

'I want to go home.'

'You will, Amy. I promise. Just as soon as we've finished.'

'I don't understand why you've brought me here.'

'It's part of the healing process. It will help you to move on.'

'Where?'

'A better place.'

'Am I dead?'

'The spirit never dies. It just moves on. Let's do some deep breathing to help you relax.'

'Okay.'

'Breathe in through your nose and out through your mouth. Slowly. Rhythmically. I'm going to count back from ten to one. When I get to one, you will be relaxed. With each exhalation, I want you to release all the tension and fear inside you. Cast it to the wind. Be rid of it forever.'

'Okay.'

Westwood counted back, watching Chloe relax in her mother's lap. When he reached one, he told her to be still and breathe deeply. Let the sunshine pour into her, and the stress flow out of her. 'Sunshine in, Stress out. Sunshine in, stress out.'

After a few minutes, he walked back to his desk and sat down. He wrote on the pad: *Do you want to jeopardise the whole thing?*

I won't be insulted by the likes of her!

If you want me to continue, you'd better leave the room.

Why?

Because we're about to take this child back to the point of her death. Do you want to kill her?

King didn't reply. He put the notepad down, folded his arms across his chest, and dared Gavin Westwood, with a well-practised look of contempt and derision, to utter another word.

CHAPTER TWENTY-NINE

'Hi, Amy. It's me again.'

'Hi.'

'Are you feeling better?'

'Yes.'

'I only want what's best for you. To help you to heal.'

'I want to go home.'

'You can't go home just yet.'

'I want to see my mum.'

'You'll see her soon.'

'When?'

'When this is over.'

'Will she'll be mad at me?'

'Why would she be mad at you?'

'For running away.'

'You followed your dream, Amy. That takes guts. I'm sure she knows that.'

'I doubt it.'

'Tell me more about this game?'

'One False Move?'

'Yes.'

'I already told you. We were just game pieces. They moved us around their stupid board.'

'I want to learn more about the Punishment Square and the Death Square.'

'Don't want to talk about them.'

'You'll feel better.'

'How?'

'It will help with the healing process. Did you ever land on a Punishment Square?'

'Course I did.'

'How many times?'

'Maybe a dozen.'

'That's an awful lot of punishment. What did they do to you?'

'Locked me in the cage, mostly.'

'What sort of cage?'

'The ones you see monkeys in.'

Westwood hesitated. He glanced at King before continuing. 'Then what did they do?'

'Made me crouch down until I couldn't feel my legs anymore. Threw buckets of iced water over me. Poked this long thing through the bars and gave me electric shocks.'

'Like a cattle prodder?'

'I don't know what it was. But it fucking well hurt. I used to scream and beg them to stop, but it made no difference. They enjoyed hurting me. The more I screamed, the happier they seemed to be.'

'That's terrible.'

'Not as bad as the whipping post. I got flogged at least half a dozen times. Twenty lashes. Then they rubbed salt into the wounds. I actually thought my back was on fire. Blood was running right down the backs of my legs.'

'You were naked?'

'They always stripped you to punish you. Even in the stocks. I got put in those three times. They pelted me with rotten fruit. A plum stone took my eye out. They thought that was hilarious.'

Westwood's voice dropped to little more than a croak. 'You're being very brave, Amy.'

'Am I?'

'I'm proud of you.'

'Thanks.'

'I want you to tell me what happened the day you landed on the Death Square.'

Silence, save the ticking of a clock and King's exaggerated sighs.

'How did they kill you?'

'With one of those guillotine things.'

'Can you describe it?'

'It was made of wood. I had to kneel down and put my neck in this big groove. They tied my hands behind my back with leather straps. Then the bastard stood in front of me with one of those scroll things and read out a load of crap about being refused a pardon. Said I'd been ordered to suffer death by guillotine in accordance with the rules of the game. He also rambled on about losing one of his better players, and that he'd be sorry to see me go. If it was up to him he'd offer me a pardon, but the opposition's word was final in such matters. Then he asked me if I had any last requests.'

'What did you say?'

'I said I hoped he rotted in hell. He told me he would pray for my soul. I could hear the other one behind me, Marlowe, fiddling with the rope securing the blade. Hear him breathing hard. I could see the board squares painted on the floor in such vivid vibrant colours. Purples, yellows, oranges and turquoises. It was as if all my senses were heightened. I saw a spider weaving a web on the bars of the cage. I could smell the damp in the air. Garlic. Shit. Polish on the guillotine frame. The fluorescent overhead light was flickering. And then I heard the blade fall. It made a whooshing sound. I didn't actually feel it hit me. I must have passed out before it struck home.'

'At least you were spared that.'

'Next thing I knew, I was floating up near the ceiling. It was great. No longer in pain. The sight was back in my blind eye. At first, I thought I was dreaming, that I'd somehow fallen asleep in the middle of a game. And then I saw what was happening below me.'

'What did you see?'

She didn't answer.

'Amy?'

'The one who called himself Shakespeare shouted at the other one to pull the rope on the guillotine up.'

'Was Shakespeare the one who abducted you?'

'Yes. The Game Master.'

'Go on.'

'The blade had failed to cut my head off. Blood was running everywhere. All over my shoulders. The bottom of my hair was stained red. It was dripping onto the floor. The Game Master said the blade wasn't sharp enough. He blamed the other one for not checking it. They argued about whose fault it was. Then the Game Master walked over to the table and grabbed the knife they used for prompting.'

'Prompting?'

'If you fell asleep in the cage, they would stab you. Not deep, but hard enough to jolt you awake. Anyway, he walked back to me and hacked my head off.'

'Thank God you were already dead.'

'I'm not sure I was. I was making this horrible noise that sounded somewhere between screaming and gargling. Blood was spurting everywhere. All over him. The wall. The floor. It took ages. He used the knife like a saw. When he was finished, he held up my head as if it was some kind of trophy. I no longer cared. I was just glad I'd never have to play their game anymore. I was finally free.'

'What happened next?'

'I was taken away.'

'By who?'

'An angel. She came straight through the ceiling like a beam of light. Materialised and turned into the most beautiful woman I'd ever seen. No wings, just a golden aura. When she spoke, this amazing light shone from her eyes. She said, "It's time." Then she held out her hand. When I took it I felt the most amazing sense of peace wash through me. Peace and warmth and light. And then we floated out the top of the building. Up and up. Above the clouds. Higher and higher.'

'To Heaven?'

'That's enough,' King interrupted.

Chloe twisted her head around. 'Who's that?'

'It's no one, Amy. It's time to leave the special place now. I want you to take my hand.'

'But I heard someone.'

'It's just your imagination.'

'But'

'You've just relived a very traumatic experience, Amy. But it's over now. Do you understand?'

'I'

'We'll go back across the bridge now.'

Chloe didn't answer.

'Amy?'

'How do I know he's not waiting for me?'

'He's not. I give you my word.'

After a long pause, Chloe agreed.

Westwood walked her back across the bridge, reassuring her, promising to protect her. 'That wasn't so bad, was it?'

'I don't like it here.'

'We'll walk back up the steps now and leave the garden.'

'Okay.'

'With each step, I want you to leave this life behind and return to your life as Chloe Hollis.'

'Okay.'

He gestured for King to leave the room. Once gone, he walked Chloe carefully away from the past and back into the present.

Chloe opened her eyes and looked around the office. 'Where am I?'

'With Mummy. You had a little nap.'

Westwood brought Mel out of her trance, telling her Chloe was in good health and suffering no abnormalities. She would have no recollection of coming to The Wellbeing Clinic once she returned home.

Mel kissed the top of Chloe's head. 'Did I doze off?'

'These sessions often make it seem that way,' Westwood said. 'It's best to give it a while before you get up.'

'I feel so much better knowing there's nothing wrong.'

'Glad to have helped.'

'Where's Charles?'

'He's still in the waiting room. You stay there and take a moment. I'll get Olivia to bring you both a drink.'

'Can I have fizzy, Mummy?' Chloe asked, her voice showing no trace of Amy's.

'You've had a lot of fizzy drinks this Christmas.' She looked at Westwood and rolled her eyes. 'She'll have squash.'

'And you?'

'I wouldn't mind a cup of tea.'

'Coming right up.'

CHAPTER THIRTY

King left the building by way of the fire escape. His mind was so engrossed in what he'd just witnessed that he drove halfway home without even being aware he was doing so. It was only a jam on the southbound bypass that dragged him back to reality. The traffic was tailed back, reminding him of the fragile state of British roads. It was an insufferable fact of life that the infrastructure of this once proud nation was at breaking point. Why didn't anyone care anymore? Lily-livered politicians were only bothered about feathering their own nests and provoking the occasional war to satisfy their jingoistic needs.

What in devil's name just happened in that room?

King's usual failsafe mechanism for dealing with paranormal activity failed. His whole belief system had been turned on its head. It was as if a giant hand had tipped him upside down and capsized his brain. Left him in no doubt that the girl had once lived as Purple-five.

Not only had she described, with unerring accuracy, her abduction, imprisonment and subsequent death, she'd done it in a voice unrecognisable as that of a child. It had been like watching a case of demonic possession in one of those ghastly horror films.

Someone honked a horn behind him, making him jump. He noticed the traffic had started to move again. Aware of his frailties, and conscious of his encounter with the tractor driver, King resisted an urge to retaliate. He slipped the car into drive and cruised home with thoughts of Chloe Hollis dominating his mind.

By the time he'd had two stiff brandies and treated himself to a Havana cigar, King felt better. He sat in a dark-red leather recliner exploring the deep caverns of his mind. His belief system was still in denial. How could death not be final? He'd always dismissed talk of spirits as drivel. Rubbish made up to facilitate a primitive need to frighten one another on dark nights.

'"I have heard, but not believ'd, the spirits o' the dead may walk again: if such thing be, thy mother appear'd to me last night, for ne'er was dream so like a waking."'

A fine quote, enhanced by King's ability to deliver the lines with the reverence and authority they deserved. Shakespeare possessed an ability to make the most trite subjects credible. He could probably turn 'Ba Ba Black Sheep' into an authentic piece of literary prose, but that didn't mean King fell into line and adopted as fact every word spoken by the great man.

He treated himself to another glass of brandy. 'It can't be true,' he told the crystal decanter as he returned it to the mahogany drinks cabinet. 'She can't know. She's barely out of nappies.'

Do you doubt your own ears?

He settled into his favourite chair, sipped his drink, and tried to come to terms with what Gavin Westwood had unearthed with his psychiatric shovel. The girl had even remembered the fictitious name he'd used on Paddington Station to lure her away. Lure all the girls away. Thomas Kowalski.

Not to mention how she'd described the botched attempt to execute her by guillotine, the cage, the stocks and the whipping post.

The girl would have to die. And soon. Hesitation was never a good friend to destiny.

What about Westwood? He knows far too much. Not to mention his unfavourable reaction to murder. Acting as if he was a paragon of virtue. Bloody lowlife hypocrite. His father had once announced that it was impossible to trust a man with a beard. King could now vouch for the dubious nature of those sporting facial hair, albeit just a moustache.

King cursed his rotten luck. He'd expected Westwood to prove it was all a load of rubbish; not to open a can of worms large enough to excite the entire bird population.

How will you kill him?

With memories of Nathan's impromptu slaughter still fresh, King rounded on his inner voice. 'I don't know! I need more time to plan.'

Time waits for no man.

'Stop throwing clichés at me.'

You should have listened to Charles when he first told you of the girl. Disposed of her without getting Westwood involved.

King opted for a quote from *All's Well That Ends Well* to settle his frazzled nerves.

'"Our remedies oft in ourselves do lie. Which we ascribe to heaven: the fated sky gives us free scope, only doth backward pull our slow designs when we ourselves are dull."'

All very well until we involve third-parties in our private affairs.

'I am master of my own affairs.'

Unless Gavin Westwood drinks too much wine and babbles secrets in the wrong ear.

'He knows better than to discuss my private affairs with anyone. His house, and the foundations which support that house, are built of glass. Let he who casts the first stone…'

If Purple-five lives on in Chloe Hollis, then what of all the others who have perished?

King's stomach dropped down a lift shaft.

There could be eighteen more kids out there experiencing similar flashbacks.

To ground himself, and still the voice in his head, King walked to the wine cellar and opened the purple trophy cabinet. He slid out the drawer containing Purple-five's severed head.

'Dead,' he slurred. 'Dead as a Dodo.'

Purple-five's remaining eye stared to one side, but he detected an accusatory glint in that orb.

'You can't be in that child,' King concluded, touching the icy bag, tracing the contours of the frozen head. 'You're Amy May Constable.'

Amy May Constable responded by regarding him like a one-eyed Mona Lisa with a squint. The gentle hum of the freezers purred in the background.

'You were always my favourite,' King told the head, as if trying to garner favour. 'Gutsy. Not like others I could mention. Your successor has something about her, but she's mouthy and common. Still, credit where credit's due, she's still rattling her chains after five years. She landed on the Death Square once, but I negotiated a pardon by offering Charles a forfeit. Suffice to say, he was a happy headmaster after a long night of sexual favours.'

Amy didn't look as if she could give a hoot about the progress of Purple-six. She seemed more concerned about the possibility of thawing out. And with good reason. Water trickled down the outside of the bag, creating a realistic illusion that she was shedding tears.

'Grief spills like molten bullets as divinity mourns,' King whispered. 'But we should not fear the silver-streaked reaper.'

He considered the statement and concluded his brain was very near to tipping point. He would need a holiday after Westwood and the girl had been dealt with. Perhaps Switzerland. The Alps. A spot of skiing to recharge the batteries.

He told Purple-five of his plans. Purple-five didn't seem interested.

'I'm going to go now. If I don't see you before, I'd like to wish you a happy and prosperous New Year.'

Purple-five didn't look in a very celebratory mood.

'Peter?'

King jumped, heart banging like a gong, sending shockwaves through his head.

'What are you doing down here?'

He held onto the freezer for support. Purple-five appeared to wink at him, further heightening his paranoia.

'Are you all right, Peter? I've been looking everywhere for you.'

'How dare you sneak up on me like that? You almost gave me a heart attack.'

'I'm sorry. I didn't mean to. Why are you looking in the freezer?'

King looked at his lover and imagined the man's head encased in ice. 'Why do you think?'

'I don't'

'I'm selecting something nice for dinner.'

'Ugh!'

'What do you fancy? Ear or a tongue?'

'That's gross.'

King slammed the freezer shut as Purple-five appeared to pucker her lips and blow him a kiss.

'What happened during the regression?'

King chose his words carefully. 'I'm at a loss to make any sense of it.'

'Did Chloe talk of a past life?'

'Of sorts,' King lied.

'What did she say?'

'I don't want to discuss it down here in front of the guests. Let's go to the lounge.'

Once seated in his leather chair, feet resting on a genuine Persian rug, fresh brandy in one hand, cigar in the other, he felt able to relay the hypnotherapy session with unerring accuracy.

'My God, it's all true,' Honeywell squawked. 'I told you so, didn't I?'

King puffed on his cigar.

'She *really* is Purple-five?'

'It seems so.'

'What are we going to do?'

King blew on the tip of his Havana. 'What do you suppose we do, Mr. Marlowe?'

Honeywell didn't seem to hear him. 'I knew something was wrong. I could see it in Westwood's face.'

'That bugger always looks suspicious. Even when he's…'

'Go on.'

Tied to the bed and enjoying oral sex. 'Nothing.'

'I want to know the true nature of your relationship with him.'

'Hostile, Mr. Marlowe. Hostile.'

'I don't want to share you.'

King tried to cluck his tongue and almost bit it. Cursing his poor coordination, he put the brandy glass on the coffee table. He arranged his thoughts into a coherent line and then attempted to articulate them while revealing none of his innermost secrets. Particularly those relating to his tempestuous sexual relationship with Gavin Westwood.

'For what it's worth, Mr. Marlowe, I don't like the man. And I don't trust him.'

Honeywell looked pleased, relieved and confused all at the same time. 'But I thought you said he could be trusted?'

'Is life not fluid, Mr. Marlowe? Opinions change, as do our goals and motivations. I now believe Gavin Westwood to be devious and devoid of shame. That's why we must tread carefully.'

'I couldn't agree more.'

'Take stock of the situation.'

Honeywell nodded. 'Yes.'

'Lay the cards on the table and see what comes up trumps.'

'Quite.'

'Then kill him.'

Honeywell's eyes widened. 'Kill him?'

King puffed on the cigar, and then rested it in an ornate glass ashtray. 'That's what I said.'

'I don't like this, Peter. I've got a bad feeling about where this might be leading.'

'You'd have a bad feeling if a genie appeared and granted you three wishes.'

'It's just… it all seems to be getting out of hand.'

King was undisturbed by his lover's fretting. 'We'll kill the girl first.'

'But'

'Tomorrow night. And take that pained expression off your face; you look like a man with a nasty bout of constipation.'

'What if the mother tells someone they went to see a hypnotist? If we kill Gavin Westwood and the child, there'll be a link. The police will be on to it quicker than you can say boo to a goose.'

'What a ridiculous turn of phrase.'

'We'll end up in prison, Peter. Please see reason.'

'Will you stop fretting. Gavin said he would program the mother to have no memory of the event. He might be a devious perverted creep on a good day, but he's an expert in his chosen field. The mother won't tell anyone about visiting The Wellbeing Clinic because she won't even remember being there.'

'How on earth are we going to kill the child?'

King ignored him, slurped the last of his brandy, and held out his glass for a refill.

Honeywell took it, a sour look in his eyes. 'We should at least wait a while. Let the dust settle. That Olivia woman kept giving me funny looks.'

'That's because Olivia's a man. She doesn't know *how* to look. Neither would you with your penis duct-taped to your thigh. I should imagine it's an eye-watering experience if it should get aroused.'

Honeywell handed him a fresh drink. 'Ouch.'

King raised his glass. '"To be, or not to be: that is the question: whether 'tis nobler in the mind to suffer the slings and arrows of outrageous fortune, or to take arms against a sea of troubles, and by opposing end them. To die: to sleep."'

Honeywell stood in the middle of the room, lips pressed into a thin line. 'Is it really necessary to kill the child?'

'Circumstance dictates necessity.'

'I don't see how killing her is going to help. From where I'm standing, it's only going to add to our problems.'

King decided to quote Westwood. The man was about as articulate as fog, but King rather liked the phrase he'd used earlier to argue the existence of former lives. 'Dead lips don't lie.'

'What's that supposed to mean?'

'For a supposedly educated man, you show a distinct lack of understanding.'

'I'

King waved a hand at him. Sometimes it was like trying to converse with a goldfish. 'Enough. I don't want your doubts and worries polluting my mind and clouding my judgement whilst I try to think.'

Honeywell turned away. 'Please don't get too drunk.'

'I need something to steady the ship tonight, or I fear sleep will be as elusive as your sense of adventure.'

CHAPTER THIRTY-ONE

King sat up in bed, moonlight spilling into the room courtesy of the open curtains. He had no recollection of coming to bed, only a thumping headache and a parched throat to remind him he'd drunk far too much brandy and smoked too many cigars. To his immediate alarm, his lover was absent. Again. Last time had been forgivable, considering Charles had been busy dismembering the rent boy. But tonight?

Perhaps you revealed some of your innermost thoughts.

This possibility brought King's dormant brain cells onto active duty. Considering one of his darkest wishes for the New Year was to erase his lover from both the earth and from his memory, he wondered if his tongue had slipped up and, well, let something slip.

As his brain scanned empty memory banks for clues to the evening's conversation, he cursed all that was heavenly for dealing him such a poor hand in life. Why couldn't he find a kindred spirit to share his life with? If pressed, he would have to admit that Charles was eager to please. Compliant. Good between the sheets. But about as exciting as a gatepost.

What about the girl? His mind whispered.

King was in no mood or state to consider her at this hour. The digital clock on the bedside table informed him it was seven minutes past three. So much for booze acting as a sleep aid. His attention was suddenly drawn to the sash window. Or, more importantly, to whatever had just moved in front of the damned thing. A shape, ill-defined and ghostly in appearance, danced rhythmically to one side of the frame.

King's heart banged against his ribs. He rubbed his eyes and peeked again. Still there. But this time it had a face.

'Who's there?' he croaked.

The figure didn't respond. Its ghostly form fluttered, as if caught in a breeze. King watched in horror as it materialised into Purple-five, her long blonde hair flowing around her face as if floating in water.

He gripped the duvet and pulled it up to his neck. 'Get away from me.'

Purple-five smiled and swayed.

'You're dead,' King squawked. 'Dead. Get away from me, you hear?'

Purple-five continued her grinning ritualistic dance. Her remaining eye seemed to milk his mind of coherent thought.

He opted for a lie dressed up in bravado. 'You don't scare me.'

'Pardon?'

King wasn't sure which terrified him the most: the apparition, or the deep male voice that seemed to be coming from it.

'Peter? What's wrong?'

For the second time in as many days, Charles Honeywell had interrupted a personal moment. He turned on the light. 'Peter? It's me. Whatever's the matter?'

King could now see that the object of his terror was just a net curtain fluttering in the breeze. 'Where in devil's name have you been?'

'To the toilet. My bladder's playing up again.'

'Who opened that bloody window?'

'You did.'

'Whatever for? It's the middle of winter.'

'You said you wanted some air.'

'Why didn't you close it? I thought it was a…'

'What?'

King clamped his mouth. Some things were better left unsaid.

After showering, and drinking two mugs of black coffee, King sat at the dining table scowling at his partner and cursing insomnia. 'Can't you do anything without being told to do so?'

'What do you mean?'

'The window.'

'You were adamant, Peter. You said to leave it open.'

'I was drunk.'

On that score, Honeywell seemed in complete agreement. 'Quite.'

'If I'd been demanding the keys to the car to take it for a drive in the swimming pool, would you have allowed me?'

Honeywell dodged the question. 'What were you so afraid of?'

'Nothing. It was just a nightmare.'

Honeywell blew steam from the rim of his mug. 'It's been… a very distressing week, all things considered.'

'That's one way of looking at it.'

'At least we know the afterlife actually exists.'

King clapped his hands together, startling his lover. 'Praise Jesus! Now all we need is the other game pieces to present themselves in dozens of children and our life's work will be complete. We'll have a posse of obsessed parents beating a path to our door before you can say "reincarnation".'

'I thought Westwood programmed the child to forget everything?'

'What of it?'

'Why don't we just sit tight and see what happens. I can keep an eye on Mel when I go back to school.'

'I'm not leaving this up to providence.'

'But we can't kill a child.'

King winced at the mewling tone of his lover's voice. 'We have no alternative.'

'She's a kid, Peter. Think about it. Even if she still remembers being Purple-five, no one in their right mind will believe her. The police pay scant attention to all that supernatural stuff.'

'I don't care what they do. I don't want them sniffing around my door. In case it's slipped your mind, we have nineteen heads residing in freezers. How do you propose we explain those to the police?'

'I'm'

'Not to mention what's concealed in the bowels of Feelham Theatre. You'll be humming a different tune if they cart you off to prison for the rest of your life. No nice fat pension to enjoy. Just a bleak prison cell, at the mercy of murderers and rapists. Is that what you want, Charles?'

'No.'

'To wake up every morning not knowing if you'll make it through another day?'

'"They whose guilt within their bosoms lie, imagine every eye beholds their blame."'

'Don't resort to quoting Shakespeare to lend authority to your weak argument,' King said. 'And, for your information, I do not hold one ounce of guilt within my heart. I have lived a life true to my spirit. Am I to be compared to a common criminal by the very man who purports to love me?'

'I *do* love you.'

'Then why do you delight in opposing me?'

'I'm not. I'm'

'Why do you sit at the very table where we break our bread and share our experiences, and accuse me of paranoia? Even a man of your limited abilities can see the child threatens the very foundations upon which we stand.'

'It *was* me who alerted you to her in the first place, remember? I'm just trying to make you see the dangers inherent in murdering her.'

'Spoken so eloquently by the man who's perfectly happy to chop a rent boy into bite-size chunks.'

'That's different.'

'Is it?'

'No one will be bothered about a male prostitute. Other than his pimp, perhaps. But a child? She's got family. People who love her. Care about her.'

'And your point is?'

'I just want you to consider the implications.'

King flapped a hand. 'We'll burn the house down tomorrow night. Pour an accelerant through the letter box and set fire to it.'

'I'm not having anything to do with this. I couldn't kill a child.'

'Why not? In light of what we know about reincarnation, just think of it as recycling.'

'I'm begging you, Peter. Please reconsider.'

'Stop allowing emotion to cloud your judgement. If you didn't know the mother, you wouldn't even be questioning this.'

'It's got nothing to do with knowing Mel. It's a four-year-old child, for Christ's sake.'

'And you're behaving like one. We set fire to the house tomorrow night. And that is my final word on the subject.' King stood up and strode from the room before Charles Honeywell tempted him to do something regrettable.

CHAPTER THIRTY-TWO

They buried Mel's father during the afternoon of New Year's Eve. She'd been in a good mood for the past couple of days, almost as if someone had waved a magic wand over her and lifted the terrible smog of the past weeks. She'd also benefited from Chloe sleeping through the night for the first time in ages.

There were just a handful of mourners at the funeral. A few friends, Uncle Tom, an old aunt who seemed to thrive on sorrow, and Mel and Tony. Chloe was staying with Kerrie-Anne for the day.

By the time the guests left the house in St Kilda's Close after eating much of Mel's leftover food from Christmas, Mel was just about ready to burst. She'd refrained from having a cigarette throughout the three-hour gathering because she didn't want to meet with disapproval from the aunt who seemed to fuss and cluck at everything like an old hen in a farmyard.

Tony took a sip from his bottle of Budweiser. 'You held up well today, all things considered.'

Mel retrieved a packet of cigarettes from a kitchen cupboard and lit up. 'I'm knackered.'

'You did great.'

'I did what I had to.'

'How are you?'

'If you're fishing to see whether I've forgiven you, Tony, don't bother. I'll never forgive you.'

'I know.'

'Have you any idea how much you've hurt me?'

'Yes.'

'How would you feel if I'd done it to you? Screwed a teacher at school to help get over Megan's death? How?'

'I'd be devastated.'

'Would you call me a whore?'

'I'

'Did you make her come, Tony?'

The question made him recoil. 'I don't'

'Did you go down on her?'

'No.'

'Why not?'

'It wasn't like that.'

'What *was* it like?'

'Nothing. A meaningless screw.'

'What does she look like?'

'Nothing special.'

'Was she married?'

'Yes.'

'So, you were quite prepared to destroy another marriage as well as your own?'

'I didn't want to destroy anything. I told you, I wasn't thinking straight.'

Mel finished her cigarette and lit another. 'You know what makes me laugh in all this?'

'What?'

'The way you judge other people. They say hypocrites are the most opinionated bastards on the planet.'

'I'm sorry.'

'I've got a simple equation for your mathematician's head. You can teach it to all those kids at your posh school. Stand them in good stead for when they grow up. You want to hear it?'

Tony didn't.

'One careless fuck can ruin many innocent lives. How does that sound?'

Tony shrugged.

'One for the curriculum?'

He stared at the floor like a naughty schoolboy.

Mel stared out the kitchen window. She hated him with every ounce of her being for what he'd done, for inflicting such damage with one careless act, but he was still Chloe's father. Whatever happened during the rest of their lives, wherever fate took them, they would always be joined together by the precious gift of a child.

'I've got to pick Chloe up at six.'

'Okay. I'll get off.'

'You can wait here. She's still your daughter. You can spend the evening with us if you want.'

'Do you mean it?'

'I don't know what I mean anymore, Tony. But I believe you love Chloe, and she adores you. I see no reason to let our troubles spoil that.'

'Thank you. Thank you so much.'

'I'd appreciate it if you could tidy up while I'm gone.'

Tony looked as if he'd just won the lottery. 'Anything.'

Mel drove to Kerrie-Anne's on autopilot. She could never let Tony back into her life. Never trust him again. Perhaps in time the pain might diminish, but the act of betrayal would always hang over their relationship like an axe waiting to fall. He'd only need to be home half an hour late from work, or get called away to a meeting, and Stephanie Wallace might as well walk naked into the room and wrap her arms around his neck.

But she had to consider Chloe. Tony was her father. A good father. And it wasn't fair to let his sordid affair spoil that. Tony could go home after Chloe went to bed. It would give them time to work something out regarding access. At least, until the courts could make a proper ruling.

She rang the doorbell and stood shivering on the doorstep. She'd forgotten to put on a coat, and her black cardigan was too thin to have any benefit.

Kerrie-Anne opened the door. 'Come on in.'

Mel stepped inside the warm hallway. 'How's she been?'

'Good as gold.'

Mel felt some of the knots in her stomach slacken. 'No more pictures?'

'No. Harriet let her dress up in her nurse's outfit. Last thing I heard, Chloe diagnosed her with a temperature and asked me if Harriet could have some Calpol.'

Chloe burst into the hallway. 'Mummy!'

Just the simple normality of her child's demeanour almost brought tears to Mel's eyes. 'Hiya, Pumpkin.'

Chloe wrapped her arms around Mel's middle. 'Are we going home now?'

'Yes.'

'I've been playing doctors.'

'I know.'

'Harriet had a temperature, but I made her better.'

'Aren't you a clever girl?'

Chloe nodded. 'I wish someone could make me better.'

'What do you mean, sweetheart?'

'My head's poorly.'

'Headache?'

'It hurts where they cut my head off.'

Mel's heart stalled. She stepped back as if the words had physically assaulted her. 'What… do… you… mean?'

Chloe blinked. 'What's wrong, Mummy?'

'What did you just say?'

'I made Harriet better.'

'Before that?'

'Nothing.'

Mel glanced at Kerrie-Anne. The childminder shook her head.

Mel told Chloe to put her coat on.

'Are you all right, Mummy?'

'Mummy's just tired. I've got a surprise for you.'

Chloe fought with the sleeves of her purple coat, twisting around in circles as she searched for the armholes. 'Another Christmas present?'

'Better than that.'

Chloe rammed her arm home. 'Nothing's better than Christmas presents.'

'This is.'

'What is it?'

'Daddy's at home.'

Chloe's eyes sparkled. 'Yay! For good?'

'Just for tonight.'

'Is Grandma Vicky still sick?'

'Yes.'

'I wish Daddy could come home forever.'

'Me, too,' Mel said, the words more truthful than she would have cared to admit. 'Me, too.'

CHAPTER THIRTY-THREE

Chloe sat on the sofa cuddled up to her father for the rest of the day. It was as if she thought he might vanish into thin air if she let him out of her sight. Mel had cooked sausage rolls and quiche for tea. Simple finger-food to sit in front of the TV with and watch *Finding Dory* for the second time that day.

Mel took advantage of Tony's visit to have a long soak in the bath. Her initial relief that Chloe wasn't experiencing any past-life experiences had been shattered by the child's claim to be suffering from a poorly head at Kerrie-Anne's.

It hurts where they cut my head off.

The words made Mel shiver in spite of the steaming water. She'd been almost convinced there was nothing wrong for the past few days. Perhaps she ought to talk to Charles again. See if he could suggest anything else. He'd been wonderful. Kind. A true friend.

Mel finished her bath, walked into the bedroom, and examined her body in the mirrored wardrobe door. She'd never been too bothered about her figure before. She'd given birth twice, and didn't regard vanity as a virtue, but it was amazing how her husband's disgraceful behaviour had highlighted every imperfection on her body. Every lump and bump and excess of fat.

They spent a pleasant evening watching TV and playing Hungry Hippos and Dotty Dinosaurs. When Tony asked if he could put Chloe to bed at eight, Mel said he could. Mel didn't expect her to go to sleep for ages, but Tony came back downstairs fifteen minutes later, grinning.

'That was quick.'

'I got about halfway through *Chicken-licken* and she snuggled up to Ruby Rag Doll and that was that. Out like a light.'

'You must have a magic touch.'

'Probably my boring voice droning on and on.'

'True.'

Tony sat down. After a few minutes awkward silence, he said, 'So, how's it been?'

'You wouldn't need to ask that if you'd kept your dick in your trousers.'

'If I could take it back, Mel, I would.'

'Well, you can't, can you?'

'I know.'

'When I picked Chloe up from Kerrie-Anne's she was complaining of a bad head. Then she said it was because *they* cut off her head.'

Tony's mouth hung open. 'Who?'

'I don't know. It's all such a mess. I'm really scared I'm going to lose her.'

'You won't lose her.'

'And you *know* that, do you?'

Tony hesitated, then said, 'I know I love you with all my heart.'

Mel finished her wine. 'God knows I want to believe you, Tony, but how can I?'

'Because I mean it.'

'How long ago did you sleep with that bitch?'

'Please stop torturing yourself and'

'Six years ago, right? I shared my bed with you every single night since. Cried myself to sleep over Megan. You watched me falling to pieces, and all the time you had your sordid little secret.'

'I'

'How many other things have you kept from me, Tony?'

'None. I swear.'

'Why should I believe you?'

'Because it's the truth. I swear on Chl'

'Don't you dare! Don't you bring our child into this. Ever!'

'Okay. I'm sorry.'

'What have I done to deserve this? First I lose Megan, then my husband, and now Chloe. It's as if I've been cursed.'

'I want to help you.'

'I can't let you back into my life, Tony. Why can't you see that you've destroyed what we had? Killed it.' She lit a cigarette. 'The sad thing is, I don't think you do. You think it will all blow over. I'll get used to the idea that you cheated on me.'

'I don't'

'You probably think Chloe's just having a little wobble. Watched something scary on TV. Had a nightmare. Or, maybe I let her have too many fizzy drinks. Too many baked beans. All those colourings and preservatives are bound to make a child think she's lived before and been murdered.'

'Jesus Christ, Mel, I've never experienced anything like this before. It's just my nature to look for a rational explanation. I love science and maths. I've never given any consideration to ghosts and reincarnation. I've always believed we're just physical matter. We live and we die. How can there be anything else? But the thought of Chloe being murdered makes my blood run cold. I'm begging you to let me help. Let me be here for you.'

'How can I even begin to trust you?'

'Because I give you my word.'

'How do I know you won't go running straight back to scepticism the minute I let you back through that door?'

'I won't.'

'Or to Stephanie Wallace?'

Tony hesitated, brow furrowed, as if his thoughts were causing him pain. And then he said, 'I know I've messed up, Mel. Messed up big time.'

'You fucked her, Tony.'

'I'

'Say it! *I fucked Stephanie Wallace*. Say it!'

Tony looked away.

'What's the matter? Cat got your tongue?'

'I wish you'd stop torturing yourself with'

'Are you for real? It's you who's done all the torturing around here. Not me.'

'I want to support you. Help you get to the bottom of what's happening to Chloe. If you don't want me around after that, I'll walk away. No questions asked. No pressure.'

'I can't let you back in, Tony. It wouldn't work. Every time I look at you, I imagine you two at it like a pair of stray dogs on heat. I imagine her touching you. Doing stuff that makes me sick to my stomach.'

'I know.'

'Stop saying that! You don't *know*. You don't have a fucking clue.'

'Sorry.'

'What are you sorry for? That you smashed my heart to smithereens?'

'Yes.'

'Or that you got caught?'

'We both need to stay strong for Chloe.'

'Like you stayed strong for Megan?'

Tony looked at his hands as if they might help him to understand why they had touched another woman. Mel was on the verge of telling him to leave. Go back to his mother and her dreadful cooking and nit-picking ways, when he bowed his head and started sobbing.

With a mixture of sadness and satisfaction, she watched him rock back and forth as his grief poured out of him. Why hadn't he done this when Megan had died? Showed her he was hurting, too? Instead of walking around in 'practical mode', rationalising, putting his job and that bitch before their marriage.

Part of her wanted to reach out and comfort him. Another part wanted to delight in his sorrow, punch the air, shout from the rooftops this was what happened to men who couldn't control their dicks.

When Tony's sobs subsided to a series of snorts and sniffs, he looked at Mel, eyes red and swollen. 'I hate myself for what I did. I just hope you can find it in your heart to let me help you. Help Chloe.'

It took Mel two more glasses of wine and twenty minutes of contemplation dressed up as idle talk, to decide. She couldn't face the coming weeks on her own. She needed someone to share the burden.

'I can't undo the past,' Tony said, 'but I can help to write the future.'

'That's quite poetic for a maths teacher,' she conceded.

'I have my moments.'

'All I've ever wanted is for you to back me one hundred percent. That's it. But on the two occasions I've needed you the most, you've gone missing.'

'I know.'

'Do you promise to support me?'

'Yes.'

'Not try to convince me that Chloe's just going through a phase?'

'I just want to do what's best for her.'

'Okay. You can stay. But I want you to listen to what I'm going to tell you, okay?'

'I'm listening.'

'The first sign you're not on my side, you can go back to your mother's for good. Is that clear?'

'Yes.'

'You can sleep on the sofa for now. I'm not ready to share a bed with you yet.'

'I understand.'

'I hope you do, Tony. I really hope you do.'

CHAPTER THIRTY-FOUR

Dressed in black jeans, a black jumper, and a black hooded jacket, Charles Honeywell parked his Ford Fiesta outside Feelham Park and switched off the engine. His hands were shaking badly enough for King to notice.

King, who was wearing matching clothes, said, 'For God's sake, what on earth's wrong with you?'

'You know what's wrong with me.'

'Then have a word with the rational part of your brain and convince it you're only doing what is necessary.'

'How can you call it that? It's a child.'

'It's no different to killing anyone. I seem to recall you got excited when you killed Turquoise-two after she landed on the Death Square.'

'That was different.'

'How so?'

'Because that was part of One False Move. And she was older.'

King rounded on him. 'So what? Age is just a number. If this child persists in babbling on about her past life as Purple-five, it will be the end of everything. You, me, the theatre. You'll see out the rest of your days as some big bugger's bitch in Wormwood Scrubs.'

Honeywell didn't respond. He seemed more interested in his leather gloves.

'All we have to do is walk across the park, pour petrol through the letter box, set fire to it, and walk away.'

'I won't ever be able to walk away from this, Peter. It will haunt my days and nights for years to come.'

You won't be around for years to come. 'Nonsense!'

'That's easy for you to say. You're not the one who will have to go into school and pretend to be in shock. People will be asking questions. Everyone will be commiserating, gossiping, weeping. I'll have to face the press. TV cameras. It will be like hell on earth.'

'Don't be so melodramatic. She's not the last teacher on earth. It will all die down in no time. People have short memories.'

Honeywell didn't seem to hear him. 'I'll have to conduct ceremonies. Go to the church and stand amongst her grieving relatives.'

'Then your propensity toward emotional outbursts should stand you in good stead.'

'I won't be able to cope.'

Trust me, Charles, you won't have to. 'Human beings have an amazing capacity to manage. To change. To adapt. It will pass. I promise.'

'I wish I shared your optimism.'

'"True hope is swift and flies with swallow's wings."'

'I'm begging you to reconsider, Peter.'

'"And fearless minds climb soonest to crowns."'

'Soonest to graves, more like.'

King gave up trying to inspire him. There was a nasty whining tone to Honeywell's voice that evoked an urge to kill. But it wouldn't do to kill the horse before he'd hooked it up to the cart. 'Let's get this over with.'

At three o'clock in the morning the park was deserted. Only the ghosts of children rode on the swings, watched over by tall oak trees dressed in shadowy robes. An owl hooted, as if heralding their arrival. Honeywell panted like a faithful ageing dog, the petrol can swinging by his side, breath forming into foggy clouds in the moonlit air.

'I enjoy this time of night,' King said, as they walked past a roundabout creaking in the wind. 'It's so full of mystery.'

'It gives me the creeps.'

'You seem to revel in negativity, don't you?'

'With reason.'

'Petulance is not endearing.'

'Neither's killing a child.'

King opted to keep his thoughts to himself. He was sorely tempted to erect a stake from fallen branches, tie Charles to it, douse him with the petrol and set fire to him.

At the far end of the park, there was a small walkway which cut straight through to St Kilda's Close. The trail was lined with tall trees that rustled and bowed as if struck with reverence for this lone couple braving the frosty night.

King reached into his pocket and curled a gloved hand around a rag left over from when the handyman had painted the freezers. Once they'd poured the petrol through the letter box, they just had to douse the rag with petrol, light it and stuff it inside.

Honeywell dropped the petrol can on the ground. He rested his hands on his knees and threw up on a grassy bank.

King waited patiently for him to cease what sounded like a crude attempt to converse with frogs. 'Finished?'

'I think so.'

'For heaven's sake, pull yourself together.'

'Can't you do the rest on your own?'

'No.'

'Why not?'

Because I want to ensure you are complicit in my crimes. Stop you getting any nasty ideas about telling tales to the police. 'Because we always do everything together. That's our arrangement.'

'But I'

'Once it's done, it's done.'

'I'm not feeling well.'

'I'm not interested in your hypochondria. Put your balaclava on.'

They both donned balaclavas and pulled the hoods of their jackets up.

'I can't breathe,' Honeywell moaned, as they arrived outside Mel's house.

Good. Hopefully, all the excitement will lead to a fatal heart attack and save me the bother of killing you. He put the rag on the ground. 'Douse it with petrol.'

Honeywell fitted the hose to the can and splashed petrol onto the strip of cotton sheet. His trembling hands ensured a liberal dose of the liquid splashed onto the path and the welcome mat. King snatched it from him before he wasted it all. He poured half the contents through the letter box, put the can down, held the rag up and ordered Honeywell to light the fuse.

Honeywell's hands were shaking so badly, it took him three attempts to ignite the rag. Finally, it bloomed orange in the darkness.

'Push the letter box open.'

For once Honeywell obeyed a simple order without the usual fuss or fanfare. King stuffed the rag inside and watched it ignite the petrol inside the porch. Flames licked the coats, savouring their fur linings. King watched a pair of slippers devoured in seconds. A scarf turned into a daisy chain of orange petals.

He closed the flap. 'Let's go.'

They hurried back to the park and along the tree-lined trail. Honeywell snorted and stumbled like an asthmatic drunk on his way home after a night of heavy drinking. King now saw his ex-lover as a dangerous, self-centred, narcissistic, pretentious, fanciful, weak liability who could no longer be tolerated.

Back in the car, King removed his balaclava. 'I think that went rather well.'

Honeywell opted for silence, save the grunting noises leaking from the back of his throat. He ripped off his balaclava and snorkelled air through a blocked nose.

'Will you stop making that horrendous noise? You sound like a pig bound for the abattoir.'

'We'll go to hell for this.'

'I'm not going anywhere, apart from home for a stiff brandy and a long sleep. If you insist on being racked with guilt, you can sleep in the spare room.'

'What if the fire doesn't kill them?'

'It will.'

'What if a smoke alarm alerts them? What if they get out?'

'They won't.'

'What if someone saw us?'

'The most any stray insomniac might have seen is a pair of dark blurry shadows. Will you stop fretting?'

'We're going to get caught.'

'We will if you continue to behave like an excitable schoolgirl.'

'I wouldn't expect you to understand.'

King's tenuous grip on patience snapped. 'Understand what, you fool?'

'How this has affected me.'

'Stop being so melodramatic.'

'You never stop to think of my feelings, Peter. It's all about you, you, you. What Peter wants. You're not the one who will have to go into that school and face everyone knowing what you've done. Speak to the police. Teachers. The school board. The governor. Politicians.'

'Don't forget Uncle Tom Cobley,' King said, in the best mocking voice he could muster at this ungodly hour.

'Sometimes, I wish…'

Suppressing an overwhelming urge to kill his partner, King waited for him to finish his sentence. When nothing was forthcoming, he said, 'What do you wish, darling?'

'Nothing.'

'Go on. Say it. Let it all out. I'm listening.'

'I wish I'd never got involved with you.'

'"Our remedies oft in ourselves do lie. Which we ascribe to heaven: the fated sky gives us free scope, only doth backward pull our slow designs when we ourselves are dull."'

'I don't care a fig about Shakespeare. He's not the one facing a lifetime in jail.'

King opted for ambiguity in his answer. 'Neither are you, my fair-weather friend. Neither are you.'

CHAPTER THIRTY-FIVE

Chloe Hollis, neither awake nor asleep, stood at the top of the stairs as the lighted rag ignited the accelerant King had poured through the letter box. She clutched Ruby Rag Doll to her chest and watched the flames devour the coats in the porch. The fur-rimmed hood of her bright purple coat turned into a ring of fire.

'Ladybird, ladybird, fly away home,' she shouted.

Toxic smoke, black and acrid, crept through the living room and up the stairs. If the small porch had been separated by a door, it would have taken longer for the fire to take hold in the main body of the house, but it was nothing more than a tiny space to hang coats and kick off muddy shoes. The builders had won awards for saving space. Unfortunately, the same could not be said for saving lives.

Chloe walked down the stairs, repeating over and over at the top of her voice, 'Ladybird, ladybird, fly away home.'

She could see her father asleep on the small two-seater sofa, legs curled up, head at an awkward angle on the arm of his makeshift bed.

'Ladybird, ladybird, fly away home, your house is on fire and your children are gone.'

Tony stirred.

Chloe approached him, arms outstretched, Ruby Rag Doll hanging from one hand. 'Ladybird, ladybird, ladybird, ladybird…' She chanted.

Tony opened one eye and saw his daughter standing beside him. The smoke was getting thicker, rolling through the lounge like a black fog. At first, his mind refused to register what he was seeing. 'Chloe?'

'Ladybird… ladybird… ladybird…'

The smoke triggered the alarm on the landing, bringing Tony fully awake. He jumped off the sofa and swept Chloe into his arms.

'Ladybird… ladybird… ladybird…'

The chair by the fire was already ablaze, offering the flames a springboard to the curtains and the artificial Christmas tree. Tony ran into the kitchen and closed the door behind him. He put Chloe down.

'Ladybird… ladybird… ladybird…'

'Chloe? Listen to Daddy!'

The child looked at him, mouth hanging open in a small O.

'I need to put you out in the garden. I want you to be a big girl and wait outside while I get Mummy.'

'Ladybird, ladybird, ladybird…'

Tony considered slapping her. Actually pictured himself doing so. Instead, he knelt down and shook her by the shoulders. She was only wearing a thin nightdress, and it would be freezing outside, but he had no choice. There was no way he could get out via the front door, and he couldn't risk leaving her alone in the kitchen whilst he went upstairs to get Mel.

'Ladybird… ladybird… ladybird…'

He shook her hard enough to jolt her head. 'Chloe? Wake up, sweetheart. Wake up for Daddy.'

Chloe clutched Ruby Rag Doll to her chest. 'What's that yucky smell?'

'The house is on fire, Chloe. You'll have to go into the garden while I get Mummy, okay?'

Chloe nodded.

He took off his jumper, wrapped it around her shoulders, and led her into the garden. He cursed the builders of St Kilda's Close for not constructing rear access to the property. There was an eight-foot wall separating it from the park, but no gate. 'I won't be long. I promise.'

'Is the Tall Man coming?'

Tony's mind stalled. 'Who?'

'The Tall Man.'

'No.'

'What if he's hiding somewhere?'

'He's not. No one can get over the wall. I promise.'

'Did he start the fire?'

'No… you need to be a big girl for me, okay? I'll be back as quick as I can.'

'Okay.'

'You stand right by the back door. I'll leave the light on so as you can see.'

'Is he going to kill us, Daddy?'

Tony looked at the terror in his daughter's eyes and almost abandoned going back for Mel. 'No one's going to kill us, sweetheart. Not while Daddy's here.'

Chloe choked on a sob. 'I'm scared.'

'I'm just going to get Mummy. I'll be right back.'

He walked back inside and closed the door. He looked at the phone on the wall, thought about calling the emergency services, dismissed it. Every second counted now as far as Mel was concerned. He was about to open the kitchen door when something exploded. There was a crash, followed by several loud popping and spitting noises. He imagined lights and baubles exploding on the Christmas tree, sending fragments of glass flying across the room.

Don't open the door.

Tony's hand stalled on the handle. It was basic common sense not to open a door leading onto a fire. The sudden rush of oxygen only fuelled the flames. Tendrils of black smoke were already leaking underneath the door. He opened it half an inch and peered through the gap. The room was ablaze, orange and yellow flames reaching right up to the ceiling. The sofa, where he'd been sleeping just a few minutes ago, was unrecognisable as a piece of furniture. Thick black smoke billowed from it, reminding him how close he'd come to perishing. One thing was certain: he wouldn't last two minutes if he tried to get through the lounge, let alone up the stairs.

He closed the door, snatched the phone from its cradle, and called the emergency services. He gave his name and informed the operator that Mel was trapped upstairs. Told her he would wait in the back garden with his daughter because he couldn't get back through the house. There was no rear access. The only way out was over a high wall backing onto the park. The operator advised him to wait by the wall. She would inform the fire brigade of their situation.

Torn between a natural instinct to help Mel and not wanting to die a hero, Tony walked back into the garden and whisked Chloe up into his arms.

'Where's Mummy?'

'Mummy's fine, sweetheart. The fire brigade are coming.'

'Is she still in bed?'

Tony didn't answer. He walked to the bottom of the garden, rocking her gently from side to side.

'Is Mummy awake?'

'Yes.'

'How do you know?'

'The smoke alarm will have woken her up.'

'What if she didn't hear it?'

'It's too loud not to hear.'

'Even if she was in a dream?'

'Yes.'

Tony gawped at the house, begging God to let Mel be all right. If anyone deserved to die in that fire, it was him. He questioned his own response. Could he have done anything any differently? Rushed up the stairs before the fire had taken hold? But his main priority had been to get Chloe out of the building. Everything else was secondary. He couldn't comprehend how quickly the fire had spread. How rapidly it had devoured everything.

'Is Mummy going to die?'

'No. The firemen will get her out.'

'I don't want her to die.'

'She won't die.'

'I want her.'

'I know.'

'I love her.'

'Me too.'

After a lengthy silence, Chloe said, in a small, croaky voice, 'You can't hide anymore, Tony-baloney. The truth will always out.'

Tony tried to respond, but his brain was as frozen as his body. He held his breath, waiting for Chloe to say something else, his heart stomping all over his chest. He could feel Ruby Rag Doll's head pressing against his throat, sandwiched between him and Chloe. He had a sudden urge to rip the bloody thing away from his daughter and feed it to the burning house.

Thankfully, Chloe said nothing else. She lay in his arms, shaking, sniffing and sucking her thumb.

After what seemed like an eternity, a siren blared through the night air.

'The fire brigade are here,' Tony announced.

'Will they get Mummy out now?'

'Yes.'

'Good.'

Tony stood shivering, hugging Chloe to him, begging God to let Mel be all right. After what seemed like hours to Tony's tortured mind, a fireman appeared at the top of the wall. He shone a flashlight into the garden. 'Mr Hollis?'

Tony looked up. 'I'm here.'

'I'll put a ladder over the wall and get you both out.'

Tony's legs grew weaker, his breath more laboured. It was as if whatever was holding him together for the sake of his daughter was no longer required.

The fireman climbed into the garden. He squatted down in front of Chloe. 'Hello, honey. My name's David. You okay?'

'Uh-huh.'

'You're a very brave little girl.'

'My wife?' Tony said. 'Is she all right?'

'She's suffered smoke inhalation, but she seems okay. The ambulance has taken her to the John Radcliffe Hospital to get her checked over.'

'Thank God.'

The fireman smiled at Chloe. 'You ready to go up the ladder with me?'

'Uh-huh.'

'Then I'll come back for Daddy, okay?'

'Not that he deserves it.'

The fireman didn't seem to notice the implication of the little girl's words. 'I'm going to carry you up the ladder and give you to another fireman when we get to the top, okay?'

'Okay.'

Tony watched David climb up the ladder with Chloe and Ruby Rag Doll hanging over his shoulder. Near the top, Chloe looked at him, eyes wide. 'You could say you've burned your bridges, Tony-baloney.' And then she was gone, whisked into the waiting arms of another fireman.

Tony's knees buckled. He crouched down, shivering and praying for an end to this nightmare.

CHAPTER THIRTY-SIX

King was in no mood to sleep. Running on adrenalin, he paced around the wine cellar in his blue and green checked dressing gown like an animal marking its territory.

'"O for a Muse of fire, that would ascend the brightest heaven of invention."'

The cellar amplified the words, rolling them around the bare stone walls, lending them a theatrical quality. He'd wanted to drive to St Kilda's Close and watch the house burn, but as usual his lover was behaving like a mouse who'd eaten too much cheese and subjected itself to unspeakable nightmares.

He'd been with Charles for over fifteen years now, but sometimes it felt closer to fifteen lifetimes. His propensity toward doubt had served as a stark reminder to King that loyalty had its limits. Charles's weakness, as far as the child and its mother were concerned, had made it all too clear that his tongue was close enough to betrayal to make his death inevitable. He'd taken to the spare room like a housewife with a migraine, and he could jolly well stay there and rot.

All the way back from the *house-warming* party, Honeywell had hopped from repentance to paranoia to self-loathing and back again like a rabbit on amphetamines. After a particularly nasty incident, when they'd mounted the pavement and narrowly missed a wheelie-bin, King had found it necessary to take the wheel and drive the rest of the way home in that diabolical tin can Honeywell had the audacity to call a car.

He stopped stalking around the basement and stood in front of the purple freezer. He addressed the door. 'Have you any idea of the trouble you've caused me, Purple-five?'

Purple-five seemed neither roused by guilt, nor interested in engaging him in conversation. He felt compelled to take her head out and hurl it across the room. Smash it into a thousand ice cubes. But he had long since learned to control his emotions after the unfortunate event at his mother's house with his first love, Big Al. Unless one was cursed with a tendency toward necrophilia, which King certainly wasn't, Big Al had proved to be neither use nor ornament after the attempt to achieve orgasm through strangulation.

'"Our doubts are traitors, and make us lose the good we oft might win, by fearing to attempt."'

Purple-five didn't seem appreciative of Shakespeare, either. No surprise. Her crude upbringing would never have put her into contact with great works of literature. The rubbish they taught in schools was of sufficient quality to inspire illiteracy. By definition, a fool was someone who repeated the same thing over and over, expecting different results. The education system seemed happy to operate by the same deluded mandate, with all the eloquence and finesse of a dung beetle.

'Why did you have to spite me?'

Purple-five exercised her right to remain silent. It wasn't lost on him that she had inhabited the body of a child connected by its mother to Charles. The link was tenuous, and inadmissible in a court of law, but there all the same. It was as if she'd somehow chosen Chloe Hollis to spite him.

'I am "pierced to the soul with slander's venom'd spear,"' King told the freezer door. 'But revenge, as you well know, dear Amy, is a dish best served cold.'

Purple-five didn't seem to appreciate humour, either.

What if the fire doesn't kill them?

Honeywell's words drifted across his mind like tendrils of smoke. He tried to dismiss them, but they came again, louder, more emphatic. *What if the fire doesn't kill them?*

He walked to the wall-to-wall wine rack, selected a bottle of Sassicaia and studied the label. Perhaps a glass or two of a decent red might help to calm his nerves. These past few weeks had been testing, to say the least.

He went to the kitchen, uncorked the wine and poured a small measure into a glass. He swirled the dark liquid around the bottom of the glass, savouring its lavender bouquet, and treated his taste buds to its finesse and grace. Calmed by the wine's delicate beauty, he filled the glass and walked into the lounge. He sat in his leather recliner and raised his glass to a photograph of his mother on top of the mantelpiece. 'Happy New Year, Mother.'

Mother stared back at him, eyes hardened by the years of abuse suffered at the hands of her uncompromising brutal husband. His mother was a true fighter. He wouldn't have been at all surprised to learn that her heart had been cast from granite. King liked to believe some of her indestructible nature had been transferred to him via the umbilical cord whilst in the womb.

He took a sip of wine and told his mother how much he missed her. He could see from the tenderness lurking behind her frosty stare that she missed him, too.

'"Death lies on her like an untimely frost upon the sweetest flower of all the field."'

His mother didn't seem moved by her son's sentimental, if not misplaced, ode to her, courtesy of *Romeo and Juliet*. He sipped his wine, recalling the endless hours spent at the family home locked in the library, with only the words of Shakespeare to offer solace.

His trip down memory lane hit a pothole as he realised his mother might also now be inhabiting the planet as someone else. Another thought, more worrying: What if she now occupied the body of someone he knew? It had been over nineteen years since her death. That left room for a considerable number of potential rebirths since then. Tens of thousands, millions, even.

By the time he'd finished his wine, he was grateful for being gay; at least it meant there was no possibility of incest. After the third glass, his thoughts had veered towards the possibility of investing in the skills of a psychic medium to see if his mother had risen from the ashes of her premature death. As his mind stumbled along a corridor between sobriety and drunkenness, he hunted inside his head for possible born-again mothers. Perhaps a waitress at his favourite restaurant. A checkout girl at the supermarket.

The cleaner.

The very thought of that duster-wielding hag being related to him almost negated the effect of the alcohol. She had the personality of a wart-hog, and the manners to match. How the devil she performed her duties without breaking something was beyond him, but she seemed to manage it and obey simple orders such as where she could and could not take the hoover.

Relief. She was far too old. At least forty perhaps more. With another glass of wine fermenting in his belly, and thoughts of his wonderful mother fermenting in his head, he decided he would indeed enlist the help of a psychic medium to shed light on his mother's whereabouts. Until this unfortunate business with Purple-five turning up as bold as brass in Chloe Hollis, he'd been of the firm opinion Mother was nothing more than dust and bones. But now everything had changed forever. Anything, it now seemed, was possible.

He walked into the kitchen and poured more wine. He overfilled the glass, leaving a small puddle of dark liquid on the table. Normally, this would have sent his cleaning obsession into overdrive, but tonight he didn't notice. He walked back into the lounge, wine dripping from the bottom of the glass like droplets of blood.

'Oh, Charles, why do you torment me so with your reckless thoughts?'

Like his mother, Charles didn't offer an answer. King imagined him sitting up in bed, besieged by the Christmas ghosts, eyes wide, terror quaking on his lips, pleading for mercy.

'The man who parts company with integrity shall join hands with uncertainty,' King slurred, quoting a play he'd once started to write. He'd abandoned the cursed thing after act one with a bad case of writer's block which had threatened to tip him towards suicide. It was only the attention of several rent boys that had saved him from complete destruction. The ritual burning of the ill-fated manuscript had also proved therapeutic, as if the characters who had caused him so much anguish were perishing in the flames.

He allowed his mind to relish a future without Charles. He could go where he liked, when he liked, and not have to watch every move he made. Charles was always accommodating of the rent boys because they offered no threat to the stability of their relationship. It was just casual sex with sadomasochist benefits. But God help equilibrium if he should dare to share an intimate moment with another man.

'"O, beware, my lord, of jealousy; it is the green-eyed monster, which doth mock…"' King said, opting for Shakespeare in preference to his own work. It was one thing to admire a great artist; quite another to emulate him. As much as it pained him to concede it, his talent for writing was often as fruitless as his talent for acting. But one thing separated him from other mortals: he was aware of his limitations, and a man aware of his limitations was a man also aware of his strengths. Like a fine wine, his creative mind was maturing.

'All good things come to those who want,' he told the empty room.

Wait.

King paid scant attention to the pedantic side of his brain. Not tonight. He had better things to do than to get into an argument with the word-weasel. Such as formulate a plan to rid the world of Charles Honeywell. Not that he wouldn't miss his former lover. They'd shared some good times together; especially playing One False Move. Those endless hours engaged in battle. Marred only by Charles's refusal to grant Purple-five a pardon after she landed on the Death Square. King had been sorely tempted to pull rank and send his lover's game piece to the cage out of spite. But he was not a man given to unfairness, and Purple-five had met her fate as sentenced.

Another thing he'd miss was his lover's cooking; his beef bourguignon was a delight, as was his steak tartare. He was also a good lover, when he put his mind to it. Considerate, complicit, and with a half-decent pain threshold to boot.

'One doesn't cast off one's worn-out coat for fear of freezing. One simply looks for another coat,' he said, the alcohol teasing his brain with renewed resolve to write another play. Perhaps a tragic tale of two lovers torn apart.

He toasted the words with a noisy slurp of wine and squinted at his mother. She would have liked his work. Encouraged him. Inspired him. Helped him.

Your mother might have been born again as a man.

King sobered at the thought. Dark, unbidden and cruel.

A rent boy, perhaps?

King slammed down his glass on the coffee table hard enough to break the stem.

Nathan was about the right age. Seventeen, eighteen, give or take a pimple.

King stood up and stomped into the kitchen. He refused to sit and listen to any more of this nonsense. He stepped out into the garden. The sudden change of temperature stilled the spiteful voice in his head. He stood for as long as his body could endure before going back inside.

Shaking in much the same way Nathan had when King had hacked off his left nipple with a razor blade, he sat at the kitchen table and wrapped his arms around his chest to get warm. The central heating kept the house at a steady twenty-two degrees, but tonight it felt set at minus-two.

One hour and two brandies later, he had the rough outline of a plan regarding the untimely demise of Charles and Gavin Westwood. Crude, and far from finished, the plan was beautiful in its simplicity. He would arrange a meeting between them. Convince Charles to let the hypnotherapist erase his memories of New Year's Eve. A private session at Westwood's home. Once there, he would shoot them both, and then arrange the crime scene to make it appear as if Charles had murdered Westwood and then turned the gun on himself.

It would need fine tuning, and some incriminating evidence to tie Westwood and Charles together, but he had several secret love letters from Westwood locked in a bureau in the study. He'd just stuff one in Charles's pocket after the shooting. None of them referred to King by name. They'd always used pet names when corresponding. The police would simply assume that Charles was Bunnykins, and close the case and mark it as misadventure.

King held onto the bannister for support as he staggered upstairs to bed. It wasn't much of a plan, but at least it would give his intellect something to work with in the coming days. Something to console himself with as he looked at Charles Honeywell's maudlin face at the breakfast table on these freezing winter mornings.

CHAPTER THIRTY-SEVEN

After spending the night at the hospital and New Year's Day at Tony's mother's, Mel's patience was wearing thin. Not that she particularly disliked Vicky Hollis, but it was sickly the way she talked to Tony as if he was still wearing short trousers. To make matters worse, her tiny two-bedroom flat was barely sufficient to house the four of them in the long term.

It was still far too early to properly assess the damage to the house, but Mel didn't care what state it was in; she would never set foot inside Thirty-six St Kilda's Close again, even if someone waved a magic wand and turned the place into her dream home. It would be forever tainted and representative of the diabolical attempt to murder her family.

With Chloe in bed, the three adults sat around the kitchen table discussing the fire.

Vicky ran a hand through her tangled grey hair. 'Why would anyone do such a wicked thing?'

Tony sighed. 'It's a wicked world.'

Mel stared at the knots in the pine table. Tony had agreed not to say anything about Chloe. It was hard enough trying to deal with the fire, without fanning the flames with talk of the supernatural.

'On New Year's Eve,' Vicky added, as if that made a difference. 'The state of the world these days makes me want to weep.'

'It was probably kids,' Tony said.

'Oh, well, that's all right, then. They'll just give them a pat on the back and send them off to Disneyland.'

Tony nodded. 'Some of them don't know they're born these days.'

Mel stood up. 'I'm going outside for a cigarette.'

'Perhaps now might be a good time to consider giving up,' Vicky said. 'Make it your New Year's Resolution.'

Mel's patience snapped. 'I've got more important things to do right now.'

'I know this is hard for you, Mel, but vanishing behind a cloud of smoke won't help. Not to mention the cost.'

Mel's need for a cigarette increased tenfold. 'I couldn't care less.'

'You have Chloe to consider. It's not fair on her… or Tony.'

'Poor Tony.'

'He hates smoking.'

'Have you asked your precious son what it is I hate about him?'

Vicky looked about to say something, snapped her mouth shut, and looked at her Tony.

'It's nothing, Mum. We're all on edge at the moment, that's all.'

Mel laughed. 'That's the bloody understatement of the year.'

Vicky looked at her son and said, 'Is there something you're not telling me?'

'It's just been a bad time for everyone.'

'Did you two *really* split up because Mel started smoking again?'

Mel rolled her eyes. 'Is that what he told you?'

'He said you had a big row about it.'

Mel felt the truth threaten to burst out of her. 'And you believe him?'

'I don't know what to believe. I just want you to be happy for that little girl's sake.'

'At least we agree on something,' Mel said, walking out of the flat and putting the front door on the latch.

She stood shivering in the communal front garden whilst she smoked her cigarette right down to the filter. Why couldn't Tony be a man for once, assume responsibility and tell his overbearing mother the real reason why they'd split up? When she returned to the flat, mother and son were still sitting at the table, the silence between them palpable. Mel knew they'd been talking about her; the words were written all over their faces.

'Is it cold out?' Vicky asked.

'You could say that.'

'I'm not judging you, Mel. Your marriage is your own affair. God knows me and Tony's father had our fair share of ups and down, God rest his soul. You have to compromise. You can get those nicotine patches for smoking nowadays. It's not that difficult. Tony said he'll support you every step of the way.'

Mel looked at her husband with what she hoped was enough venom to poison him. 'Is that right?'

Tony looked away.

'If you want to know the real reason we split up, I'm sure Tony will find it in his heart to tell you. I'll tell you this much, though: it has nothing to do with smoking.'

Vicky's eyes swivelled to her son like gun barrels. 'Is that right?'

'Now's not the time, Mother. It's complicated.'

Mel laughed. 'It's not. It's really quite simple.'

'I'm not going to discuss it now,' Tony said. 'We've got enough to worry about with the fire and everything.'

Chloe saved Tony from further embarrassment. She appeared in the kitchen doorway, eyes wide, Ruby Rag Doll clutched to her chest. 'Ladybird, ladybird, fly away home.'

Mel took a few steps towards her. 'Chloe?'

'He's coming.'

'Who?'

'The Tall Man.'

'What the hell's she talking about?' Vicky asked.

Tony put a finger to his lips. 'She's sleepwalking.'

Mel crouched down in front of Chloe, heart pounding. 'Who's the Tall Man, Pumpkin?'

'Shakespeare.'

'William Shakespeare?'

Chloe nodded.

'But he died a long time ago.'

'No one dies.'

'No?'

'We all go round and round. Like the wheels on the bus.'

Mel was about to reach out, pull Chloe close, when she spoke again. 'I've landed on the Death Square.'

'Wake her up!' Vicky demanded.

Mel ignored her. 'What's the "Death Square," Pumpkin?'

Chloe smirked. A nasty sarcastic sound that had to right coming from a child. 'I think you'll find it's all in the name.'

'Is this how?'

'All in the game, even. Marlowe refused to pardon me.'

'Who the bloody hell's Marlowe?' Tony whispered.

Mel leaned close enough to almost touch noses. 'Did Marlowe kill you?'

'Guilty as guillotines.'

Mel remembered the picture Chloe had drawn at Kerrie-Anne's. Remembered it in all its gory vivid detail. In that one moment, she understood everything.

'What's your name?'

Chloe sighed. 'You know what my name is.'

'Amy?'

Chloe nodded. She dropped Ruby Rag Doll and put her hands behind her back. 'Please, don't hurt me.'

'No one's going to hurt you. Mummy's right here with you.'

Chloe didn't seem to hear her. She knelt on the cold linoleum floor, head up, as if her chin was resting on something solid. Her breathing came in short ragged gasps. She closed her eyes, squeezing them into slits.

'Wake her up,' Tony said. 'Wake her up, Mel.'

Mel stared, unblinking, stomach clenched, as a large, red mark appeared on Chloe's neck.

Mel tried to act, but she couldn't move. It was as if she was part of some never-ending nightmare.

'Help me, help me, help me…' Chloe yelled, gargling the words.

'Stop it!' Tony shouted. 'Stop it, now!' He ran to his daughter and scooped her up in his arms.

Vicky stood beside Mel, one hand clutching her throat. 'What in God's name is wrong with her?'

'It's nothing, Mum,' Tony said. 'She's just having a nightmare.'

'I saw her neck! What's happened to her?'

Tony walked to the bedroom, hugging Chloe, rocking her from side to side.

Vicky turned to Mel. 'What's going on?'

Mel didn't answer her. How did you explain to a grandmother that her granddaughter had been executed by guillotine in a past life? It would have been simpler to explain the complete history of evolution in one simple sentence.

CHAPTER THIRTY-EIGHT

King did not react well to the news that the fire had destroyed the house but not the intended targets. He was even less inclined towards grace when the bearer of that news was the man he wanted dead by the end of the month.

'What do you mean, they survived?'

'What I say,' Honeywell chirped, seemingly unable to contain the joy in his voice. 'Mel phoned. Said Tony and Chloe got out before the fire really took hold. The fire brigade rescued her from the bedroom.'

'Is this your idea of a joke?'

'I'm just'

'Have you sensed my good mood and decided to destroy it with the worst possible news imaginable?'

'It's the truth.' Honeywell's voice adopted a more sombre tone. 'Mel told me she's not returning to work in the foreseeable future. Perhaps a period of reflection might be in order, Peter. Act in haste, and all that.'

King tossed a half-eaten slice of toast onto his plate and poured himself a cup of tea. 'We should have broken in and doused the whole of the downstairs with petrol.'

'I'm surprised Tony was there. I thought they'd split up.'

'Stop using proletarian language. "Split up" is a meaningless term which makes no sense. Unless referring to log cutting, perhaps.'

'I'

'Where are they now?'

'At Tony's mother's.'

King resisted an urge to poke his lover in the eye. 'And I'm supposed to know where that is, am I?'

'I don't know myself. I'm not a close family member, Peter. Just a friend.'

King didn't care for the pout on Honeywell's lips. 'Then, in your elevated capacity as a friend of the family, you'd better find out where they are.'

'I can hardly ask where the mother lives, can I? It'll seem out of place.'

'Not if you feign concern and insist on visiting.'

'It might sound intrusive. Perhaps we should just wait a while and let the dust settle. We don't want to'

'And what do you suggest we do whilst this "dust" settles? Have a few cosy nights in by the fire toasting marshmallows?'

'It wouldn't hurt.'

'Let's rewind, Charles. Remind ourselves who it was that started fretting about the child.'

After a pause, and another unsavoury pout, he said, 'Me. But we don't want to go rushing in and make any more mistakes, do we?'

'The only mistake I made was listening to you.'

'I thought we could start a new game of One False Move.'

Derailed by the sudden change of subject, not to mention the sheer stupidity of the suggestion, King said, 'How in Dickens' name are we supposed to concentrate whilst Mary Poppins and her spooky brat are still on the loose with tales to tell?'

'I don't think they will'

'Phone that bitch and find out where she is.'

'But what will I say?'

'Tell her you've got something for the brat. A personal message from Father Christmas if it helps. Just make sure you get the address.'

'Someone ought to go to the theatre and check on the girls. It's been a few days since'

'When did you suddenly become their welfare officer?'

'I'm just saying.'

'Fussing, more like. Those ill-bred types are hardy enough when they have to be. Something in the genes. If you trace the bloodlines back far enough, I'm sure you'll find them to be direct descendants of mountain goats.'

'We can't just leave them to starve.'

'We can. Now, do as I asked.'

Honeywell mumbled something under his breath as he left the kitchen. King consoled himself with thoughts of Gavin Westwood and Charles Honeywell both lying dead in the hypnotist's lounge. A lovers' spat escalating into violence and murder. The experience would lend his new play a realistic edge. Give him the added advantage of knowing his main characters' motivations and traits. The headmaster and the hypnotist, driven by lust, greed and an insatiable urge to control. His mind bubbled with the ramifications of such a plot.

'It is a fine line that draws itself between reality and fantasy,' King whispered, driven to a sudden bout of creativity. 'Entwined like an invisible thread, stitching together a montage of fevered jealousy and rage.'

He retrieved a notepad from a kitchen drawer, sat at the breakfast bar, and scrawled the words onto the paper while they were still freshly baked. He studied them. They seemed somewhat muddled. Bereft of the creative structure and genius of Shakespeare. The great man's words always seemed to flow like a gentle stream over smooth pebbles.

Death knocks louder than opportunity.

What on earth did that mean? He had no idea, but wrote it down. Inspiration often came in riddles. One had to be patient with one's muse; that fickle friend prone to bouts of sulking and contemplative silence. He'd learned that lesson the hard way after beating his head against the bedroom wall once after a nasty case of writer's block. He'd spent a week in bed suffering migraines and severe bouts of depression in equal measure.

Honeywell returned to the kitchen and plonked his mobile on the breakfast bar.

'Well?'

'Went straight to voicemail.'

'Did you leave a message?'

'I thought it best not to. I didn't want to seem too pushy.'

'You do realise that this needs to be treated with urgency?'

'I know. But'

'Why do you give me the impression of someone under the influence of apathy?'

'I can't make her answer the damned phone.'

'No need to take that tone.'

'Everything I do is wrong.'

'Grow up, Charles. For someone who is the headmaster of a school, you seem to have adopted the whiny persona of your charges.'

'I'm just fed up of being pushed around. You treat me as if I'm some menial servant. We're *supposed* to be lovers.'

'Angst doth ring its bell the loudest.'

Honeywell blinked and looked at King as if he'd just offered him a ride on a space rocket. 'Is that Shakespeare?'

'No; it's mine.'

'You wrote it?'

King scribbled it down on the pad. 'Yes.'

'It's… good.'

'You say that with trepidation.'

'No. It's genuinely good.'

'Perhaps you think me incapable of great art?'

Honeywell didn't need to answer. His eyes drew shades and claimed no one was home.

'I can be whomever I want to be, Charles. I am not damned by limitations.'

'I know. You're very…'

'Talented?'

'Yes.'

'Knowledge is the ink that shall furnish my pen. I shall write of impassioned nights beneath a gluttony of stars.'

Honeywell cocked his head to one side, seemingly less certain of this fresh outburst from King's muse.

King forgave him his ignorance. 'I'm going to write a new play.'

'Have you got time for such a lengthy project?'

'I shall make time.'

'You'd have an awful lot more time if you forgot about Chloe Hollis.'

'Do you enjoy chasing your own tail like a demented dog?'

'I just want you to see reason, Peter.'

King looked at Honeywell's half-closed eye sitting in its nest of bruises. The damn thing appeared to be winking at him. 'I see something before me, and it bears no relation to reason.'

'I don't think'

'"Giddy Fortune's furious fickle wheel, that goddess blind, that stands upon the rolling restless stone",' King said, opting for the safety and wisdom of Shakespeare. He emptied his plate of half-eaten toast into the waste bin, rinsed his hands under the tap, dried them, and took a four-inch paring knife from the drawer. He slipped it into the pocket of his dressing gown and returned to the breakfast bar.

'So, let's recap. You think we should just leave our future resting in the hands of a child?'

'We've already set fire to the house, Peter. The authorities will be treating it as attempted murder. At the very least, we should stay away from that family for the foreseeable future.'

King held up his hands, palms out. 'What do you see, Charles?'

Honeywell frowned. 'Hands.'

'Exactly. Hands that toil to bring joy. Hands that nourish and support the very foundations of our relationship.'

'I'

'Show me your hands, Charles.'

'Why?'

'Humour me.'

Honeywell held them out, palms up, as if about to seek spiritual enlightenment.

'You can learn a lot from a man's hands,' King said. He touched the left palm with the tip of his index finger. 'Some even claim to be able to predict the future by reading the lines.'

Honeywell gawped at his hands, glasses perched on the end of his nose. 'Just an old wives' tale, if you ask me.'

King agreed. 'Gypsy nonsense designed to steal money from the deluded. Why don't you let me have a go at reading yours?'

'Me? No. I don't think'

'Lighten up, Charles. It's just a bit of harmless fun. Sit down. Put your hand on the breakfast bar.'

Honeywell's eye, the one that wasn't set to a permanent wink, regarded King as if he'd just invited him to a duel at dawn. 'Are you serious?'

'Yes.'

He surrendered his palm.

King traced the curved line running from the centre of his lover's hand to the heel. 'Hmm.'

'What is it?'

'I see these hands have never seen an honest day's toil.'

'I helped to build a wall once.'

'Hadrian's?'

Honeywell chuckled. 'It *was* a very long time ago.'

'Your lifeline is rather short.'

'My hands are small.'

You're confusing that with your mind. 'It might be prudent to tread carefully. We don't want you to meet with a nasty accident, do we?'

'True.'

'Close your eyes.'

'Why?'

'I want you to relax. Get in touch with your inner feelings.'

'How's that going to help with reading my palm?'

'Humour me.'

Honeywell closed his eyes, although the injured one seemed to still be peeking through the blackout shades of the bruise.

King ran the tip of his index finger over his lover's palm.

'That tickles.'

'Shush. Don't spoil the moment. I'm tuning into your life. I see a fork at the end of your lifeline.'

'What does that mean?'

King took the paring knife out of his dressing gown pocket. 'It means you will face a big decision soon. One that will cause much soul-searching.'

'Oh.'

He raised the knife. 'Be sure to do the right thing.'

'Okay.'

King brought the knife down with as much force as he could muster. He drove it through Honeywell's hand far enough for the tip of the blade to hit the tiled breakfast bar.

At first, Honeywell didn't react. It was as if the pain receptors in his brain had been temporarily switched off. Then, a scream rolled out of his throat like something dredged up from a drain.

'Now, listen carefully. Find Mel Hollis and her child, or I will plunge this knife into your heart. Is that clear?'

Honeywell's breath hissed from his lips as if his mouth had turned into a steam press.

King pulled the knife out, drawing with it a small river of blood. 'Now get to it, before I really lose patience with you.'

CHAPTER THIRTY-NINE

After spending three torturous days at Tony's mother's, Mel felt as if she was losing her mind. If Vicky Hollis asked her one more time what she was going to do about Chloe, she wouldn't be held responsible for her actions. She lay awake on the camp bed, pain rolling up from the base of her spine to her shoulders. Tony snored beside her.

She rolled off the bed and spent a few moments on her hands and knees stretching her back, waiting for the stiffness to subside. She then made her way across the living room, switched on the main light and retrieved her cigarettes from her handbag.

Tony groaned and rolled over. Sod him! Hopefully, the light would wake him up. She opened the living room window, lit up, and blew smoke into the freezing air. The cigarette soothed her nerves. Helped to calm her.

After a few minutes, Tony propped himself up on one elbow, squinting at her. 'What time is it?'

'Don't know.'

'Are you all right?'

'Do I look all right, Tony?'

Tony studied his watch. 'It's only twenty past seven.'

'So?'

'I thought it would be nice to have a lie in. Make the most of it before terms starts again.'

Mel flicked her cigarette butt out the window and closed it. 'Don't make me laugh. I've hardly slept since I took Chloe to Feelham Theatre.'

'Maybe you ought to ask the doctor for something.'

'Fabulous idea. Then if Chloe has one of her episodes, I'll be zonked out on sleeping tablets.'

'It was only a suggestion.'

'Half the reason I can't sleep is because I'm having to share a bed with you.'

'Sorry.'

'Will you stop bloody apologising?'

'I can't do right for doing wrong.'

'What do you expect? You even lied to your mother. Telling her we'd split up because I'd started smoking again. Have you any idea how weak and pathetic that sounds?'

'I'

'Why couldn't you tell her the truth?'

'Because…'

'Afraid Mummy might see what a nasty selfish brat she has for a son?'

'Something like that.'

'She looks at me as if I'm a social leper. As if it's me who's driven a wedge between us.'

'The less she knows, the better. Believe me.'

'You're a coward, Tony.'

Tony offered no argument. He flopped back on the bed and stared at the ceiling.

'I'm not staying here. I'm not spending another day with her looking at me as if I'm an unfit mother. God, I'm so tempted to wipe that self-righteous look off her face. Tell her what really happened. How her precious son decided to fuck some slag at work whilst his wife was in meltdown.'

'You'll never forgive me, will you?'

'And now my daughter's suffering from bugger knows what and I can do nothing to help her. Not to mention someone tried to burn down our house. Pardon me if I'm not in a very forgiving mood, Tony.'

'Chloe is *our* daughter. Not just yours.'

'Ten out of ten for observation. So, are you going to tell your mother what really happened?'

His silence told Mel all she needed to know. 'I'm leaving. I'm not taking the blame for this anymore. I'm sick of your mother's questions, and I'm sick of your lies.'

'But you've got nowhere to go.'

'If you say so, Tony. If you say so.'

Tony clambered off the bed. 'Please, Mel. Don't do this.'

Mel ignored him and lit another cigarette.

'You'd better open the window to let the smoke out.'

Mel snorted. 'Maybe the smoke doesn't want to go out.'

'We can get through this. If we stick together, we can work it out. Be strong together.'

Mel reluctantly opened the window. 'You wouldn't know what *strong* was if it leapt up and bit you on the nose.'

'Don't'

'I want to be on my own.'

'For God's sake, Mel. Where will you go?'

She didn't answer.

'You're not thinking straight.'

'Tell me something I don't know.'

'But you've hardly got any clothes.'

'I'll buy some.'

'You're cutting off your nose to spite your face. At least let me drive you.'

'There's no need for that. I'm taking the car.'

'You're not having the Golf.'

'It's just as much my car as it is yours.'

'I need it for work.'

'So do I.'

'This is ridiculous.'

'I'm taking the car. And I'm taking Chloe somewhere your stupid mother can't keep fretting and pestering her.'

'She's only'

'I'm only what?' Vicky Hollis stood in the doorway waving a hand in front of her face.

'Go back to bed, Mother,' Tony said.

'You two woke me up with your rowing.'

'You don't have to worry about that anymore,' Mel said. 'I'm leaving.'

For the first time since Mel had known her mother-in-law, the woman looked lost for words. 'Why?'

'Because it's best for everyone. We can't stay cramped up here like this. It's not fair on you. It's not fair on Chloe.'

'But where will you go?'

'To a friend's.'

Tony stepped closer to his mother as if seeking safety in numbers. 'What friend?'

'I'll tell you when I get there. Now, if you'd both excuse me, I'd like to get dressed.'

'Oh, for God's sake, Mel. See sense.' She turned to her son. 'Make her see sense.'

'He already has,' Mel said. 'Believe me, he already has.'

Tony coaxed his mother into the kitchen with the promise of a pot of tea.

Mel dressed in a pair of blue jogging bottoms and two oversized jumpers. One green, the other red. The fruits of Tony's trip into town to buy some emergency clothes. She went into the bedroom, turned on the light and woke her daughter.

Chloe looked at her mother, eyelids heavy with sleep. Ruby Rag Doll was covering her mouth with her woollen hair. 'Mummy?'

'Come on, sweetie. It's time to get up.'

'Why?'

'We're going for a little ride in the car.'

'Where?'

'To Granddad's house.'

'But Granddad's dead.'

'We're going to look after his house for a while.'

'Is Daddy coming, too.'

'Not for now. Daddy's staying with Grandma Vicky.'

'Why?'

'Grandma Vicky's not well. Come on. It'll be fun. And it's out in the country.'

'Is it a farm?'

'No.'

'Are there any cows?'

'There's a farmer's field if you carry on up the lane.'

'Why didn't we ever go to Granddad's house when he was alive?'

'It's a long story, Pumpkin. I'll tell you all about it one day.'

'When are we going back to our house?'

'When it's fixed.'

'Grandma Vicky told Daddy you might have started the fire by smoking.'

'Did she now?'

'Uh-huh. But that's not true, is it?'

'No. And she has no business saying so.'

'I don't like Grandma Vicky much. She's bossy.'

'Well, Grandma Vicky won't be at Granddad's house, will she?'

'Nope.'

Mel lowered her voice to a whisper. 'No witches allowed.'

Chloe giggled. 'I still love her, though.'

'I know.'

'I love you, too, Mummy.'

'I love you more.'

'More than the sky?'

'More than the whole universe.'

They rubbed noses for the first time since before their ill-fated visit to Feelham Theatre.

As Chloe dressed in her new jeans, trainers and bright pink jumper, she turned to Mel. 'Will the Tall Man know where Granddad's house is?'

Mel's breath caught in her throat. 'No.'

'He wants us to die, Mummy.'

'He can want what he likes. He'll have me to deal with first.'

Chloe continued to dress in silence, as if she knew Mel felt as empty and hollow as her words.

CHAPTER FORTY

As Mel pulled up in the gravel lane outside Rose Cottage, her initial burst of bravado, fuelled by resentment towards Tony and his mother, had vanished. She'd had to wait in town almost two hours for the estate agents to open to get a key to the house. Mel had treated them to croissants from Dalton's bakery. She'd also purchased a coffee for herself, and made Chloe's day by allowing her to have a bottle of Fanta orange.

The large detached building had a strange ghostly quality. The rendered walls, once white, were now filthy and peeling in places.

You're making the biggest mistake of your life. Go back to the flat. Swallow your pride and go back.

'Is this Granddad's house?'

'Yes, Pumpkin.'

'It's old, isn't it?'

'Old as the hills.'

'What does that mean?'

Reverse back up the lane and leave before it's too late. 'It's just a saying.'

'Is it as old as Daddy?'

'Older.'

'It's a… lonely place, isn't it?'

Mel was once again struck by the adult nature of Chloe's words. It was as if she'd bypassed childhood. 'A bit.'

'Why do you want to live here, Mummy?'

I don't. Oh, God, I don't. 'It's only for a little while.'

'How long?'

'I'm not sure.'

'How long's a piece of string, eh?'

Mel turned around. 'Where did you learn that?'

Chloe shrugged and fiddled with her new coat. Pink, with big toggles and a detachable hood. She hadn't liked it anywhere near as much as her purple one with the fur-rimmed hood. Mel had almost sent Tony back into town to get a purple one, but she hadn't been in any mood to argue with him over a coat; he was in a bad enough mood as it was that day, moaning about the shops and people's never-ending need to 'scavenge' just because it was Christmas.

'I'm cold, Mummy. When are we going inside?'

'In a minute.'

'You don't like it here, do you?'

Mel told the biggest lie she'd ever told in her life. 'I don't mind it.'

'Why don't we go back to Grandma Vicky's?'

Because I'd end up throttling her. 'The flat's not big enough for all of us.'

'I liked my room.'

'I didn't like mine.'

'Granddad's house looks really cold.'

'It'll be all right once we light the fire.'

'Has it got radiators?'

'I don't think so.'

'Does it have smoke coming out of the chimney?'

Mel shuddered. 'Yes.'

'Daddy told Grandma Vicky you smoke like a chimney.'

And he gossips like an old woman. 'Did he now?'

'I don't want you to smoke, Mummy. It's bad for you.'

Mel switched off the engine and took the keys from the ignition. 'Come on, let's get inside.'

The front door opened straight onto the living room. As they stepped inside, the smell of damp was overbearing. Unopened mail littered the doormat, spilling into the twelve foot square room. Mel switched on the light and closed the door.

'It stinks,' Chloe complained, pegging her nose between her thumb and forefinger.

'We'll just have to give it a good clean, then, won't we?'

'It's yuk! I want to go back to Grandma Vicky's.'

'Well, we're not,' Mel snapped. 'So we'll just have to make the best of it until I can find somewhere better.'

Apart from a large widescreen TV sitting on a mahogany cabinet, most of the room looked frozen in time. Still the old pink and green floral-patterned settee and two matching chairs, the pine dresser with its display of plates and cups, the red and grey leather foot stool, the hideous gold and green Axminster carpet, and the wallpaper depicting leaves and vines.

The open fire had been boarded over and replaced by a coal-effect electric fire. Mel almost whooped for joy. She switched it on and was treated to an instant red glow from the three bars, along with a pungent smell of burning dust.

'Why don't you sit on the sofa whilst Mummy has a look in the kitchen?'

Chloe looked at the settee as if it might eat her. She rocked Ruby Rag Doll as if trying to comfort her.

'Chloe?'

'Ruby wants to go home.'

So do I, Mel's mind screamed. 'I know. But you're both going to have to be big girls until Mummy gets sorted out.'

Chloe sighed. 'Story of your life.'

'What did you say?'

Chloe stared at the doll, a small V-shape knitted at the top of her nose.

'Chloe?'

'Huh?'

'What did you say?'

'Nothing.'

'You did.'

'It was Ruby.'

'Ruby doesn't talk.'

'Does.'

'Ruby's a toy. She can't speak.'

'She can when Grandma Audrey comes to visit.'

Mel's blood froze. 'Is… she… here… now?'

Chloe looked at the doll and shrugged.

'But you said'

'Ruby's cold.'

Mel didn't press matters. 'Tell you what, we'll get some hot chocolate and marshmallows later when we go into town.'

'I want my Tigger hot water bottle.'

'I'm afraid it's gone, Pumpkin. He…'

'Died in the fire?'

'Yes.'

'Can we buy another one?'

'As soon as we get straightened out. We'll go into Oxford and do some proper shopping.'

'I miss him.'

'I know.'

'And Daddy.'

'Mummy's just going to the kitchen. I won't be long.'

'Okay.'

'Good girl.' Mel walked to a chipped and scarred door at the far end of the lounge. Mindful of the huge step leading down into the kitchen, Mel switched on the light. The fluorescent strip light blinked and hummed into life.

Mel took a deep breath and looked around the room. The sink by the small window was piled high with dirty dishes. The green and white-checked curtains drawn across the small window were filthy and stained. Two of the oak base units had no doors, and the glass cabinet on the wall above the kitchen table was smashed. Silver shards dangled from the frame like deadly stalactites.

'Jesus,' Mel whispered, as she surveyed the derelict scene.

Come on, Mel, dinner's on the table, her father's voice piped up in her head, so loud and clear that, for a moment, she thought his ghost was actually in the room with her. *Cabbage and sprouts to make you grow up into a big strong girl.*

She used to love it when he was at home. The place seemed to come alive. Proper meals on the table. Roast beef. Yorkshire puddings. Apple pie and cream. He was a wonderful cook. They would talk for hours, just the two of them sitting on the sofa, her father smoking his pipe and telling her stories about his time at sea on a submarine. Sometimes, when her mother was lying down upstairs with one of her migraines, he would sing 'Yellow Submarine' to her, and make strange noises which imitated a ship's bell and the claxon. He would tell her of trips to faraway places, where all the people lived forever, and they rode on pigs' backs and mowed the grass with hungry goats.

Once, she'd asked him where he went to when he sailed to sea. He'd sat silent and thoughtful for a long while before answering. 'Anywhere the wind blows, Mel. Anywhere the wind blows.'

Sometimes, he'd let her read passages to him from her favourite book, *Black Beauty*. She'd loved the story. From Black Beauty's early life on the farm where he grew up with his mother, being treated with love and kindness, to his later life and experiences with other owners who had not been so kind. How she'd wished to have such a lovely caring mother as Black Beauty's.

Now, she went to the sink and looked inside the base unit. Apart from a dozen scouring pads that lay in a puddle of filthy brown congealing liquid, the only cleaning product was an old bottle of Vim. Did they even make that stuff anymore? She made a mental note to get an arsenal of cleaning products from the supermarket when she went shopping for food.

She looked at the fridge-freezer standing against the wall near the back door. She couldn't bring herself to look inside. She would just dump everything into black bags later and leave them outside for the dustmen.

Next to the fridge-freezer, halfway along the wall, there were two doors standing side by side. One led upstairs to the bedrooms, the other down to the basement. Just thinking about the basement made her feel as if her whole body was being molested by clammy hands.

'This place is as dead as door knobs.'

Mel's legs buckled at the sudden sound of her child's voice. She spun around to see Chloe standing in the doorway, Ruby's face pressed to her ear.

'Jesus Christ, Chloe! Don't make me jump like that.'

'Don't make me put you down in the basement again, Smelly-Mellie.'

CHAPTER FORTY-ONE

Charles Honeywell seemed in a buoyant mood for a man with only one functional hand. The other, encased in enough bandaging to suggest it might have fallen victim to a bomb blast, rested by his side.

King made a mental note to tread carefully. A wounded animal was a dangerous animal, and he thought he detected a note of deceit in those eyes. 'You seem chipper.'

'I've managed to contact Mel.'

King almost abandoned caution and threw his arms around his lover. 'Where is she?'

'At home.'

King imagined her sitting amongst the burnt-out ruins at St Kilda's Close. 'She can't be. The place is uninhabitable.'

'She's gone to her father's house.'

'Father? Marvellous. Now we have another obstacle in the way.'

'He died just before Christmas.'

'Good. What about her mother?'

Honeywell shrugged. 'She mentioned nothing about a mother. I assume she's also deceased.'

'The truth is oft blinded by assumption,' King said, pleased by the sound of his spontaneous originality.

Honeywell looked at his bandaged hand. 'I'm sorry, Peter. I'm doing my best.'

'Where is this house?'

'Rokemarsh. It's out in the sticks. About an hour away.'

'That's all we need. I detest the countryside. All muck and mire and little else. Is the child with her?'

'Yes.'

'The husband?'

'No. She said she needs a break from him. It might be irreconcilable.'

'Excellent.'

'What do you plan to do?'

For once, King resorted to honesty. 'I'm not sure. Drive out to Rokemarsh and see how the land lies. What's the address?'

'She didn't say.'

King eyed his lover's good hand and imagined plunging a dagger through it, preferably one with a poisoned tip. 'Why didn't you ask?'

'I didn't think to… I'm sorry.'

'How in devil's name are we supposed to find her without an address?'

'I'

'Ask the satnav where she lives? Knock on every door in the village and announce our intention to eliminate the bitch?'

'I'm sorry. I'll call her back.'

'For goodness' sake, wake yourself up, Charles. Your constant need for instruction is wearing out my brain.'

'I'm not thinking straight with all this going on. And my hand hurts like mad.'

'Your statement lacks logic. The mad are incapable of feeling pain. Inflicting it, perhaps, but not experiencing it.'

'I need to go to the doctor.'

'Whatever for?'

'A tetanus jab.'

'Don't be absurd. That paring knife was as clean as a surgeon's.'

'It's better to be safe than sorry.'

'It's better to be a man, Charles. Accept your punishment and move on.'

'I did nothing to deserve punishment. You had no right to stab me.'

'"To offend, and judge, are distinct offices and of opposed natures."'

'I'll make that call.'

King dismissed him with a wave of his hand. As soon as he'd located Mel Hollis, Charles could go to negotiate the Pearly Gates with St Peter. He'd now decided that Gavin Westwood and Charles Honeywell would die in a suicide pact. It had a certain theatrical ring to it which satisfied his artistic nature. He would make them both write heart-wrenching suicide notes to this effect before they died. It might prove poignant to lay them side by side, letting their blood merge in one final act of union.

'It's been a hard week,' King told the empty kitchen. One which had seen his belief system turned upside down by Purple-five's unquestionable return. It was almost as if she'd been conjured from the pen of one of those awful horror writers. Or, worse, had stepped straight from a scene in a Christmas pantomime.

She's behind you!

If he had his way, pantomimes would be banished at Christmas, along with baubles, gaudy lights and tinsel. He liked the festive season, but it had been forever tarnished by man's unerring ability to turn it into an orgy of overindulgence and extravagance. Where in the Bible did Jesus say that everyone should drink themselves into a stupor and eat enough food to feed the five thousand? Where in the Bible did Jesus say everyone who owned a theatre must put on a hideous pantomime every year which bore no relation to the Virgin birth?

'Jesus would spin on the cross at such a bastardisation of His values,' King said, pleased with the fluency of his muse. 'Mesmerisation: A tale of love spurned, mind control and retribution.'

An image of a quill gliding effortlessly across paper was so strong in his mind that he actually visualised it sitting on the breakfast bar. Another flash of inspiration: he would dress as Shakespeare to write his masterpiece.

Perhaps you are his reincarnation.

King was about to scoff, but then remembered Purple-five's unquestionable return. 'Are we one and the same?'

'"One and the same" what?' Honeywell said.

King jumped. 'None of your business. I'm thinking aloud. I hope your interruption brings good news?'

'She's staying at a place called Rose Cottage. I've googled it. It's down the end of a lane where the Rokemarsh road forks with Berrick Salome.'

King felt all his stars align. 'Good. We'll take a look tonight.'

'What are we going to do?'

'Nothing for now.'

'Do you really have to kill them, Peter?'

'We'll see what transpires. Rose Cottage, you say?'

'Yes.'

'"What's in a name? That which we call a rose…"'

Honeywell didn't look very impressed by this latest quote from *Romeo and Juliet.*

'Rose is a rather nice name, don't you think? Warm and comforting. Reminds me of blood-red lips and stiletto heels.'

'How is that warm?'

'By virtue of imagination, Charles. By virtue of imagination. I'm going to have a lie down. Don't disturb me unless it's vital. I want to meditate; transcend the conscious mind and see if I can't tap into my muse in preparation for writing my new play.'

'Can I ask what it's about?'

King didn't care for the doubt lurking in his lover's eyes. It was just as well he wouldn't be around to read the finished masterpiece. 'Tragedy, Charles. Now, if you'll please excuse me.'

King did such a fine job of transcending the conscious mind that he fell asleep whilst visualising a candle. The flickering flame in his mind's eye lulled him into a state of relaxation so deep that he crossed the threshold into sleep before he'd had a chance to contact his muse.

Eight hours later, he was in the midst of a dream vivid enough to induce palpitations. It portrayed a rerun of Purple-five's death by guillotine, but instead of the mechanism failing to take off her head, it had detached it with ease, sending it rolling across the floor in a trail of blood. It came to rest against the leg of the playing table.

In the true tradition of dreams, it had skipped a frame, and the head had then appeared on top of the table, sitting in the middle like some hideous decoration. Only it was no longer the one separated from Purple-five's body; it now belonged to Chloe Hollis and, from what King could tell in this strange land of impossible plots, it didn't seem too happy with the day's events.

'I will follow you wherever you shall go,' Chloe promised.

King tried to snort derision, but only upset his adenoids. 'Your idle threats don't scare me.'

'Peter?'

A man's voice. For one crazy dream-state moment, he actually thought God had spoken to him.

'Peter? Wake up. It's half-eight.'

'Who's there?' King said. 'Show yourself.'

'It's me... Charles.'

King looked at Chloe's head, as if his lover might be hiding inside it. Without warning, the head exploded, sending a kaleidoscope of blood and brain matter airborne. King screamed and flailed his arms, trying to protect his face from the gore.

'Peter? Peter, wake up!'

Hands upon him now. Strong. Shaking him. Honeywell's face above him, almost angelic in the glow of the ceiling light.

'Where am I?'

'You've been dreaming. It's half-eight.'

It took a short while for this piece of news to digest. When he realised they were supposed to be driving out to Rose Cottage, he sparked into life. 'Jesus Christ, why didn't you wake me sooner?'

'I tried, but you were completely out of it.'

'Have you not heard of the word *persistence?*'

'I'm sorry.'

King sat up on the four-poster bed and swung his legs over the side in one movement. It was an action he immediately regretted as his head didn't seem to travel with him. 'You shall be the death of me.'

'Would you like a drink of water?'

'I only intended an hour's meditation. Now, thanks to you, we're way behind schedule.'

'We're only driving to Rokemarsh. It won't take that long.'

'I want to see Gavin Westwood afterwards.'

'What on earth for?'

'Business.'

'What business?'

'You'll see when we get there. Get my phone. It's on the dining table. I need to make a call whilst I get ready.'

For once, Charles Honeywell obeyed an order without argument. He fetched the phone and left King to attend his private business.

Once ready, his mood had lifted slightly. Gavin Westwood had agreed to let him visit the flat and bring Charles with him. King had neglected to tell Mr. Westwood of his true intentions, and had let the reason for this impromptu visit rest under the vague heading of "a fruitful proposition that might be of benefit to all three parties".

The drive to Rose Cottage took just over forty-five minutes. They parked halfway down the lane and walked the rest of the way. Two lovers, hand-in-hand, out for a romantic stroll beneath the moonlit sky.

After studying the house for a few minutes, King decided to strike within the next few days. He would gain access to the building by fair means or foul, kill the occupants, and set fire to the place. A proper job this time. No faffing around with pouring petrol through the letter box. Rose Cottage would be razed to the ground before the fire service got anywhere near it. And Mel and

Chloe Hollis would be long dead before the fire got anywhere near them.

King was so delighted with this latest thought he almost threw his arms around Charles Honeywell and peppered his cheek with kisses. Instead, he opted for the simplicity of words. 'It's a beautiful night.'

Honeywell's teeth rattled together like maracas in a cave. 'Is it?'

'See how the stars align?'

Honeywell looked up. 'I've never really studied astrology.'

'You don't need to. Just understand that fate is forever moving, forever changing, forever shaping our destiny.'

CHAPTER FORTY-TWO

It took Mel the best part of two days to get Rose Cottage licked into shape. She bought new bed linen, winter duvets, enough food to feed an army, and most of the cleaning products available in Tesco's, including a mop and bucket and a Henry vacuum cleaner. She also treated them both to a wardrobe of new winter clothes, two pairs of boots each, and a pair of pink dolly shoes for Chloe.

Chloe helped her mother clean the kitchen sink, standing on the same small red plastic step Mel had stood on years ago when she'd helped her father peel vegetables. After they had been subjected to four buckets of hot water laced with disinfectant, the black-and-white floor tiles now looked 'clean enough to eat off', as her father used to say when her mother wasn't around to spoil their time together.

Henry the hoover sucked most of the dirt from lounge, stairs, and two double bedrooms. She'd had to change the bag three times; and she'd filled six bin liners with perished and out-of-date food. The hard work had seemed to make Chloe happy. Helped to take her mind off her father.

Although reasonably settled by day three, the house still lacked the comforts of home. But at least it was warm, clean and habitable.

Mel and Chloe were huddled together on the sofa watching cartoons.

'Why hasn't Granddad John got a DVD player?'

'I don't think he ever watched DVDs.'

'Huh? Everyone watches DVDs.'

'Maybe he just preferred the telly.'

'Can we get a new DVD?'

'Course.'

'I miss my Disney films.'

'We'll get new ones,' Mel promised. 'You're going to Kerrie-Anne's tomorrow. We'll pop into town after.'

'*Finding Dory*?'

'Absolutely.'

'Why am I going to Kerrie-Anne's?'

'Mummy's got to see some people about the fire.'

'To find out who lit it?'

'To see who will pay for the damage.'

'Like a bank?'

'Sort of.'

'When are we going to go back home?'

'I don't know.'

'I miss my bedroom.'

'Me, too,' Mel lied.

'Granddad John's is too cold.'

'Even with the new duvet?'

'Uh-huh. And the bed smells.'

'Anything else, Goldilocks? The mattress too lumpy?'

Chloe giggled. 'I'm not Goldilocks.'

Mel stroked her hair. 'Are so.'

'I'm Chloe Hollis. Thirty-six St Kilda's Close, Feelham.'

'Wow! That's impressive, young lady. Would you like some hot chocolate?'

'Can Ruby have some, too?'

'Tell you what: why don't you share yours with her.'

'Okay.'

Mel went to the kitchen and set a pan of milk to boil on the stove. She put two heaped teaspoons of Cadbury's chocolate powder into each of their mugs and stared out the small kitchen window. She watched shadows falling across the lane. Just past four, and already the light was haemorrhaging from the sky.

She remembered going up the lane when she was young to fetch eggs from Miss Tomms who owned the big house at the top of the lane. She kept chickens and ducks and geese. Mel had been terrified of the geese; they always seemed angry, hissing and waddling after her like a gang of angry thugs. But the eggs had been worth it. Golden yolks. Dipping the soldiers her father toasted over the open fire on the end of a long two-pronged fork. There wasn't a toaster in circulation that could make toast to match her father's. And now he was gone. Forever erased from the earth. Nothing but a memory.

She watched a car pull up outside a house halfway down the lane. Warwick Lane had no streetlights, but the house where the car had pulled up had a security light. A man stepped out of the car. He was well over six feet.

The Tall Man.

Mel told herself not to be stupid. Her imagination was working overtime. Writing a script that suited her paranoia.

So, why's he just standing outside in the freezing cold? Why doesn't he go inside?

Suddenly convinced it really was the Tall Man, all the strength drained out of her legs. They were going to die. All alone, with no one to help them. The nearest police station was twelve miles away in Oxford. Even if she dialled 999 they would be long dead before anyone got to Rose Cottage.

Something hissed and spat. For one terrible moment Mel thought it was the Tall Man, venting his wrath and getting ready to strike.

'Mummy?'

Mel shrieked and spun around at the sudden sound of Chloe's voice.

'The milk's boiling, Mummy.'

'Huh?'

'The milk!'

Mel gawped at the saucepan, struck mute by terror. She grabbed the handle and lifted it from the stove. Forgetting it didn't have a heat-resistant handle, she reacted to a sudden flare of pain by throwing the thing in the vague direction of the sink. It bounced off the edge of the worktop and landed on the floor, spilling its bubbling contents.

'Shit, shit, shit.'

'Are you all right, Mummy?'

Mel ran the tap and put her hand underneath a cold jet of water. 'I'm fine.'

'Did you burn your hand?'

'A bit,' Mel said, once again staring out the window. The man was no longer standing by his car.

'Do you want me to help you?'

'It's all right, Pumpkin. You go back to the lounge and watch TV. I'll clean up and make the hot chocolate in a minute.'

'Okay.'

Mel drew the curtains, but not before she'd had a final look along the lane. Empty. Dark. Lonely. Exactly how she felt.

Jesus Christ, Mel, get a grip.

By the time she'd mopped up the milk, treated her hand with Sudocrem, and made two mugs of hot chocolate, she'd almost managed to convince herself she was overreacting. What next? Hide under the bed every time the wind blew?

She walked back into the lounge and put the drinks on the coffee table. Chloe smiled. No menace lurking behind that smile. Just a wonderful innocence.

As Chloe returned her attention to the cartoons, Mel tried to rationalise her fears. Put them into some sort of perspective. But how could she when there was no logical explanation for any of this? The doll. The Tall Man. The drawings. Chloe's past-life memories. It was as if she was being stalked by death itself. The more she told herself to calm down, the more anxious she became. At first, she didn't hear Chloe talking to Ruby Rag Doll and responding in a barely audible voice.

'Mummy hurt her hand,' Chloe told the doll.

'Silly Mummy.'

'But she's all right.'

'Carelessness costs lives.'

'What does that mean?'

'What it says on the tin.'

'Chloe?' Mel said, suddenly aware of the strange conversation going on between her daughter and the doll sitting in her lap.

Chloe ignored her. 'What tin?'

'It's just a figure of speech.'

'What's that?'

'Questions, questions, questions.'

Mel put a hand on her daughter's shoulder. 'Chloe?'

Chloe stroked the doll's woollen hair. 'You say funny words, sometimes.'

'Words are wisdom.'

'What's wisdom?'

'Knowing when to cook your goose.'

'I like chicken.' Chloe announced.

'Not Goosey-loosey?'

'No.'

'I like gin.'

'What's gin?'

'It's a spirit.'

'Like a ghost?'

'It's a drink.'

'What's it made of?'

'Tears.'

'Yuk!'

'Chloe?' Mel interrupted. 'That's enough. Stop it!'

'Listen to old grumpy drawers.'

'Mummy's not well.'

'Is that so?'

'Uh-huh.'

'She never did have a sense of humour.'

'Stop that right now,' Mel said. 'Do you hear me?'

'Get her! Crying like a baby over spilt milk.'

Mel raised her hand. 'Stop it. Stop it right this minute.'

'What you going to do, Smelly-Mellie? Hit me?'

Mel's hand hovered near Chloe's face, shaking. 'You shut your mouth. You're evil.'

'Sticks and stones, Smelly-Mellie. sticks and stones.'

'I'

A loud knock on the door interrupted Mel.

'I wonder who that could be?' Chloe said, in that awful rasping voice. 'Maybe it's the Big Bad Wolf come to gobble up the two little piggies.'

Chloe giggled. 'I thought there were three little piggies.'

'There were. But one's been a naughty piggly-wiggly at school.'

The knock came again. Three times. Louder. More urgent.

'Maybe it's the Tall Man come to chop off your head.'

Mel shuddered.

'I know you're in there, Mel.' A man's voice. Familiar. Shouting through the letterbox, competing with the wind.

'Tony?'

'Please let me in. I just want to talk to you.'

'There's nothing to talk about.'

'Please… it's freezing out here.'

'Let him freeze,' Chloe said, in that small croaky voice.

Chloe's interruption made up Mel's mind for her. She couldn't stay here on her own any longer. She would either go mad, or do something she would regret for the rest of her life. Or both. She opened the door and let him inside.

'Daddy! Daddy!' Chloe shrieked, all traces of Grandma Audrey gone from her voice. She threw the doll on the sofa and ran up to her father, throwing her arms around his waist.

'Hiya, darling.'

'I missed you, Daddy.'

'I missed you, too.'

Mel closed the door and bolted it. She didn't see the man crouched in the bushes at the end of the lane watching the house.

CHAPTER FORTY-THREE

King wished he'd been able to use Gavin Westwood's recording equipment to film the demise of his lover. The beauty of the occasion was already falling prey to the flimsy nature of memory.

Charles had left the world as he had lived a coward. Westwood had been far more spirited. Hopping between threats and promises, he'd claimed to have evidence that could lock King away at Her Majesty's pleasure for the rest of his life. King had been in no mood to pay heed to bluffs and threats; especially from a man who derived sexual pleasure from abusing hypnotised patients. He'd simply taken aim and put two bullets in his chest.

Charles had reacted to the killing by running towards the front door.

King had aimed the gun at his back. 'Where in devil's name are you going?'

'I want no part of this.'

'Oh, but you're already a part of it, Charles. Stop right there, unless you want a bullet in your back.'

Honeywell turned around. 'For goodness' sake, Peter. See sense. Someone's going to hear all the commotion and call the police.'

'I don't care. You've only got yourself to blame for getting embroiled in a love affair with that pathetic excuse for a man.'

Honeywell's jaw slackened. 'I don't even know him.'

'Liar.'

'For God's sake, Peter, you *know* I don't know him.'

King plucked the love note from his pocket which Gavin Westwood had sent to him in more pleasant times. 'Words do not lie, Charles. This letter clearly states his feelings towards you. Frankly, it fills me with revulsion. Call me old fashioned, but I still believe in romance. This is just full of filth and depravity.'

'It's not mine.'

King handed the note to him. 'I beg to differ.'

After a few moments gawping at the piece of paper, he handed it back. 'I've never seen it before.'

'Either your eyes lie, or your tongue does. Have you no morals?'

'I'

'I have neither the time nor the inclination to argue with you. You are now surplus to requirements. I suggest you accept your fate like a man and make your death a simple and pleasant experience.'

Honeywell sank to his knees. 'Please, Peter. Please, I'm begging you…'

'Do stop mewling like a cat.'

'But I love you.'

'"No sooner met but they looked, no sooner looked but they loved, no sooner loved, but they sighed, no sooner sighed but they asked one another the reason."'

'I love you with all my heart.'

'Your love no longer matters to me. All I require of you is to sit in that leather chair over by the window whilst I prepare the scene.'

Honeywell crawled to the chair and hoisted himself into it with all the grace of a dying bull.

'Everything must die,' King declared, smearing the love letter with blood from Gavin Westwood's wounds. He handed the paper to his nemesis. Honeywell had turned a colour to suggest he was already transitioning to spirit.

'I don't want it.'

'Would it help to change your mind if I tore your testicles out with my bare hands?'

He took the note, hand trembling. 'Why are you being so cruel? I've done nothing but love you.'

'Nonsense pours from your mouth like pus from a running sore.'

'But it's true,' Honeywell wailed. 'I've given everything to you. Loved you. Protected you. Killed for you.'

'Then God shall reward your efforts.'

'I don't want to die.'

'We're all destined for the grave. Perhaps you should take heart from Purple-five's rebirth. You might come back as my cat.'

'You don't like cats.'

King grinned and raised the gun. 'No; I don't suppose I do.' He squeezed the trigger as Honeywell opened his mouth, no doubt to protest and beg for his worthless life. Some people had no shame. The bullet blew the side of his face away, sending a shower of bone and brain matter against Westwood's white walls. Some of the gore appeared to form into a question mark, as if Honeywell was enquiring about his demise from the other side.

King didn't have time to hang around for long and appreciate his handiwork. He put the gun in Honeywell's right hand and curled the man's index finger around the trigger. '"These violent delights have violent ends, and in their triumph die, like fire and powder, which, as they kiss, consume."'

He thought the scene befitting of a tragedy. Love's elusive dream destroyed by man's endless pursuit of the unattainable. His mind fashioned a suitable piece of his own prose. Poetic in nature, pleasing to the ear. 'Blood doth run like ribbons of scorned love.'

He savoured the taste and texture of his undeniable talent. His new play would start with these wonderful lines. Set the scene perfectly. Lead to the acclaim and the adulation he so richly deserved after all these years in the literary wilderness.

With this in mind, he let himself out of the flat and walked almost two miles before calling a taxi to take him home. The driver had exercised his right to show his ignorance by attempting to engage King in a conversation about football. A subject he had no interest in. King had resorted to offering the man a generous tip if he promised to keep his crap-flap shut for the rest of the journey.

He'd spent the next two days going over the crime scene in his mind, looking for potential mistakes. There would be evidence of his numerous visits to the flat, but he never intended to deny that he knew Gavin Westwood. They were friends. Which made it all the more hurtful to think his lover was carrying on an affair with a trusted associate.

The long restless nights were the hardest to deal with. Alone in bed, the cold empty space where Charles once slept seemed both poignant and frightening in equal measure. He missed his lover's warmth. His humility. His calming nature.

How he wished, in those long slow hours of early morning, that Charles was still there with him to ease his pain and reassure him. When he did finally manage a few hours' sleep, nightmares besieged him. Charles eating breakfast with half his head missing. Charles beside him in the bed, soaked in blood. Charles's head in the freezer with Purple-five's, one eye winking at her as if they shared the greatest secret on earth.

It wasn't often Peter King cursed his vivid imagination, but in the aftermath of each nightmare, he dearly wished he possessed the intellect of a toad. To make matter worse, his reconnaissance trip to Rose Cottage had been plunged into disarray by the return of the woman's husband in a taxi. He'd had to seek refuge in a bush. His mood hadn't been helped when the Hollis woman had let her wayward husband inside.

To top it all he'd been convinced he was sharing his hidey-hole with a rat. After being driven to distraction by rustling and scraping noises, he'd abandoned the mission and returned home.

There was little doubt he would have to eliminate the husband before the main event, because he wanted to spend some quality time alone with Mel Hollis and the child before sending them skywards. He was reluctant to admit he might derive pleasure from killing Purple-five for a second time. The girl had shown resilience during the numerous games of One False Move, but it gave him a sense of pride knowing fate had allowed him to be part of such a rare phenomenon.

He would need to keep Rose Cottage under surveillance for a while. Watch the movements of the husband. Check the lie of the land.

Not in that blessed bush, though, at the mercy of rodents and footrot.

King shuddered. He would park at the bottom of the lane where it narrowed to a dirt track. Stay warm. Stay wise. Stay alert. He was a survivor. A lone warrior. A man of both pen and sword.

Poker, more like!

King smiled. His muse's occasional bursts of wit would be most helpful in the coming weeks. 'I am but as I am,' He declared to a row of saucepans sitting idle on a shelf. 'I choose to be free to choose, and for that alone, I shall be free.'

He allowed his mind to bask in the glow of future favourable reviews of his play. Perhaps he might even find it within himself to play a leading role.

'I am Cornelius, and death is my heir.'

King bowed, and strutted around the kitchen, lost in a maze of fantasies and possibilities.

CHAPTER FORTY-FOUR

Chloe had taken advantage of her father's return by making him read her a dozen bedtime stories. After a good hour and a half, with Chloe finally asleep, he'd sneaked out of the bedroom with Ruby Rag Doll tucked under his arm.

Mel looked at the doll with barely disguised contempt. 'You got it, then?'

'I feel mean taking it away from her.'

'Think of it as being cruel to be kind.'

Tony flopped down on the sofa. 'She'll get upset when she realises it's gone.'

'I don't care.' Mel eyed the doll as if it might spring to life at any minute and babble in her mother's long dead tongue. 'I want you to take it down the basement. There's a manhole cover in the middle of the room that opens onto the sewer. Put it in there.'

'Bit extreme, isn't it?'

'You wouldn't say that if you'd heard the way Chloe spoke to the bloody thing.'

'What did she say?'

Mel told him what she could remember of the bizarre conversation between her daughter and the doll. 'Anyway, you were there when she talked about your affair.'

Tony looked away. 'Do you *really* believe it's your mother?'

'Yes.'

'How's that even possible? It's a doll, for Christ's sake.'

Mel lit a cigarette. 'Just get rid of it, Tony. Please.'

Tony walked to the kitchen. 'If that's what you really want.'

Mel imagined the basement door swinging open, emitting its rotten pungent smell of death and decay. Its rank stale odour of lies and cruelty. 'And shut the kitchen door behind you before you go anywhere near that basement.'

As she waited for Tony to return, she wondered if she could ever look at him again without imagining Stephanie Wallace's legs wrapped around him. Fear the worst every time he was five minutes late home. All she'd ever wanted was to be happy. Get married, have children, a nice house. Simple things. She didn't want riches, parties, fast cars. She much preferred a simple home-cooked meal to a fancy restaurant. Was that too much to ask after her ruined childhood?

'I lost my child. Isn't that enough?' she whispered.

Cruelty has an insatiable appetite. Enough is never enough.

And wasn't that the truth? Not content with snatching Megan from her, it now had its sights set on Chloe. She'd tried so hard not to dwell on the unfairness of it all. Remain strong for her daughter. Not give in. But every day the tide swept her further and further out to sea, leaving her more and more powerless to fight, lost, confused, helpless.

Ten minutes later, Tony walked back into the lounge, interrupting Mel's thoughts. 'All done.'

'Shut the kitchen door.'

'It smells a bit ripe down there.'

'Who cares? We won't ever have to go down there again.'

'There's huge tins of coffee and'

'I know what's down there!'

'Just saying.'

Mel put her cigarette out. 'Sorry. I'm just on edge.'

'Have you been crying?'

Mel touched her face, surprised to feel it wet. 'I don't…'

'Would you like a glass of wine?'

'That would be nice.'

After two glasses of wine, and half an hour lost in thought, Mel said, 'My mother's fucking evil.'

'Do you want to talk about it?'

'My whole life's been a bloody nightmare. You were supposed to be my salvation, Tony. Make it all better. So much for knights in shining armour, eh?'

'I'm sorry.'

'Stop apologising. Sorry is just a word. You need to show me.'

'I know.'

After a slight pause, Mel said, 'My mother hated me. I was always in the way as far as she was concerned. Especially when my dad was away at sea. She was nothing more than a whore. The summer she died was sweltering. One of the hottest on record according to the radio. My father went back to sea on June third, two days after my birthday. I'd spent most of that morning praying something would happen to make him stay at home. I even wished he'd break a leg or catch flu. Anything to stop him leaving.

'But God wasn't granting wishes for little girls. He let my father go back to his submarine, whistling as he walked out the front gate. I can't describe how I used to feel watching him leave. It was as if my whole world was being tipped into a stinking bog.

'My mother started drinking soon after he left. A large tumbler of gin with a tiny splash of tonic. I took my cue and went to my bedroom. I could hear her in the kitchen, talking on the phone to someone, probably one of her men friends. I was trying to draw my dad a picture of me and him sitting by the river. "Fishing for tiddlers" as he used to say. He loved the peace and quiet of the river. Said it was a "place where you could get your heart beating properly".

'I showed Ruby Rag Doll my picture. In my imagination, she told me it was the best drawing in the world. After about an hour, my mother came into my room. Not to offer me something to eat. Or ask me if I wanted to go for a walk, or to help tidy the house like normal mothers do. It was to tell me she had friends coming over . It was time to get down in the basement.

'The first time she ever put me down there I thought she was joking. I got belted for daring to laugh. She slapped me so hard across the face that my feet left the ground. I never laughed when she was within striking distance again after that. Not even when she was sloshed and trying to be funny.

'I grabbed Ruby, the blanket off my bed, and walked down into the basement without a word. It was pointless to ask for anything like food. After the first few times she locked me in there, I plucked up the courage to pinch a can opener from the kitchen and hide it.'

'How old were you when she first locked you in the basement?' Tony asked.

'Seven. Nine, the last. Sometimes it would go on for ages. The week she died, I'd been down there for three days.'

'What did you do for all that time?'

'I used to make up stories for Ruby. Adventures on a magic train that could take you anywhere you wanted. Even up in the clouds to meet fairy-tale princesses and visit their castles. Sometimes, I'd just sit and cry for hours. Or imagine life without my mother. Just me and my dad. How happy we'd be without her around to spoil things.'

'I can't begin to'

'Three days doesn't sound long, does it? But time's a strange thing when you're sitting in a cold damp creepy basement with spiders in the rafters and rats scurrying around in the sewer. I didn't know whether I'd been down there for three hours or three days when the police came.'

'Who called the cops?'

'A neighbour. Apparently, a paperboy told him the front door was open and there was a terrible smell in the house.'

'I'm so sorry, Mel. I had no idea…'

'It wasn't my fault. That bitch can blame me all she likes, but it wasn't my fault. She was drunk. Her eyes were all red and puffy, like she'd been crying, but it was the booze. I told her I was cold. Do you know what she said?'

Tony shook his head.

'She told me to do some exercise and stop sulking like a spoiled brat. I begged her to let me out. I knew all her "guests" had gone, because the house was quiet. But she seemed determined to make me suffer. She kept tugging at her hair as if trying to make herself think straight. She had a bottle of water for me. I didn't want water. I wanted food. A bath. My bed. Was that too much to ask?

'She kept going on about how I was never grateful. How I needed to learn to respect my elders. She kept waving the bottle of water about, as if it was the greatest gift on earth. Her hair was standing out in wild, frizzy clumps. I was sitting on a crate by an old wine rack. My knees were knocking together so loud I was sure she could hear them. I knew what was coming. She was going to whack me over the head with that bottle of water. It doesn't sound much, a squash bottle filled with water, but it felt like a brick. Trust me. She'd already attacked me with one before.

'She lifted her foot up to step into the basement. A big, exaggerated movement, like an astronaut walking on the moon…'

After a few moments silence, Tony prompted her. 'What happened, Mel?'

'It wasn't my fault. I'd been playing with Ruby on the steps. Pretending we were on the magic train. I panicked when I heard her unlocking the door. Left Ruby on the steps. She brought her foot down right on top of the doll's head. Her legs just seemed to give way. She fell forward and bounced all the way down to the bottom.

'At first, I thought she was just pretending. God knows why. My mother never had a playful bone in her body. But as time passed, I realised she was really hurt. I kept looking at the open doorway, willing myself to move, to get out of there, take Ruby and run. But I couldn't move. It was as if my backside was stapled to the wooden crate with splinters.

'Ruby was pinned beneath her arm. There were flies buzzing around her. I didn't leave the basement. I just sat on that crate, rocking back and forth. That's how the police found me. Gawping at my mother's twisted dead body.'

'Jesus, Mel, why didn't you tell me about this before?'

'It's hardly a chat-up line, is it? I know it sounds stupid, but I think my mother's spirit somehow got trapped in that doll. I didn't see the bloody thing again until Dad gave her to me in that old suitcase.'

'Jesus!'

Mel was quiet for a moment, and then she said, 'I wonder if that bitch somehow cursed Megan.'

'You can't think like that. Megan had a heart defect. It was nothing to do with your mother or the doll.'

'I wish to Christ I'd never given the bloody thing to Chloe. I should have thrown it away. Burned it. Got rid of it.'

Tony pulled Mel close. 'It's over now. Done. The sewer's probably the best place for it.'

Mel wished she could find comfort in his words, but it was far from over. The Tall Man was still out there. Watching and waiting, controlling every beat of her heart and every thought in her head.

CHAPTER FORTY-FIVE

After a week spent observing Rose Cottage the way a cat might watch a family of nesting rodents, King finally felt ready to pounce. Well, perhaps pounce was a little optimistic, considering he'd parked the car two miles away and walked to his destination in a pair of shoes clearly inadequate for hiking. Still, all things considered, it had done him good to focus on something other than events at Gavin Westwood's flat.

The authorities had refused to release the body of his lover for burial until their investigation was complete. He'd been horrified to learn that this could take weeks. It chilled his heart to think of poor Charles lying on a cold slab, pathologists pecking at his carcass like vultures. Did they have no respect?

At least the Hollis family seemed to behave with monotonous regularity. Hubby left for work at seven every morning and returned home around six. Supper at seven. TV. Bed. A banal pointless existence based upon years of conditioning. Mel Hollis hadn't yet returned to work. No doubt still licking her wounds after almost getting barbequed at St Kilda's Close. She stayed at home all day with the brat, occasionally walking to a local shop for supplies.

To break into the Hollis's VW Golf, King had secured a piece of equipment from an internet site which was almost beautiful in its simplicity. A slim jim. A thin strip of metal made from sprung steel, about two centimetres wide and sixty long. It acted on the rods and levers controlling the door mechanism.

Grateful for the darkness of the lane at 6 a.m, King, clad in black parka and black jeans, slid the slim jim down between the window and the doorframe of the driver's door as per internet video instruction. It was amazing what one could learn to do on the web. There were even videos available teaching you how to wire a crude bomb, which interested him for reasons not yet apparent.

He'd practised the manoeuvre with the slim jim dozens of times on Charles's Fiesta, which had been returned to him three days ago, so it was with a certain degree of expertise that he approached breaking into the Golf. Once the slim jim was in position, he popped the lock by jerking thc bar sharply to the right. He pulled the metal out and put it back in the pocket of his parka.

With a quick look along the lane, wary that these ghastly rural places might still use the services of a milkman, King leaned into the car and unlocked the back door. He closed the driver's door as quietly as he could and then let himself into the back.

Locked inside, he wedged himself facedown between the front and back seats. Now, all he had to do was wait for Hollis to wave goodbye to his family for the last time and make him drive to the country lane where he'd parked his own car.

Time ticked by like a tortuous dripping tap. By the time he heard the creak of the hinges on the garden gate, his whole body was numb. There was also a nasty rick in his neck that would need treating with an icepack when he got home. To make matters worse, his rattling teeth sounded like a pneumatic drill digging up a road to his fractured mind.

Hollis bid farewell to his family at least half a dozen times. Talk about excessive. To shut up his chattering teeth, King made the mistake of biting down on his tongue hard enough to draw blood. Now, he had a stinging pain in his mouth to add to his growing list of woes.

Hollis climbed in behind the wheel, threw a briefcase and his mobile phone onto the passenger seat, and strapped himself in. He drove to the end of the lane, ignorant of the deadly cargo waiting to pounce behind him. As he was about to pull out onto the main road, King struck. Battling numb legs and a stiff neck, he got up and warned the driver to do exactly as he was told, or risk losing his head.

Hollis didn't seem to heed the warning. He stalled the car, making it lurch forward. 'What the fuck?'

King thrust the gun into the man's neck. 'Shut up and drive. Do as I ask, or you will never see your family again.'

'But'

'Are you mentally challenged, Mr. Hollis? Do you have an inability to follow simple instructions?'

'No.'

'Good. I want you to turn right and then take the next left.'

Hollis restarted the car. 'Where are we going?'

'Somewhere nice. Now, drive!'

King directed him to where he'd parked his own car, and ordered him to pull over.

Hollis applied the handbrake, and then released the one on his tongue. 'Who are you? Why are you doing this?'

'A little bird tells me you're a schoolteacher. Is that correct?'

Hollis nodded.

'Good school?'

'Yes. I'

'Teach all the children right from wrong?'

'I suppose.'

'Fill their heads with state-controlled rubbish?'

'I'

'What do you teach?'

'Maths.'

'I've never seen much point to riddles and puzzles. They used to teach us our times tables at school. By rote. Programmed to trot out answers like robots. I'd take art over algebra any day. The poet is inspired, the playwright enlightened, but you, dear friend, are a state-sponsored liar. I'm offering you one last chance to confess your crimes.'

Hollis didn't answer.

'Sulking won't help you.'

'I'm not'

'Do you believe in God?'

'No.'

'You should. I've heard He can be a great source of comfort in times of trouble.'

'If you want money, I'll give you everything I've got,' Hollis babbled. 'Take me to a cashpoint machine. I've got over three grand in the account.'

'I don't want your money, Mr Hollis.'

Hollis emitted a pitiful sob.

'"He that dies pays all debts." Do you know who said that?'

'No.'

'Stephano. *Tempest.* Act 3, scene 2.'

The man's silence spoke volumes for his ignorance. 'You're not familiar with the works of William Shakespeare?'

'Some.'

'"He lends out money gratis and brings down the rate of usance here with us in Venice." Ring any bells?'

'No.'

'Shylock. *The Merchant of Venice.*'

'Just tell me what you want. Please. I'

'I don't want anything. You're in the way, Mr. Hollis. It's as simple as that.'

'In the way of what, for Christ's sake?'

'My destiny.'

'But I don't'

'This isn't personal. It's what you might call *necessary.*'

'But why?'

King almost lost patience and clubbed him over the head with the gun. It was an absolute travesty that this man was entrusted with the education of children. 'I've already told you. You're in the way. It's your wife and child I want, Mr Hollis. Not you.'

At the mention of his precious family, Hollis seemed to abandon all reason. He twisted his head around, mouth working like a rabid dog. 'You leave them alone. I'm warning'

'I don't think you're in any position to issue orders, Mr. Hollis. In case it's escaped your attention, I'm the one with the gun.'

'You'

King tired of trying to reason with a fool. He squeezed the trigger and ended the conversation. The bullet hit Tony Hollis in the left-hand side of his neck, rupturing the jugular vein and sending a thick hot spurt of blood across the car. Hollis clutched his wounded neck, made a brief but futile attempt to stem the flow of blood, and then slumped forward, head resting on the steering wheel. King fired again. Back of the head.

'"What ugly sights of death within mine eyes!"' King said, as his eyes gained access to the inner workings of Hollis's mind. 'That's *Richard the Third*, in case you're wondering.'

He stepped out of the car. Blood had splashed onto his face and chest. God alone knew what infections a man of such dubious character might harbour in his bloodstream. He could have hepatitis.

Or HIV.

This last thought brought a handkerchief from the pocket of his coat. He dabbed furiously at his face. He opened the driver's door and dropped the gun into Hollis's lap. The nine millimetre pistol was the second weapon from his father's collection he'd had to forfeit. At this rate, his mini arsenal would soon be reduced to an air pistol and a rather useless catapult which his father had used to scare cats from the garden.

He leaned across the body, grabbed the briefcase and phone from the passenger seat, and slammed the door. The phone might yield some useful numbers, not least Mel Hollis's. The briefcase was a token trophy; something to remember Hollis by on those long cold winter nights when memory might be his only source of solace.

He removed his coat and stowed it in the boot of the BMW. He drove home in a strange state of euphoria, once more master of his own destiny. He would burn the coat, along with the rest of his clothes, once he'd had a shot of brandy to steady the ship.

CHAPTER FORTY-SIX

When Tony hadn't arrived home by seven-thirty that evening, Mel's mind naturally wondered if he was in the arms of Stephanie Wallace. By eight, she was sure he was. Her mind's eye elected to show her all the gory details of his infidelity.

'Come on, Pumpkin, it's gone eight. You've got to go to bed.'

'But I want to see Daddy.'

'Daddy's been held up at work. You'll see him in the morning.'

'But'

'No arguments, Chloe. Not tonight. Mummy's tired. I'll send him up to give you a kiss when he gets home.'

'Don't want a kiss when I'm asleep.'

'It'll be a magic kiss,' Mel tried. 'You'll feel it in your dreams.'

Chloe trudged up the stairs as if her feet had turned to rocks. She climbed into bed and cuddled a new pink bunny Mel had bought her to replace Ruby. Naturally, there wasn't a soft toy on earth that could replace Ruby. Chloe had spent the best part of two days looking everywhere in the house for her. She didn't believe Ruby had been 'accidentally' put out with the rubbish. After two sleepless nights, Mel had resorted to reading stories and stroking her daughter's hair until she fell asleep.

Tonight, it took two readings of *Dumbo,* and half an hour's stroking before she tiptoed out of the room. It was almost half-nine by the time she sat down with a glass of wine and a cigarette. By now, her apprehension about Tony had turned into concern.

She tried his mobile again. It went straight to voicemail. She tried again. Same. She swallowed half her wine in one go and called Vicky Hollis. After a rather frosty stand-off, Mel accepted her assertion that Tony wasn't at the flat.

Mel had tried Tony's mobile three more times before getting ready for bed. She'd also checked the front and back doors a dozen times to make sure they were all locked and bolted. The windows were all single paned. It wouldn't take an intruder much effort to smash one and break in.

Sitting on the settee, wrapped up in her duvet, Mel took a sip of wine and vowed to stay awake all night, alert to every sound, every movement.

Better swap the wine for black coffee, then.

A shadow on the wall appeared to move. Mel's heart stuttered.

Don't be silly. It's nothing. The reflection of the lamp. The bulb just flickered.

Mel's mind went into overdrive. She imagined Ruby standing on the other side of the kitchen door, an evil grin pasted on her chops, a large kitchen knife gripped in her stumpy hand.

There was a sudden knock on the front door, loud and insistent. Mel screamed, convinced the Tall Man had come to kill them.

Here comes a chopper to chop off your head.

Another loud rap on the door, followed by a man's voice calling her name through the letter box. 'Mrs Hollis? It's the police.'

She knew the man could see her cowering on the sofa. She felt torn between burrowing beneath the duvet and running upstairs.

'We need to speak to you, Mrs Hollis.' A woman's voice now. Soft, compassionate. 'It's about your husband. I'm afraid we have some bad news.'

Mel gawped at the letter box as if it was capable of spouting lies.

'Would you like me to put my ID through the letter box?'

Mel peered through a gap in the curtains and saw a police car parked in the lane.

'Mrs Hollis?'

Mel opened the door. 'What the hell's happened?'

The woman introduced them. 'I'm PC Murray. This is Detective Inspector Cartwright. May we come in, please?'

Mel stepped aside and let them in. She closed the door. She felt as if she'd been sucked inside a giant bubble, no longer in step with time. Her hands fluttered around her throat as if they were considering strangling her.

PC Murray removed her hat. 'Would you like to sit down?'

Mel thought the woman looked too young to be a police officer. A pretty girl, with dark, bobbed hair. 'No… I…'

DI Cartwright took over. 'Can you confirm you are Mel Hollis?'

'Yes. What the hell's happened?'

He referred to a notebook. 'We had a report of an abandoned car in Spraggett's Lane around nine-thirty this morning. It was discovered by a farmer attending his cattle. A red Volkswagen Golf, 1.4. I'm afraid a male body was found inside the vehicle.'

Mel's knees buckled. 'Oh… my… God…'

'He was identified by his driver's licence as Antony Paul Hollis, of Thirty-six St Kilda's Close, Feelham.'

Mel struggled for breath. 'That… can't… be… right...'

'I'm afraid he suffered gunshot wounds to the neck and head. A firearm was recovered at the scene.'

Mel felt like screaming at him, telling him the Tall Man did it, but how did you explain to the police that your daughter had been murdered in a past life, and this was all somehow connected?

'Would you like PC Murray to make you a cup of tea?'

Mel gawped at him. Why did people always offer tea, as if it had some magic healing power? The ability to make bad news more bearable.

'Mrs. Hollis?'

'I…'

Cartwright nodded at Murray. She walked through to the kitchen.

Cartwright fiddled with his earlobe. 'I know this has come as a terrible shock. I want you to know that we'll do everything in our power to get to the bottom of this. Find out what happened.'

You don't need to. I already know, Mel thought.

'Perhaps you ought to sit down, Mrs. Hollis.'

'My daughter's asleep upstairs,' Mel told him. 'What the hell am I supposed to tell her?'

Cartwright didn't seem to have an answer to that. He snapped his notebook shut. 'Would you like PC Murray to stay with you for the night?'

'I'll tell you what I want. I want my husband to walk through that door and tell me this has all been a sick joke. And then I want you to tell me you've caught the sick bastard who's been trying to kill my family.'

Cartwright seemed unable to provide any of these things. Instead, he once again offered Mel the services of the young constable. 'It might help to be with someone. To talk. Make tea. Help with your daughter when she wakes up.'

Mel nodded. Not because of anything DI Cartwright had suggested, but because of what might be lurking in the shadows outside Rose Cottage waiting to fulfil its dreadful prophecy to destroy their lives.

CHAPTER FORTY-SEVEN

Bathed and rested, mind soothed to a meditative state by Beethoven's 'Moonlight' Sonata and several glasses of his finest cognac, Peter King reflected on the day's events. Apart from his ruined coat, it had gone reasonably well.

After examining his face in a magnified mirror for shaving wounds that might invite infection, he'd added copious amounts of Dettol to a scalding hot bath and spent the next half an hour letting the water take care of his numerous aches and pains.

Not long after his bath, a DI had called at the house to inform King of his findings regarding Charles and the hypnotist. The man had pock-marked skin, a nose possibly fashioned in a boxing ring, and eyes that appeared to be squinting through smoke. As far as King was concerned, the DI didn't look as if he could investigate a case of fleas in a dog kennel.

No, King wasn't aware of the two men being romantically linked. No, he wasn't aware of any animosity between the deceased. No, he wasn't surprised to learn of their relationship. Charles was his own man. Free to do as he pleased. They had what one might call 'an open relationship.' It was a poor man indeed who sought to control another's actions and deeds.

Driven by the detective's obvious ineptitude, King had told the squinty-eyed frog of Charles's susceptibility to bouts of depression. His suicidal tendencies. Dramatic outbursts. Detective Inspector Rumble had left the house with a subservient humbleness that bordered on sickly. King didn't expect him to return. The case was straightforward enough, even for someone of Rumble's limited ability.

Let's hope he doesn't 'rumble' the truth.

King smiled. His mind was in fine form tonight if not a little cheesy.

A thought. So sudden and charged with particles of doubt as to ruin his evening. What if one of those nosy coppers interviewed that dreadful transvestite, Olivia, in her now redefined role as a witness? And what if Olivia told the police of Mel Hollis's visit to Gavin Westwood's practice?

King sat bolt upright in his leather recliner. Even one of such diminished ability as Rumble might see something amiss in this tragic hotchpotch of apparent suicides. All roads led to him. And forensic science was adept at finding clues in the most unlikely of places. As paranoia gripped him, a mental list of things to dispose of grew in his mind. The petrol can they'd used at St Kilda's Close. Everything in the boot of the car. Anything they might have touched after returning home from their brief flirtation with arson. All clothes. Charles's car itself, which was probably hosting enough evidence to get him locked up for the rest of his days. Not to mention Olivia. She would have to go to meet her maker and explain to Him why she was no longer as He had made her.

Driven to act, King went to the kitchen and sat at the breakfast bar with a pen and an A4 notepad. He listed everything that might incriminate him in a court of law. By the time he'd finished, he'd filled two sheets.

He walked back into the lounge and poured himself a cognac large enough to sooth a rhinoceros with a tooth abscess. But the alcohol only fuelled the paranoia. The second one brought the paranoia under control, but replaced it with something worse: murderous intent. This was all Charles Honeywell's fault. If he hadn't come home whingeing and whining about the Hollis girl, none of this would have happened.

'Why dost thou forsake me?' He asked a picture of Charles sitting on an occasional table near the window. Charles was beaming at the camera, suntanned, smiling, unaware of his ill-judged future love affair with Gavin Westwood. Portuguese sunshine glinted off his spectacles, reminding King of a truly wonderful holiday in the Algarve.

'I loved you. Gave you everything. Invested my life in you. Took you into my home, fed you, clothed you, wined and dined you, taught you the intricacies of love's sweet and fragile nature.'

Driven by a sudden urge to write his play, King retrieved the A4 pad from the kitchen, and scrawled his thoughts down underneath the list of things to eliminate from his life. His fevered thoughts made the words unreadable.

'Inspiration must breathe,' he slurred. 'And tonight she breathes from my heart. From my soul.' King tasted the words, decided they were comparable to some of Shakespeare's finest, and scrawled them down on the pad. The ferocity of his writing tore ragged holes out of the paper, but King did not see this in his state of euphoric creative flow.

'My love has been thwarted, tainted, but whilst I live, whilst I breathe, whilst I feel, I shall remain a man of passion, a man of fire.'

A vision of St Kilda's Close popped into his head, halting the creative process. And then, to further complicate inspiration, Rumble's froglike features emerged from the flames like the ugliest phoenix known to man.

King ploughed on regardless, lapsing into plagiarising Shakespeare. '"They whose guilt within their bosoms lie, imagine every eye beholds their blame."'

Lapse over, he continued in his own form. 'You left me, sir, to float in the vacuum of a deep dark abyss. The blackest of holes in the spacest of spaces. But, alas, you underestimated my resilience. You were blinded by your greed. Your misguided desires. And it is you who shall fall as surely as Beelzebub's grace.'

King abandoned the pad, walked to the table, and picked up the solid-silver frame containing Honeywell's picture. It seemed to have an aura shimmering around it. A golden halo of light. And, more alarmingly, two heads.

'Be warned those who cast stones, for it is they who will have their fragile hearts shattered.'

The Honeywell twins seemed to mock him from their Portuguese sanctuary. King hurled the frame at the fire. His intention to feed it to the flames was thwarted by the new artificial fire. Nothing more than a realistic computer image cast onto glass. The picture smashed and fell face down on the hearth.

Betrayal was one of man's strongest suits. Trumped only by greed. Charles Honeywell had been a man of simple needs, but his capacity to betray had put him in allegiance with some of the most treacherous men in history. Brutus. Judas Iscariot. Tony Blair.

Honeywell didn't seem too disturbed by such comparisons. King walked over to the broken photo frame and stomped on it until his legs ached. Satisfied that he'd ground the glass to powder, and Honeywell's features with it, King left the lounge, staggered through the kitchen, and down the cellar steps holding onto the handrail for support.

Once amongst the familiarity and comfort of the freezers, some of his rage evaporated. He staggered up and down in front of the freezers like a drunken sergeant-major inspecting troops on a parade ground.

'Purple, orange, yellow and turquoise,' he slurred. 'You have lent colour to my life. A vibrant hue.'

The freezers stood to attention. All nineteen heads present and correct.

'I miss you all,' he declared. 'You should be proud to know you have been part of history. Part of something greater than the sum part of its total sums.'

He studied the floor, frowning. 'I hold you all in the highest e-shteem.'

Esteem, his mind corrected.

King tried to say the word several times, practising like a child reading from its first infant's book, but gave up when his tongue insisted on adding a H after the S. He stopped in front of the purple freezer and leaned against the door, head swimming in a soup of sentimentality. He'd never loved a woman in his life, apart from his mother. But all things considered, Purple-five had been a special girl. His purple heart.

Until Chloe Hollis ruined everything. Sitting there in Gavin Westwood's office, barely out of nappies, recounting details of Purple-five's life with a child's mouth and an adult's tongue.

He opened the freezer door, pulled out the drawer, and stared at Purple-five's head swirling in tendrils of icy mist. 'Has time yet to be written by the stars that guide our fortunes?'

Purple-five gawped at him with her remaining fish-slab eye, lips parted, as if about to whisper untold secrets. And then, in a sudden flash of knowing, all became apparent. He and Purple-five were forever joined in an inseparable union. Right back to the beginning of time. Purple-five and Chloe Hollis were only the tip of the iceberg. They had all lived a billion lives in a billion worlds.

With this enlightened thought in mind, and an unexpected surge of love in his heart, he walked back to the kitchen and retrieved a carrier bag from beneath the sink. He returned to the cellar, put Purple-five's head inside the bag and retired to the master bedroom.

He didn't undress. This was not a sordid tacky relationship rooted in sexual gratification. It was something special. Something forged throughout the history of the universe. Something that would be written about with care and sensitivity when he penned his new play.

He put the head on the pillow left vacant by his erroneous ex-lover, and then lay down beside it. He wished Purple-five the very best of luck for the New Year, and then fell asleep with a smile on his lips and a human head thawing on the pillow beside him.

CHAPTER FORTY-EIGHT

If you'd asked Mel Hollis how she'd spent the last five days since learning of her husband's murder, she would have been hard-pressed to tell you. After the dreadful experience of identifying Tony's body, she'd picked Chloe up from Kerrie-Anne's and returned to Rose Cottage.

Chloe now possessed twenty-two cuddly toys, none of which seemed to be an adequate replacement for Ruby. DI Cartwright had informed her three days after the identification that the case had now been upgraded to a murder enquiry, and they were looking at possible links between Tony's death and the fire at St Kilda's Close. Mel had been tempted to ask him if he was always in the habit of stating the bloody obvious.

Kerrie-Anne had agreed to let Chloe stay with her for the weekend. Give Mel some breathing space. Mel had told Chloe that Tony had died in a car accident. It was the best she could do under such tragic circumstances. Chloe, for now, only seemed concerned that her father wasn't ever coming home.

A police liaison officer had brought Mel enough paperwork to threaten a rainforest. Leaflets for coping. Information about counselling. How to talk to children about death. Services available. Numbers to call. Not one of them offered advice on how to deal with the Tall Man, past lives, and a rag doll possessed by her dead mother.

Mel had already made one decision. An easy one. She would sell Rose Cottage and the fire-damaged house in St Kilda's Close as soon as possible. Move as far away from Oxfordshire as she could. The Outer Hebrides seemed appealing right now.

Somewhere they could start again where nobody knew them or anything about their dreadful past.

Barnaby Bunny, the latest soft toy to go on trial as Ruby's replacement, was clutched to the child's chest. 'Why do bad things happen to good people, Mummy?'

Mel stopped stroking her daughter's hair, struck once again by the adult nature of her daughter's words. 'I don't know, Pumpkin.'

'It shouldn't be like that.'

'I know.'

Chloe stared at the ceiling for a short while, and then said, 'I think the Tall Man killed Daddy.'

'Daddy died in a car accident.'

Chloe ignored her. 'He's going to kill us, too.'

Mel wanted to hold her, reassure her, promise her no one would do any such thing, but how did you say something you didn't believe yourself? 'Who *is* the Tall Man, Chloe?'

Chloe seemed thoughtful, and then said, 'He's bad. And he cuts off people's heads.'

Mel shuddered.

'He's angry.'

'About what?'

'Me.'

'Why?'

Tears turned her blue eyes to marble. 'I don't know.'

Mel changed the subject before Chloe became too distressed. 'Are you looking forward to seeing Kerrie-Anne tomorrow?'

'Not really.'

'But you like Kerrie-Anne.'

'I want to stay with you.'

'It's only for the weekend. Just so I can sort things out.'

'What things?'

'Boring stuff.'

'Like what?'

Your father's funeral. 'Finding somewhere to live.'

'Aren't we staying here?'

'Not for ever.'

'What about St Kilda's? I like my room there.'

'We'll get you a bigger one when we move.'

'With a TV?'

'Maybe.'

'Can I have a puppy?'

'Now you're pushing it. Dogs need a lot of looking after.'

'I'll walk him.'

'A dog would pull you over if it saw a cat.'

'Not if it was a Yorkshire terrier like Toto.'

'Toto?'

Chloe gazed at the ceiling. 'Toto was funny. We took him to the seaside once, and dad let him off the lead. He ran across the beach and bit a lady's bum.'

'That's one naughty dog.'

'He was just playing.'

'Biting a lady's bum?'

'Uh-huh.'

'Was this when you were Amy?'

Chloe didn't answer.

'Pumpkin?'

'Huh?'

'Toto? Was this your dog when you were Amy?'

'Amy?'

Mel looked at the puzzled expression on her daughter's face and changed the subject. 'Would you like your bedtime story now?'

'I want to sleep with you.'

'I need you to be a big girl and sleep in your own bed.' Mel didn't want to tell her she was sleeping on the sofa, terrified that the Tall Man would break in and murder them in their sleep.

'I'm scared.'

Me too. 'Don't be. Mummy's right here with you.'

'I want Daddy back.'

'I know you do.'

'Daddy's nice.'

'I know, Pumpkin.'

'I miss him.'

So did Mel. More than she ever believed possible. It was funny how death had somehow wiped the slate clean. Forgiven his infidelity. Turned him from villain to hero. Love rat to missed husband. 'Would you like to go on holiday in the summer?'

'Not without Daddy.'

'We could go abroad.'

Chloe shook her head. A tear spilled onto her cheek. 'I don't want to. I want to sleep in your bed.'

Mel relented. At least they now had a DVD player and some new DVDs. 'Okay. You can come downstairs with Mummy for a while. We'll snuggle up on the sofa and watch *The Little Mermaid.*'

'Really?'

'But I want you to promise you'll go to bed straight after.'

Chloe looked less certain. 'Okay.'

And so Mel carried Chloe back downstairs, made hot chocolate, and snuggled up on the settee beneath the duvet.

'I wish I had King Triton's magic trident,' Chloe said, as Ariel's father appeared on the screen.

'Why?'

'Then I could kill the Tall Man.'

Mel shuddered. She glanced behind her at the window, and then spent the rest of the time alternating between watching the film and listening for signs of intrusion.

CHAPTER FORTY-NINE

At the same time as Chloe Hollis was snuggled up to her mother beneath a duvet, King was getting dressed in a black suit, white shirt and black tie. He thought he made a passable police detective. Detective Inspector Norris was inspired in part by the relentless interrogations of Rumble; a man displaying all the hallmarks of a dog with a butcher's bone. Apparently, the crime scene had thrown up some very interesting clues which needed further investigation. King had felt some of his self-confidence slip. Even more so when Rumble had refused to elaborate, teasing him with hearsay and innuendo.

To make matters worse, if there could be such a thing, he'd made the grave error of taking Purple-five's head to bed with him whilst under the influence of grief and brandy. The result had been to wake up with a thumping headache and a thawed head lying beside him on the pillow.

Purple-five had not been a beautiful girl whilst alive. Even less so in death. It was fair to describe her as the most gruesome thing he'd ever had the misfortune to lay eyes on. Skin hung from her skull in grey rotting clumps. Such was the macabre ugliness of the thing, he thought he'd awoken next to the head of one of Macbeth's three witches suffering the ravages of advanced leprosy. After the initial rush of horror and confusion, he'd resealed the head in a clear polythene bag and returned it to the freezer in a markedly poorer state than when he'd taken it out.

Never a believer in omens, and even less so in superstitions, King would, however, later reflect that waking up next to a decomposed head was a sign of bad things to come. He should have returned to his bed after returning Purple-five to her final resting place, locked the door and busied himself reading *Macbeth* or *Hamlet* until the moon grinned in the black face of the night sky.

Fate never gives warnings. It acts on impulse. So it was with an optimistic outlook he'd met Olivia in a wine bar in Oxford to discuss the terrible events at Gavin Westwood's flat. He'd been careful to lure her with a snippet of undisclosed information. Dangle some juicy bait for the fish to nibble on. He didn't have the faintest idea what that information was, because, quite frankly, there wasn't any, but Rumble the Frog had given him some valuable lessons in how to create an aura of mystery and intrigue based upon nothing but supposition.

After three margaritas, and several trips outside to puff on a cigarette, Olivia had become casual in manner, flirty, deeper of voice, less inclined to talk about Westwood, and, in a certain light, in need of a shave. King had played along, teasing her with his eyes, cajoling her with playful words.

By the time they'd left Henry's Wine Bar, Olivia had abandoned decorum and gone straight for seduction. It wasn't any less than King had expected. His natural charm was impossible to resist, even to a human hybrid of such hideous proportions as the delightful Olivia.

King had suggested driving to Waverly Wharf, going for a stroll along the banks of the River Thames and enjoying the peace and charm of the night sky beneath a thousand stars. Once parked in an isolated spot, Olivia had asked King what he'd learned about poor Gavin's death.

'That it might have been an accident. Not murder and suicide as first suspected.'

'Really?'

King treated her to a smile which had cost well over a thousand pounds to produce at Feelham Dental Practice. Whiter than a polar ice cap and capable of lighting the interior of the BMW on its own. 'Yes. They say it might have been some sort of sexual game that went horribly wrong.'

'How gruesome.'

King agreed, although it had a certain erotic appeal in the right setting.

'And you had no idea they were… seeing each other?'

'It came as a complete shock.'

'Gavin never talked about him.'

'People are but mysteries.'

Olivia adjusted her bust. 'That's lovely.'

King went for the kill. 'You have beautiful eyes.'

The complimented eyes blinked rapidly. 'Thank you.'

Too wide apart to draw genuine praise, King thought. 'Like mirrors to heavenly thoughts.'

'Oh, that's beautiful. Did you make that up?'

'I wouldn't dream to plunder another man's work to garner praise.'

'Are you a poet?'

'Amateur,' King conceded. He then spent the next five minutes quoting couplets from Shakespeare's more obscure work, bathing Olivia's ego in flattery.

'You're so clever.'

King held off strangling her for a minute. Praise was praise, even if it came from someone you were about to murder. He was wishing he'd brought his pad and pen to the meeting, so that he could sit down afterward and see what transpired.

'Do you like me, Peter?'

'Of course.'

'As a friend?'

King waited a few moments before answering. He didn't want to appear too eager. 'Perhaps I see something more than friendship.'

'You know I'm a *real* woman?'

King almost laughed. 'Yes.'

'I'm not a man in drag. People often confuse my sexuality with transvestism, but they couldn't be more wrong. I might have been born in a male body, but my feelings, my essence, my longing is all female. I *am* a woman.'

'I'm bisexual, Olivia. I adore the female form every bit as much as I do the male form. I married a woman once.'

'Really?'

No, you half-baked bun. Women repulse me, especially ones with porcupine legs and five o'clock shadows. Not to mention false boobs. 'Yes. Ten years. Unfortunately, she had other ideas about fidelity and ran off with a double-glazing salesman.'

Olivia reached out and rested a hand on King's thigh, giving it a gentle squeeze, murmuring sympathetic guff about how King deserved so much better.

King swallowed hard and readied himself to kiss the nearest thing he'd ever kissed to a woman. The eyeliner and the false lashes only added to the hideous cocktail. He'd have sooner taken his chances puckering up to a bulldog.

He would later consider the importance of detail. His attempt to throttle Olivia whilst kissing her proved a costly mistake. Buoyed by his ability to seduce anyone, even one so challenging as this, he'd overlooked *she* was really a *he*, and, as such, possessed far more strength than he'd given her credit for. She'd fought with all the hallmarks of something begot from a hellcat and a bull.

Nursing a bloody nose, a swollen eye, and a gouged face, he'd watched in disbelief as Olivia had clambered out of the car, fallen to the ground, and crawled away in her laddered tights.

King, driven by pure adrenalin and impulse, started the engine, slipped the car into drive, and ploughed into the kneeling seductress. There was a nasty thud, followed by a crunching noise that made him think of the giant grinding bones in *Jack and the*

Beanstalk. This was followed by several bumps and screams as he ran over the rest of her body.

Not leaving anything to chance, he'd then reversed over the motionless Olivia before colliding with a bollard and leaving Waverly Wharf in a state of high octane paranoia. What if someone had seen? Written down his registration number? Called the police?

By the time he reached the bypass, his mind was ablaze with a pathological hatred of technical advancement. Every action, every word spoken, was instantly recorded by those cursed smart phones. It would only take some courting couple, or an idiot walking a dog, and that would be Olivia's messy demise posted all over one of those ghastly social media sites before you could say *cheese.*

To make matters worse, the dent in the BMW would require professional attention. All he needed was an eagle-eyed paint monkey to notice something was amiss, and Rumble would be on the case quicker than a frog on a lily pad.

He'd stopped on the way home at a local BP garage and used a jet wash to clean the underside of the car. Twice. And then took it through the carwash. Once parked in the safety of his double garage, he'd hoovered the inside and scrubbed the rubber mats. He was neither expert nor fool, but he knew the car would never stand up to a forensic investigation. Perhaps he ought to report it stolen once he'd dealt with the Hollises. Take it to a country lane and set fire to the damned thing. Recover his losses from the insurance company.

Now, in a far more controlled manner than he'd fled the grisly scene at Waverly Wharf, King rolled along the gravel lane and pulled up outside Rose Cottage. He recited his name, Detective Inspector Stephen Norris, and the nature of his business, the terrible loss of Mel Hollis's husband, over and over in his head like a mantra.

Satisfied he could pass muster as an authentic copper, he stepped out of the car into a blast of freezing cold January wind. He thrust his hands into his coat pockets, touching the plastic library card he would produce should Mel Hollis ask for ID. He wasn't in the least concerned about the authenticity of the card; once she opened the door, all the little piggies would be roast beef.

Surely that should be roast pork.

King scowled. Whilst mostly welcome with its bouts of flamboyant creativity, his inner voice could switch to annoying and pedantic in the blink of an eye.

CHAPTER FIFTY

The knock on the door came as Mel was on the verge of dozing off. She jumped up and spilled the duvet onto the floor. Her mind fled in a dozen different directions at once.

'Who's at the door, Mummy?'

'Maybe it's the police,' Mel said. But at this time of night? Without prior warning? DI Cartwright had told her to make sure the house was secure at all times. Not to let anyone in unless she knew them or they had identification. He'd even promised to send duty officers down the lane occasionally whilst out on patrol.

'Mummy?'

'I don't know, Pumpkin.' She stared at the door, as if the letter box were a giant magnet and her eyes were cast from steel. The knock came again, louder, more insistent.

Mel peeled back the curtain. There was a large dark-coloured car parked outside.

'Mrs Hollis?' A man's voice, loud, competing with the whining wind.

Chloe stiffened. 'Who is it, Mummy?'

'Mrs Hollis? It's the police. I need to speak to you about your husband's death.'

Mel put a finger to her lips to silence Chloe. The finger was shaking so badly it jabbed the tip of her nose.

'I can see you, Mrs Hollis. I just want to talk with you.'

Chloe stared at the door, eyes wide. 'It's him.'

Mel struggled for breath. 'Who?'

'The Tall Man. It's the Tall Man.'

'My name's Detective Inspector Norris. I'm from Thames Valley Police. If you want to see my identity card…'

'Here comers a chopper to chop off your head,' Chloe chanted. 'Here comes a chopper to chop off your head… here comes a chopper to chop off your head… here'

Mel grabbed her daughter from the settee and swung her up into her arms. She walked into the kitchen on legs that felt hollow. As she closed the door, she heard several loud raps on the front door. She checked the back door was locked and bolted for the fiftieth time that evening.

'What are we going to do?' Chloe asked, tears streaming down her face.

'Mummy's going to put you down for a minute, okay?'

'What if the Tall Man gets in?'

'He won't.'

'He will.'

'The doors are locked.'

Chloe didn't look convinced. 'What if he sets fire to the house?'

More knocking, muffled by the closed door. His voice still carried through the letter box, but now had threats attached to its initial pleasantries. 'Open this door, now!' A slight pause, followed by, 'Do you think it right and proper I conduct my business standing on a freezing cold doorstep?'

Mel considered running out the back door, but the nearest house was fifty yards away. He would catch them. Her legs felt barely able to stand, let alone run with Chloe in her arms.

The sound of breaking glass made up Mel's mind. She imagined him coming in through the front room window, axe in hand, glass glittering like jewels on his tall menacing body.

'He's coming, Mummy. The Tall Man's coming.'

Call the cops. Her mind screamed. *For fuck's sake, call the cops.*

Good advice if you weren't stupid enough to leave your bloody phone on the coffee table in the lounge.

Go and get it.

The sound of the Tall Man cursing and making threats put paid to any last acts of bravado. She had only two choices now. The basement or upstairs.

What's it to be, Smelly-Mellie? Her mother's voice whispered in her head. *Upstairs, downstairs, or in her lady's chamber?*

There was nowhere to lock themselves in upstairs. The bathroom catch was broken, and the two bedroom doors only had latches. She grabbed Chloe's hand and walked to the basement door. There was a large silver key jutting out of the lock.

Something smashed in the front room. Feet stomped across the floor. 'Mrs Hollis?'

Mel unlocked the door and stepped into the basement for the first time in over thirty years.

'Don't make me search the house for you, Mrs Hollis. I only want to talk to you about how I blew your husband's head off. It won't take more than a minute, I promise.'

Mel switched on the basement light and tried to shove the key in the lock.

The kitchen door opened. 'Are you in here baking apple pie and sugar dumplings, or whatever tickles your proletarian palate?'

Mel dropped the key. She screamed and beat the door in frustration. 'Shit, shit, shit.'

'Mrs Ho-llis?' King called, the word spliced in two like a taunting playground chant.

Chloe scooped the key up, put it back in the lock, and secured the door in one swift movement. Mel sank to her knees and wrapped her arms around her daughter.

King banged on the door. 'Are you in there, Mrs Piggly-wiggly?'

Mel stifled a sob, pleading with God to make him go away. The handle rattled, followed by a loud thud. 'Open the door, Mrs Hollis. I only want to talk to you.'

Mel shook her head, clinging to Chloe and biting down on her lip hard enough to draw blood.

'Or maybe you've gone upstairs to hide under the bed. Is that it, Mrs. Hollis? You want to play hide-and-seek with me?'

Mel heard him stomp up the stairs. Her heart matched him stride for stride.

'Coming, ready or not.'

'What are we going to do, Mummy?'

Mel had no answer to that. She stood up. 'Let's go down the steps. Away from the door.'

'What if he breaks the door?'

Then we'll die in this stinking basement, just like my mother did. They say life moves in fucking circles. 'He won't.'

They walked hand-in-hand down the steps, a mother and her young daughter, trapped, with no means to defend themselves.

The old wooden crate by the wine rack was still in the same place it used to be when Mel had spent endless hours whiling away the time with nothing more than Ruby Rag Doll and a vivid imagination. She sat on the crate and hoisted Chloe onto her lap. She hugged her as tight as she could without hurting her. Chloe's hair tickled her face. At least with Chloe facing away from her, the child couldn't see the terror in her eyes. They stayed this way, rocking back and forth, as Mel searched her mind for a way out.

The sewer pipe.

Mel was almost tempted to give it a go. She didn't have a clue where it led to, other than the main sewer, or if it was even possible to get through it. She instantly dismissed the idea. They would probably drown in a disgusting mire of sewerage if they attempted to use it as an escape route.

She looked at the door. Rotten. A few good kicks and it would break free of its hinges. Shadows played tricks on the walls, casting witches on broomsticks and dinosaurs. She remembered her mother standing at the top of those steps, taking that exaggerated step up before bringing her foot down on Ruby Rag Doll.

An idea. Crude at first, without form. More of a whisper in her head. *Make him fall.*

How was she meant to do that, exactly. Rescue Ruby Rag Doll from the sewer and sit her on the steps?

'I'm scared, Mummy.'

'I know, sweetheart. But I want you to be brave, okay?'

Chloe nodded.

Make him fall.

Mel suddenly remembered the large bottles of cooking oil her father brought home from the navy. There were at least half a dozen stored on the shelving units.

Mel lifted Chloe off her lap. 'You wait here. Mummy needs to do something.'

'What?'

'I'm going to make the steps slippery.'

'Why?'

'So he'll fall if he comes through the door.'

'Will he die?'

I fucking hope so. 'I don't know.'

Mel hurried to the storage rack and grabbed two bottles of oil. She poured some of the contents across the small patch of landing at the top, and the remainder down the first half a dozen steps. She then added the contents of another two bottles.

By the time the task was complete, Chloe was shaking so badly she looked as if she might literally fall apart. Mel picked her up, sat on the crate, rocked back and forth. There was nothing else she could do now except wait.

There was a loud thud, followed by, 'Looks like the little piggies were hiding in here all along. You could have come clean, Mrs Hollis, instead of wasting police time. You do know it's a criminal offence to pervert the course of justice, don't you?'

Mel hugged Chloe tighter, trying not to respond.

'Are you going to open this door and talk to me, or do I have to arrest you for wasting police time?'

Game's up, Smelly-Mellie. What goes around, comes around.

'Is little Chloe-woey in there, too?'

Chloe broke free of her mother's grasp and ran to the bottom of the steps. 'You don't scare me,' she shouted, her voice older, deeper, defiant. 'You think you can hurt me, but you can't.'

'My, my, if I didn't know better, I'd say Purple-five had risen from the grave.'

'You're nothing but a pathetic sadistic twat.'

Mel stood behind her daughter, barely able to comprehend what she was hearing.

'Sticks and stones, Purple-five,' King shouted. 'Sticks and stones.'

What came out of Chloe's mouth next stopped Mel's heart.

'"How weary, stale, flat and unprofitable seem to me all the uses of this world!"'

King thumped the door. 'Don't mock me, girl. Don't you dare take Hamlet's name in vain.'

'What's the matter, Mr. Game Master? Too close to the truth?'

'You'll be sorry you said that, Purple-five.'

Chloe's hands clenched. 'Fuck you!'

'I'm going to kill you. Slowly this time, you ungrateful bitch. Gouge out your eyes, cut out your spiteful tongue, slice off your ears.'

Mel put a hand on her daughter's shoulder. 'Chloe?'

Chloe ignored her. She stared at the door, head tipped back, breath coming in short gasps. 'You can never kill me.'

'Is… that… right?'

'"The common curse of mankind, folly and ignorance, be thine in great revenue."'

A noise came from the other side of the door that belonged to an enraged animal. And then King's laboured voice. 'Open the door now, and I'll spare you.'

Mel said, 'Come away from the steps. He might have a gun.'

'He's a fucking coward.'

'Please.'

Chloe stepped back and allowed her mother to pick her up. The child's eyes appeared almost black in the shadowy light of the basement. Saliva, white and frothy, dribbled down her chin. Sweat glistened on her forehead as if she was in the grip of a fever.

Mel walked to the shelving unit and squeezed into a small space between the wall and the unit. 'Keep quiet, okay?"

Chloe wiped her chin with the back of her sleeve. 'Is he going to chop off our heads?'

How the fuck did you answer that? 'No.'

'He hates me.'

'I won't let him hurt you, okay?'

Chloe nodded, bottom lip trembling.

After several loud thuds, the door flew open and banged against the wall. 'Looks as if you might need a locksmith for that door, Mrs. Hollis.' King's shadow stretched down the steps like a grim reminder of Chloe's name for him. 'You see how much easier this would have been if you hadn't obstructed a police officer.'

Mel held her breath, trying not to give herself away.

'I wonder where the little piggies are hiding.'

Please, God, make this work!

After a few moments, King said, 'All right, have it your way.'

Please, God. Please.

King stepped onto the landing. His right foot instantly slipped over the edge of the first step. To correct his balance, his left foot tried to find purchase in the oil, spilling him further forward. A gunshot echoed around the basement as he tumbled forward. He dropped the gun as he fell. It came to rest about halfway down, spinning in the oil.

Mel watched her adversary crash down the last few basement steps. He cried out as his head cracked against the concrete at the bottom, leaving him in a twisted heap, one leg bent up underneath his body.

And then silence.

When he still hadn't moved after several minutes, Mel walked across the basement with Chloe in her arms. She stood a few feet away from his motionless body.

'Is he dead, Mummy?'

'I… think… so.'

'What if he's just pretending?'

Mel didn't have an answer to that. A small puddle of blood had spread out beside his head. Only one problem: he was blocking off the steps.

He might be playing dead to lure you into a trap.

Mel could see the gun glistening on the steps in a puddle of oil, tantalisingly close.

She made a snap decision to pass Chloe over the top of him. She whispered in her ear, 'I'm going to put you on the steps. I want you to go carefully because of the oil, okay?'

Chloe nodded.

'Go on your hands and knees. Don't think about the Tall Man. Just remember Mummy will make sure he doesn't touch you.'

'Okay.'

'When you get to the top, go into the kitchen and wait there for me, okay.'

'Uh-huh.'

'Good girl.' Mel strained every muscle lifting Chloe over the body. She held her breath as she watched her daughter crawl up the concrete steps, slowly, methodically, as if they were cast from ice. She looked so small, so innocent, so vulnerable.

Chloe reached the top and scrambled into the kitchen.

Your turn.

Mel's feet felt encased in concrete.

One foot in front of the other.

Why were words so easy, and actions so hard? She noticed a large bruise on the Tall Man's face. Blood trickled from his nose. And then, as if conjured from her worst nightmare, his face morphed into that of her mother. Wild red-rimmed eyes staring east and west. Chipped yellow teeth. Hair splayed out as if caught in a strong wind.

It was all Mel could do to suppress a scream. She closed her eyes.

Your mother's dead. Dead and buried in Feelham Cemetery forever.

If this thought was meant to comfort her, it didn't. She opened her eyes. The Tall Man was back in all his twisted glory. She forced herself to step over him, her stomach riding on a rollercoaster.

Two steps up now. Within touching distance of the gun.

You don't even know how to fire a gun.

Four steps. Feet slipping in the oily coating. She grabbed the greasy handle of the gun. Picked it up. The cold metal felt alien, full of threats.

'"Hell is empty, and all the devils are here."'

The voice, thick and slurry, made Mel cry out. Her left foot lost its grip, and she fell to her knees. She looked over her shoulder as the Tall Man propped himself up on one elbow. She tried to crawl up the steps, but the surface refused to allow traction.

The Tall Man screamed as he tried to unravel his twisted leg. He looked at Mel with eyes forged in hell. The scream gave way to a series of laboured pants. Bloody spit bubbled on his lips.

Mel gave up her fruitless attempt to get away. She sat on the step and pointed the gun at his head, gripping the handle with both hands. 'Don't move.'

His lips peeled back. 'What shall I compare thee to?'

'I'll shoot you.'

The Tall Man didn't appear disturbed by threats. A laugh, thick with phlegm, gurgled in his throat. 'Is that right, Mrs. Hollis?'

Mel bit down on her lip. 'Yes.'

'You have all the integrity of a stewed prune.' He rolled onto his front and edged towards the first step, using his elbows to propel himself.

'Stay there.'

He slithered forward. 'I suppose you're proud of your little plan to thwart me?'

'I'm not proud of anything.'

'You do realise it's a criminal offence to attack a police officer attending his duties?'

'Come any further, and I'll shoot you.'

He edged closer. 'I don't think you will, Mrs Hollis. I don't think you're even capable of shooting the breeze.'

'Do it!' Chloe shouted, in that alien, grown up voice Mel recognised as Amy. 'Do it, now!'

'Ah, Purple-five. I wondered when we would see your true colours. No pun intended.'

'Shoot the bastard,' Chloe demanded.

Mel's finger tightened on the trigger.

'You know the rules, Purple-five.' Blood stained his teeth and dribbled down his chin. 'You landed on the Death Square.'

'And now it's your turn,' Chloe said.

King crawled forward, almost within striking distance of Mel. '*Et tu, Brute*?'

Mel fired. The bullet took away half of King's cheek and one of his eyes. The remaining one stared at Chloe for a few seconds before he slumped forward, chin smashing into the concrete step. Mel fired again. This time the bullet hit him in the top of the head, rendering him permanently mute and motionless.

'Mummy! Mummy! Mummy!' Chloe screamed.

Mel dropped the gun and crawled up the remaining steps. When she reached the top, knees scraped and dripping with blood and oil, she wrapped her arms around her sobbing, shaking four-year-old little girl.

'It's over, Pumpkin. It's over.'

EPILOGUE

By late spring, Chloe Hollis was sleeping reasonably well again. Mel had always been aware of how resilient children were, but Chloe's ability to recover from such a traumatic series of events astounded her. The child rarely spoke about what had happened at Rose Cottage, and she'd had no more past-life recollection. Not that Mel wasn't thrown into a panic every time Chloe had a bad dream or seemed upset. It would take many years for Mel to relax again, but at least each new day put the horrors of that Christmas further into the past.

Chloe had a new rag doll. Sally. As yet, Sally had shown no signs of being possessed by Grandma Audrey. Long may it continue. Mel prayed that the evil witch would stay in the sewer where she belonged for all eternity.

Naturally, Chloe missed her daddy. Mel took her to Feelham Cemetery every Sunday to lay fresh flowers on the grave. Chloe told him how much she loved him and what a great daddy he was. She would also recount everything she'd done that week, even telling him all about Mel as if she wasn't there.

Mel missed him, too. More than she could have ever imagined after discovering the truth about Stephanie Wallace. Chloe had no recollection of the affair. She didn't even remember Ruby talking to her, although she did occasionally say she missed the doll. She swore that Sally would never get thrown out by mistake like Ruby, especially when they moved.

Mel had found a temporary flat to rent on the outskirts of Feelham. She planned to stay there until Rose Cottage was sold and she had the means to buy another house. She'd been looking on the internet at properties along the south coast. Brighton.

Chichester. Bournemouth. Far enough away to wipe the slate clean and start again. Feel safe, without painful reminders of the past waiting around every corner.

DI Cartwright had told Mel they had evidence to suggest Peter King had murdered Tony, as well as Charles Honeywell, Gavin Westwood and Olivia Watson. They'd also recovered nineteen heads from upright freezers in King's basement. The long process of identification was under way. Three had been positively identified from dental records, but the others were still unknown.

Mel was still struggling to come to terms with the fact that Charles Honeywell was King's lover and complicit in all the murders. Upon hearing the news, Mel had been violently sick. She couldn't stop thinking about all the times she'd confided in him. The years she'd worked with him at Feelham Primary School. How he'd taken Chloe to see Gavin Westwood. And all along, he'd been King's lover and accomplice.

The police had rescued four girls from the bowels of Feelham Theatre. All were suffering the effects of dehydration after six days without water. They'd had to resort to licking condensation off the walls. One was unconscious and had to be resuscitated twice in the ambulance on the way to hospital.

Chloe's hysterical reaction to going inside Feelham Theatre now made perfect sense to Mel. It must have terrified the poor child. Mel always avoided going anywhere near the place when she went into town. It was like some great monolith shrine to evil as far as she was concerned. If she had her way, it would be knocked down and turned into a memorial garden for all the poor girls who'd lost their lives in Peter King's sick, depraved game.

One girl, Tanya Whichello, had sent a letter to Chloe telling her what a brave and special little girl she was, and how she would always remember her. Over the course of the following few weeks, Mel and Tanya had talked on the phone. Tanya was back at home living with her parents. She'd enrolled at college to train as a hairdresser. Maybe one day, when Chloe got married, she would let Tanya do her hair for the wedding. Chloe had thought that was the best thing ever, and she'd made her mother promise to stay friends with Tanya. It was the very least Mel could do.

Mel sat on the small hard sofa in the rented flat with Chloe snuggled up next to her. They were watching *Finding Dory* for the thousandth time. Mel knew the story backwards and upside down by now, but it was such a simple joy to be sitting in safety with her daughter and just doing what normal people do.

'I love you, Mummy.'

'I love you, too. A million times over.'

After a slight pause, Chloe said, 'I'm glad the angels helped me to choose you, Mummy.'

Tears stung the back of Mel's eyes. This one simple statement held such a complex and intricate meaning. Life wasn't just a random act of chance. There were forces at work beyond this world, arranging the pieces, bringing to justice those who had committed despicable acts.

'Me, too, Pumpkin. Me too.'

ACKNOWLEDGEMENTS

Huge thanks to:

David McCaffrey, Maggie James and Jipsy Lee for beta reading the book.

Bloodhound Books for all their help and support, especially Fred, Betsy, Alexina , Sarah Sumaira and Clare.

Tracy Fenton and everyone in THE Book Club on Facebook.

25156997R00181

Printed in Great Britain
by Amazon